the CAMPFIRE
collection

the CAM

PFIRE

collection

SPINE-TINGLING TALES TO TELL IN THE DARK

Edited by: Eric B. Martin

CHRONICLE BOOKS
SAN FRANCISCO

To maintain the authentic style of each writer included
herein, quirks of spelling and grammar remain unchanged
from their original state.

Library of Congress Cataloging-in-Publication Data:

    The campfire collection : spine-tingling tales to tell in
    the dark / edited by Eric B. Martin.
    p.   cm.
    ISBN 0-8118-2454-3 (pbk.)
    1. Outdoor life—Literary collections.
    2. Nature—Literary collections.   3. Outdoor life.
    4. Nature.   I. Martin, Eric B.
PN6071.087C36 2000   99-40570
308.8'036—dc21   CIP

Printed in the United States of America.

Book and cover design by JEREMY STOUT
Composition by SUZANNE SCOTT

Distributed in Canada by Raincoast Books
8680 Cambie Street
Vancouver, British Columbia V6P 6M9

10 9 8 7 6 5 4 3 2 1

Chronicle Books
85 Second Street
San Francisco, California 94105

www.chroniclebooks.com

INT

Pa

Th

T

Introduction

I get scared.

I don't get scared at movies or on city streets or in a dark house, alone. I get scared outdoors. I used to seek fear out, when I was a kid growing up in Maine. My best friend and I would go on walks through the woods at night. This was in the summer, on an island where his family rented a house. There were no roads, no cars, no electricity. From the house you could follow a thin trail toward the center of the island. The trees were so thick that they formed two living walls on either side, and the branches crowded close, almost touching our shoulders. We'd walk for a while with flashlights, then turn them off and stand quiet and still in the path, squinting into the trees. There was nothing out there but tiny scraps of moonlight and Maine and the million trees and the sounds of our breath.

And that. Did you hear that?

What?

That.

My friend was a faster runner than I was, but every now and then I'd beat him back to the house.

Since those days I've sat around hundreds of campfires, in mountains and deserts and on beaches, in Maine and California and Texas and Mexico, staring into the blue-black middle of a flame, chasing after that thrilling kind of fear again. And sometimes it can happen. It can happen in that quietest part of the night, when everyone is about to go to sleep, but instead someone leans forward and says in an even, still voice: listen, let me tell you a story.

The seventeen pieces in this collection are the stories I always wish I have with me, to tell or hear or read alone, in the wild, far from home. In finding them and reading them, I've realized that the longed-for sensation of that island in Maine was about more than fear. It was fear commingled with the awe and respect that comes from loving the outdoors.

Each of these stories is an outdoor story, in one way or another. Some of the stories are true. Some are screamers, some are chillers, some will make you wince or smile or frown. Many of them are the work of the best writers of our times. All of them will stay with you, and all of them are dangerous.

So: listen, let me tell you a story. . . .

—*Eric Martin*

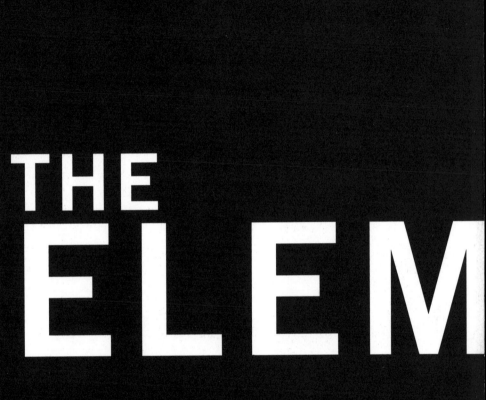

THE
ELEM

PART I

ENTS

The Snow-Shoers

by George R. Stewart

Stewart's Ordeal by Hunger, *published in 1936, is probably the best known account of the Donner Party's disastrous crossing of the California Sierras. The so-called "snow-shoe party" was the first group of several groups to try and make a break from Donner Lake west through the Sierra winter. About half of them, mostly women, survived.*

That morning of Wednesday the sixteenth was clear and freezing. The wind had worked around somewhat to the east giving hope of fair weather, and the cold night had left the snow dry and feathery, so that it did not stick to the snow-shoes. There was no more reason for delay. Those who were departing faced danger and bitter hardship, but as they looked into the wasted faces of those who remained they realized that, even should they themselves escape, they might never again see their wives and children. The parting was one of double sorrow.

They filed off across the snow, shuffling clumsily in the heavy foot-gear. At each step they sank a foot deep into the light snow. The women, for greater freedom of movement, had made their skirts into loose trousers, so that except where bearded faces showed from beneath the mufflings, men and women looked alike. The fourteen with snow-shoes plodded on first; then went "Dutch Charley" and the two Murphy boys stepping on the footsteps of the others. The hope of these last was that the passage of so many snow-shoes would beat down a path and allow them to walk. But the scheme did not work well, so that the three followers kept breaking through and floundering. Slowly the long line filed out of sight among the pine trees.

On the first day the party made slow progress. Three weeks before, when they had been able to walk on the crust, they had gone from the cabins and across the pass in one day, but now they were weaker, and the snow-shoes held them back. They made camp at evening not much beyond the head of the lake, about four miles, and ironically, in full view of the smoke from the cabins. "Dutch Charley" and Bill Murphy had turned back during the day, but Lem had struggled on. It was obvious, however, that he could not keep up as he had planned; so the others improvised snow-shoes for the plucky lad out of some pack-saddles which had come with Captain Sutter's mules and had been abandoned along the road.

Camping in the snow was in itself a problem. It was too deep for them to clear out a snow-pit and build a fire on the ground, but either from their own ingenuity or from knowledge picked up from some mountaineer they hit upon the right method. They cut logs of green wood about six feet long, and with them made a platform on the snow; upon this they kindled a fire of dry wood. If the foundation logs were of good size, they would not burn through during the night. By crowding around the fire, sheltered beneath their scanty supply of blankets, the snow-shoers got through the night miserably enough.

Next day they faced the pass itself. With their snow-shoes, their wintry costumes, and the packs on their shoulders, they reminded Mary Graves, toiling in the lead, of some picture she had seen of a Norwegian fur-company on the ice pack. The climb was heartbreaking work, but sometimes they could get along without snowshoes as they worked gingerly up the bare, slick rock-surfaces where snow would not lie. At the top some one jested, a bit grimly, that they were about as close to heaven as they could get. Nevertheless, some of them admired the magnificent scene which lay unrolled as they looked back to the east over the now frozen lake, past the smoke of the cabins, and on to the distant mountains beyond. A few steps westward, and that whole vista sank from view. That night they camped, exhausted, a little west of the pass, estimating that they had made six miles. The snow was twelve feet deep.

On the third day they had the advantage of a slightly downhill course. Nevertheless, the strain of two days of constant labor without sufficient food was beginning to tell on them. And they now faced another enemy, for as they crossed the treeless expanse of Summit Valley the white surface dazzling in the sun brought on snowblindness. Brave little Stanton was the worst affected; he was the weakest, too, and gradually fell behind, out of sight. The emigrant trail was of course buried deep under the snow, but even though Stanton failed, the Indians knew the way. Who could miss it in any case? For the great, broad valley of the Yuba ran straight ahead toward the west. Snow flurries broke upon them with a cold wind blowing furiously. Again they estimated six miles when they camped without Stanton. An hour later he struggled in.

The fourth day repeated the third. Fierce squalls of snow swept down on them; it grew so cold that their feet started freezing. Stanton still lagged. In their weakened condition they began to fall prey to hallucinations. Mary Graves saw haze in a gorge to the right. The others assured her that it was merely mist, but she insisted that it was smoke, and even made them fire the gun for a signal. Five miles was the most that they could do. By this night they were down somewhere near Yuba Bottoms, under the high dome of Cisco Butte.

The fifth morning was clear with a cold wind from the northeast. They left the river and struggled uphill four miles to the divide. Stanton came in about an hour late, as before.

On this fifth night they were camping not far from the place at which Reed and McCutchen had turned back five weeks before, and there they were only about five miles from this cache of beef and flour which the two fathers had left at Curtis's wagon in Bear Valley. But they of course knew nothing of all that. So far they had got along well enough, and had made the five miles a day which they had counted. But they must now have begun to realize that even at Bear Valley they would not be out of the snow. From its depth at the place where they were, they could only suppose that the snow belt must still extend ahead of them for many miles. They saw about them, even from points of look-out, only heavily forested mountains, deep in snow. Their packs contained food for only one more day.

The morning of their sixth day broke. It was Monday, the twenty-first of December, the shortest day of the year. Christmas week! That morning Eddy dug into his little pack to see if there was not something which he could leave behind to lighten his load still further. To his amazement he found half a pound of bear's meat. To it was attached a bit of paper bearing a note written in pencil and signed "Your own dear Eleanor." She had robbed her own insufficient stores to save her husband, and in the note she urged him to cherish her gift for the last extremity; some feeling told her, she wrote, that it would be the means of saving his life.

But by this sixth morning one member of the company was finished. Little Stanton, who had once been in the warm, safe valley of the Sacramento, who had come back that the women and children might be fed, who had three times led the way across the pass in the snow—Stanton was through. Fatigue, snow-blindness, and slow starvation had worn him down. He had made mistakes, but he had lived as a hero; it remained to die as a gentleman.

That morning as his companions were setting out, he sat by the camp-fire smoking his pipe. Mary Graves approached, and asked if he was coming.

"Yes," he said, "I am coming soon."

They went on.

Stanton's chivalry had spared them any qualms about deserting him. Nevertheless his loss almost immediately brought difficulties. He had doubtless trusted to the Indians to guide them through, but to follow an unmarked trail across snow-covered mountains, especially when they had traversed it only once before and then in the opposite direction, was entirely too much of a task for these half-civilized Indians of the plains. Moreover this section of the trail followed no river course or marked ridge, but worked along and across the valleys of small streams. Each of these began by flowing west and looked as if offering the proper route, but they all soon bore off subtly to the south, leading not toward Bear Valley, only a day's march distant, but toward the canyon-scarred, tangled country along the American. It was a perfect place for getting lost.

And almost immediately they made a mistake. Instead of keeping well up on the slope and working along it, they turned off and went downhill toward the south and away from Bear Valley. On this day they used up the last of their provisions. At night Stanton did not come in.

Tuesday morning broke upon a camp without food except for Eddy's hoarded bear meat. They went on about a mile. Then snow began to fall. Starving and confused, they halted partly because they could not travel safely in the storm, partly in fear that they were already lost, and partly in faint hope that Stanton might still come up to guide them. They stayed there for the rest of the day, but he did not come.

Next day, weaker from a day and a half of fasting, they climbed to a high point for observation. Eastward rose the buttes along the Yuba whence they had just come. Northward were ugly, forbidding mountains. Westward was a high ridge blocking the way. If there was any visible choice, it was toward the south.

They camped on the height, and the next day, starving, went down a valley for three miles. Then snow began to fall, not another flurry but the beginning of a real storm. This was their ninth day of travel broken only by nights spent crouching half-frozen in the snow around whatever fire they could build. Most of them had not eaten for more than two days, and in their weakened condition they could not go on much further. The situation must be faced. They halted, huddled together in the storm, and consulted as to what, if anything, could be done. All of the men except Eddy were completely dispirited and favored turning back. Eddy and the women declared that they would go forward, come what might. Then some one said that they must all die of starvation. It was not to be denied—unless they found food. Then came a pause.

During the last two days, as they had marched half-mad with hunger, what strange thoughts had begun to grow in their minds?

They had begun, perhaps, as they looked about with maniacal cravings for food, to regard their comrades as offering certain new possibilities. Man might eat beef—good! Man might eat horse, too, as the need came, and mule. He might eat bear and dog, and even coyote and owl. He might also—and the relentless logic drove on—yes, man might also eat man.

All about lay the deep snow, and more snow was falling. They had hungered two days and more, and had no prospect for food except that which, however much they had thought of it, no one had yet put into words.

The pause lengthened, and then Patrick Dolan voiced it—they should draw lots to see who should die to furnish food for the others. Eddy seconded. But Foster objected, and of all motions such a one most surely must require unanimity. And even if they drew lots, how would they accomplish the deed? Was a man to butcher a man like an ox, or cut his throat as if he were a sheep? They had not come to that.

But another idea came to Eddy's mind. He himself was stronger than most of the others by nature, and even more by virtue of his supply of bear meat. If they struggled on blindly in the snow, some of them would surely drop before he did, and might be eaten. But such a way was not Eddy's, and his proposal shows the flame of the man. Let two of them, he said, take each a six-shooter, and fight till one or both were killed. Thus a man would have a chance for his life, and if he lost, would die in hot blood, not slaughtered like a pig. It was a man's way. But again some one objected, for the scruples of civilization were dying hard.

Eddy finally suggested all that was left to do, and a way which was in face much safer for him—they should struggle on until some one died. It would not take long now, to judge by the looks of some of them.

They dragged themselves ahead through the storm. Death dogged their steps. Each one was to his comrade that which might perhaps be food. Whom could a man trust, or whose eyes could he meet? Could a man without hypocrisy help another through a drift, or except with ugly hope inquire how he felt? Antonio the Mexican was far gone. So was "Uncle Billy" Graves; his sixty years were telling. He was of no strength to bear up with men and women half his age, his own daughters among them. Perhaps it would be Antonio or "Uncle Billy." But they both managed to keep going, until at last all halted. The storm was blowing upon them what seemed an actual torrent of snow. In the gathering darkness, stumbling with weakness, having only one hatchet, with some of their number already collaps-ing, they found the task of collecting wood almost too much for them. If those who had to cut and carry the logs for the firm platform chose skimpy ones, they were scarcely to be blamed; they did what their weakness allowed. Even after the green logs were laid together, the numb-fingered men had the greatest difficulty, as the wind swirled and the snow drove, in getting the fire kindled at all. At last the flame lived; they cherished and built it up until it roared finely, their only cheer on Christmas Eve. But some of them were far gone.

Antonio the Mexican, who had followed the train as herdsman of the cattle, lay by the fire sleeping in a heavy stupor. He breathed difficultly and unnaturally. Once as he moved in his sleep, he threw out an arm so that his hand fell into the fire. Eddy, lying nearby and awake, himself exhausted, saw what had happened, but supposed that the pain would arouse the sleeper, and in any case if Antonio were not aroused—so much the better. But the hand doubled up and shriveled with the heat, and finally Eddy, arousing himself, drew it from the fire. Eddy lay down, but Antonio's breathing became a rattling sound and he flung out his arm again; the watcher, realizing that nothing mattered any longer for Antonio, saw the hand shrivel in the flame until it burned to a coal. Cold, fatigue, and hunger had done their work.

Again there was food in camp, but before any one made a move to eat, a worse crisis was upon them. Antonio had died around nine o'clock, and an hour later the storm increased in fury. Wind, hail, and snow beat down with an incredible fury upon the thirteen who still remained. The only way to save themselves from freezing was to pile more and more wood upon the fire. The unusual heat of this great fire soon ate into the too small foundation logs. Gaps opened up between them, and the snow melted away. The fire, platform and all, began to settle into the hole which its own heat produced. At the same time the supply of wood which they had expected to last the night became exhausted, and some one staggered off against the weight of the storm to cut more fuel, or perhaps new foundation logs. As he worked, the head flew from the hatchet and was lost in the deep snow.

It seemed the final piling up of calamities. Even if they broke off dry wood for fuel, they could not maintain a fire without a foundation for it. And the fire was settling visibly. The snow beneath it had turned to slush and water. By midnight they found themselves about eight feet deep in a circular well in the snow with ice-cold water beginning to rise in the bottom; it was like feeling the chill of death actually creeping up toward their ankles. Several of them were almost done for. "Uncle Billy" was sinking into the stupor before death. One of the Indians sat nodding next to the snow-wall, almost frozen. With the ingenuity of desperation, the few who still maintained their wits and a little strength set the half-wet logs on end and built up the fire on top, as if on stilts. It burned there, a precarious reliance against the power of the storm. With the icy water around their feet, they cherished their fire burning above it.

Suddenly the half-frozen Indian who sat by the snow-wall roused himself, made a sudden clumsy push forward to get next to the fire, and upset it. The flame winked out; the embers hissed once. The poor people huddling about broke into a most pitiful wail of mixed prayer and lamentation. They were unstrung, and some no longer in their right minds. Most of them were past the point of even trying to save themselves.

At this juncture only Eddy's knowledge of woodcraft saved them. As they were, he knew all would be frozen to death in a few hours. Prodding the stupefied men and women into action he gradually aroused them, and got them to climb out of the well. Then in the full force of the storm they spread a few blankets on the snow. On these they seated themselves in a circle facing in towards the center, and over them Eddy laid other blankets forming a tent-like mound. It was a device which he must have learned from some mountain-man. Apathy was already upon some of them, and so slowly did they act that before they could be herded into the shelter "Uncle Billy" Graves had died. Death came easily to him; he was past caring; but as he died he told his two daughters, it is said, to save themselves by using his body.

Once the starving wretches were crouched together beneath the blankets, Eddy himself crept in and completed the circle. They were then, as he had known, safe from freezing. The snow soon covered them, shutting off the wind better than the closest of tents. Even their starved bodies emitted still some heat, and this being conserved by the close space and by the covering of snow, soon raised the temperature.

Through the night the snow roared on, and the morning broke on Christmas day. It scarcely brought light to the indescribable scene beneath the blankets. Jolly Patrick Dolan was the one who was going now. Instead of falling into apathy he became delirious. His words were wild and unconnected, but he was seized with the dementia of pressing ahead and reaching the settlements immediately. He began to struggle, and finally escaped from the blankets into the storm. Then he called upon Eddy to follow, saying that Eddy was the only one of the party who could be depended on. After that, falling into complete derangement, he pulled off his boots and most of his clothing, and called upon Eddy to follow him, saying that they would be in the settlement in a few hours. Eddy went out after him, and tried to force him back, but was not able to master Dolan's delirious strength. Later, however, Dolan came back of his own accord and lay down outside the shelter; they then dragged him again beneath the blankets. For a while his agony was upon him, but as they held him tightly he gradually became quiet and submissive again. After that he fell into a calm sleep, and then toward dusk, without awakening, died.

Through Christmas night the storm still raged, and the company, now reduced to eleven, lived on as they could. Probably only the stronger ones were suffering. Most of them were half sunk in coma; after four days without food, the worst pangs of hunger had passed. Nothing human remained, but the spark of animal life glowed dully on. Madness was close upon them. They dreamed maniacal dreams of hunger, and awoke trying to sink their teeth into the hands or arms of their companions. At times they wailed and shrieked.

The youngest of them all was the next to fail. Lemuel Murphy, only a boy of thirteen, became delirious in the night, and talked wildly of food. He raged so that all of the others had to help at holding him. Still they crouched and lay beneath the blankets.

Saturday morning broke, the day after Christmas. They had now been beneath the blankets for more than thirty hours, and the situation was becoming no longer endurable. To light a fire in the brunt of the storm outside was still impossible, but in desperation Eddy attempted to get one started beneath the shelter of the blankets.

He used some gun-powder for tinder, and by accident blew up the whole powder-horn. He was badly burned about the face and hands and two of the women also suffered.

But the grim will to live still held. It outlasted the storm, and when the clouds finally broke on Saturday afternoon, Eddy, a little stronger than the others on account of his bear meat, crawled from beneath the blankets and set to making a fire. But all the wood was soaked, and even their clothing offered scarcely a dry shred. They discovered, however, that Mrs. Pike's mantle had a lining of cotton and some of this seemed fairly dry. They exposed it to the sun's rays, struck sparks into it with flint, and finally managed to blow it into a glow. After this they set fire to a large dead pine tree, and gathered weakly around rejoicing at last in the comfort of the flame.

Then they took the final step. The taboos of civilization had held against five days of starvation, but now the will to live was the stronger. Eddy held off, and strangely enough, the two Indians refused the food, and building themselves a fire at a little distance sat stoically beside it. The others cut the flesh from the arms and legs of Patrick Dolan's body, roasted it by the fire and ate it—"averting their faces from each other, and weeping."

Then they broke off boughs and laid themselves on these crude beds on top of the snow around the burning pine tree. The flames leaped up to the branches of the tree, and after a while great limbs began to burn off and fall among the men and women below. The poor creatures were too apathetic even to care, and lay among the showers of sparks; only by luck no one burned to death or was brained by a falling limb.

They offered some of the food to the plucky boy, Lemuel Murphy, but he was too far gone. The delirium had left him now, and he was quiet, sunk into a stupor. Mrs. Foster, his elder sister, sat cherishing and soothing him, his head in her lap. Night fell; the tree blazed luridly, and a quarter moon swung in the sky, casting a wan light over the deep snow. At moon-set he died.

That morning (it was Sunday the twenty-seventh) they set about the matter more systematically. They remained in camp during this and the next two days. Once the taboo was broken, things were easier. The Indians, too, joined with them. They stripped the flesh from the bodies, roasted what they needed to eat, and dried the rest for carrying with them. They observed only one last sad propriety; no member of a family touched his own dead. But the strain was scarcely less for that. For as she sat by the fire Mrs. Foster suddenly realized that spitted upon a stick and broiling over the coals she saw the heart of her cherished younger brother.

The Birthday Boys

by Beryl Bainbridge
from *The Birthday Boys*

Bainbridge's historical novel recounts Captain Robert Scott's doomed expedition to the South Pole. In July of 1911, before their fatal dash to the pole, three men from the expedition set out into the Antarctic winter to collect the eggs of Emperor Penguins, for science. Most of the eggs were smashed and the three men found themselves struggling to return to the expedition's winter camp at Cape Evans, some seventy miles away.

It took two hours to get the blubber stove lit; just as it began to burn more strongly a blob of boiling fat spat into Bill's eye. He reckoned his sight had gone and thrust his arm against his mouth to stifle his groans. It was well-nigh unbearable not being able to do anything for him beyond uttering platitudes and watching him suffer.

Cherry was a tower of strength. Going outside, he plugged up as many of the gaps in the walls as he could find. His fingers were now easier, he said, and he put it down to the oil in the broken eggs in his mitts.

When we'd eaten and were a little warmer we discussed our situation. I was all for making another descent to the rookery, yet I knew it was out of the question—Cherry and Bill were almost at the end of their tether, we had one tin of oil left for the return journey, and our clothing was in rags. Bill said we ought to rest up, wait for calmer weather and then make a run for home. "We've reached rock-bottom," he said flatly, pressing a wad of cotton rag dunked in cold tea to his injured eye. "Things must improve."

That night I dreamt I was on that other ghastly run, the St. Paul's Journeys, an initiation torture devised for new cadets on the *Worcester*. The victim had to sprint the length of the lower deck and back, and then to his hammock under the top hammocks of the older chaps who hit him with boots, rope, knotted towels, anything that hurt. I could hear my heart thumping in my chest as I ran and the shouts of those bully-boys above me. All my youthful enthusiasm and ideals had melted away, replaced by cunning and an animal necessity to go to ground. Then it became very quiet—the other fellows vanished, and there was nobody but me standing there, eyes wide with terror. A sob burst from me—or so I thought. I woke instantly, to a terrible suffocating silence. The next moment I heard a second, greater sob, a fearsome gulp of sound fit to swallow the universe.

Scrambling out of my bag I opened the igloo door, at which the world suddenly cracked wide open, the wind shrieking about my ears, a solid wall of black snow crushing me to my knees. As if under water I dog-paddled those few yards to the tent, came up against the provision boxes, felt for that neat row of finneskö, that canvas sack containing a copy of *Bleak House* and the poems of Tennyson, the tin of sweets I'd brought to celebrate Bill's birthday. I crawled back, calling for Cherry, and twice I was flung on my face by the force of the wind. "The tent's gone," I shouted.

Cherry and I laboured for what seemed like years transferring the gear to the igloo. All but crazy from the pain of his eye, Bill could do no more than lie in the doorway and blindly shovel the drift from the entrance.

I don't know what the other two were thinking while we sank into hell. I know that there were two halves of me, one which raced ahead working out ways of getting back to Cape Evans by means of digging holes in the ice and using the ground sheet as a covering, and the other which longed to curl up in the igloo and acknowledge we were done for.

It wasn't that I'd given up hope, rather that the loss of the tent and inhuman fury of the hurricane tearing at the canvas roof, so that it rattled as though we were under continuous rifle-fire, had the same hallucinatory effect as the auroral display of our outward journey and drove me into dreams. I relived the moment when I opened the igloo door and heard that mighty crack of the elements, and sometimes I saw a giant chick emerge from a giant egg, and sometimes I watched a cork pulled from a cobwebbed bottle labelled "Emergency", its plume of escaped vapour whirling up and up until it fashioned itself into the shape of a turbaned genie whose blue eyes flashed bolts of lightning. Over and over, as though words could drown the roar of that awful wind, I murmured those lines of Tennyson:

> Oh that 'twere possible
> After long grief and pain
> To find the arms of my true love
> Round me once again.

And I had such regrets, for I'd never known an untrue love, let alone one of the other sort, and the only arms that had ever tenderly held me were those of my mother.

By degrees, I pulled myself together. I think at the beginning we sang to keep our spirits up: hymns, ballads, bits of Evensong. Cherry gallantly tried to warble "Silver Threads Amoung the Gold", but when it came the line, "Darling I am growing older" his voice trailed away at the realisation there was every possibility such a process was beyond his expectations. I remembered the requirements deemed necessary for the Gold Medal for cadets, and duly bawled them out: "A cheerful submission to superiors, self-respect and independence of character, kindness and protection to the weak, readiness to forgive offence, desire to conciliate the differences of others, and, above all, fearless devotion to duty and unflinching truthfulness." At this, triggered by some secret memory of his own, Cherry clutched my arm and began to laugh. Then the roof went. The topmost rocks of the walls fell in upon us, together with a blanket of drift.

The fact that we were almost into our sleeping bags saved us, that and the ridge above us which in some measure deflected the wind howling towards the Ross Sea. Cherry dived forward to help Bill, who shouted, "See to yourself!" and Cherry still persisting, "Please, Cherry, please." All the urgency and worry in the world was in his voice, for he held himself responsible for our ghastly dilemma.

Somehow we burrowed deeper into those wretched bags, pulling them over and round until we lay on that wild mountainside cocooned in ragged shrouds, nothing between us and the hidden stars but that swirling, maddening blizzard.

I think we dozed a good bit; the temperature had risen with the storm, and we were kept almost snug by the snow that fell upon us. Every now and then I kicked out at Cherry to see if he still lived, and all of us heaved up at intervals to jerk the drift away. We didn't eat for two days and two nights, apart from handfuls of snow to ease our raw throats and a boiled sweet apiece in honour of Bill's birthday.

On the Monday there was a lull in the storm. Though it was still blowing we could talk without shouting. We asked each other how we felt . . . Pretty well, thank you, all things considered; if Bill's eye was better . . . Oh, yes, much better, thank you; if Cherry's hands were on the mend . . . Thank you, yes . . . The swelling is much reduced. None of us enquired how we were going to survive.

The wind further abating, we got out of our bags and searched for the tent. I don't think any of us really thought we'd find it, but we went through the motions. We were lucky in that all our gear was intact, save for two pieces of the cooker and a pair of Cherry's socks which had been snatched from his finneskö. At last Bill said we must cook ourselves a meal, though it was a curious fact we had little desire for food; our bodies had taken such a beating and we were so diminished from lack of sleep that eating seemed too great an effort. We struggled through the preparations, stretching the ground sheet over us and somehow huddling beneath it, lighting the primus, holding the broken cooker in our hands, waiting an age for the snow to melt. Then, the pemmican beginning to heat and the smell rising, our appetites returned and we gobbled that meaty mess seasoned with penguin feathers, dirt, burnt blubber and reindeer hairs, and voted it the best dinner we'd ever had.

I went out afterwards to look again for the tent, though I imagined by now it had blown half-way to New Zealand. There was a small glow of light on the horizon, but the sky to the south was heaped with black clouds and I feared another blizzard would soon be on top of us. I was clambering sideways, slithering down the slope below the ridge, when I lost my footing and rolled clear to the bottom, and there, furled like an umbrella, lay the tent.

"Nothing will convince me this is all down to chance," I told Bill. "I really believe we've been saved for a purpose."

"We still have the journey back," he reminded.

"We'll make it," I said. "There's something else God has in store for us, something glorious. I'm sure of it."

"You may be right," he said, staring at me gravely, his one good eye so filled with concern that I turned my head away.

That night we packed the sledges ready for an early start. Cherry'd come a long way since he boarded the *Terra Nova* unable to say boo to a goose, and we had quite a fierce argument over the gear. Everything we carried was so swollen with frozen moisture that the weights had trebled, and he was for leaving most of it behind. Bill wouldn't hear of it; he said the Owner would never forgive him if we failed to return without every item. Later, Cherry confided that when the tent blew away he made up his mind to ask Bill for the morphia and put an end to it all. "My dear chap," I said, "he would never have agreed."

"I believe I did ask him," he said, "but he couldn't hear me on account of the wind and you yelling that gibberish about devotion to duty."

For six days the weather did its worst. Time and again we were forced to make camp as yet another blizzard raged about us. And by now our bags were in such a deplorable condition—we'd stopped bothering to roll them up and simply lashed them, coffin-shaped, onto the sledges—it hardly mattered whether we were in or out of them. As for sleeping, we got most rest on the march, falling into blissful dozes interrupted by our bumping into each other, at which we woke and comically cried out, "So sorry! Good morning, is everything all right?" We wasted a lot of our conscious hours working out how many years of our life we would give for a long, warm sleep.

Cherry thought two, and subsequently changed it to five, but that was when his bag split down the middle.

On the 28th the temperature was -47, and a crimson glow spread across the Barrier Edge. We wouldn't see the sun for another month but already the light was lasting longer and sometimes the sky turned blue. On the 29th, which was my birthday, though I didn't let on, we came in sight of Castle Rock. Cherry whooped with joy, and a piece of his front tooth spat into the snow. The cold had killed off the nerves in his jaw, and whenever he shouted his splintered teeth sprayed out in crumbs.

Two days later we were within five miles of Cape Evans. Over breakfast, a mug of hot water thickened with biscuit and a blob of butter, Bill said, "I want to thank you for what you've done. I couldn't have found two better companions, and what is more, I never shall."

Neither Cherry nor I could reply; our hearts were too full for words.

It may be that the purpose of the worst journey in the world had been to collect eggs which might prove a scientific theory, but we'd unravelled a far greater mystery on the way—the missing link between God and man is brotherly love.

Bill said we shouldn't go into the hut, not immediately; we ought to put up the tent and sleep outside. I had thought someone might be on the lookout for us, but there was no one in sight; even the dogs ignored our approach. We could hear Handel's *Water Music* on the gramophone. We stood there, trying to shift the harnesses from ourselves, moving like sleep-walkers.

Then the door opened. "Good God!" somebody called, and caught in a triangle of blinding light we froze, three men encased in ice.

The Other Side of Luck

by Greg Child

from *Thin Air: Encounters in the Himalayas*

In 1983, Greg Child, a well-known climber and writer, attempted the ascent of Broad Peak in the Himalayas of Pakistan with his partner Peter Thexton. On this trip, it was the extreme altitude that taught Child the madness of mountains.

Throughout the calm, clear morning of 25 June we watched the figures of Alan, Andy, Roger, and Jean leave their high bivouacs and head towards the summit of Broad Peak. A thousand feet below them, the two Polish women followed their tracks. Even through an 800 millimetre lens they appeared as mere specks beneath the rocky black pyramid of the main summit. The slant of the sun highlighted their tracks as they zigzagged across the great snowy terrace. They negotiated a small serac, then a steep chute, then gained the col at 25,591 feet between the main and central summits.

"They'll be on the summit in two hours," Doug forecasts.

As the figures move south on the long summit ridge they disappear behind a rocky promontory. Below them we see the Polish women turn around and descend from 24,500 feet, evidently deciding that the time is not ripe for them to push on. As the women descend they sway and stumble with fatigue. From a distant part of the mountain a savage crack rents the air as a huge avalanche cuts loose and blows up a thick cloud of debris.

Soon it will be time for us to leave for Broad Peak too. Pete and I decide to leave in the later afternoon to climb Broad Peak's initial couloirs by moonlight and reach Camp One while the snow is firmly frozen. Doug and Steve, with Don and Gohar, decide to leave at dawn on the 26th, after a full night's sleep. An hour before sunset, as the afternoon begins to gather and the light on the peaks around base camp softens to a gentle glow, Pete kisses Beth goodbye and we bid the camp farewell, heading across the glacier. Out in the centre of the icy wastes I pause to photograph K2, majestic and clear in the twilight.

"There'll be plenty of time for that," Pete says, hurrying me along toward the base of the three-crowned giant ahead of us.

Between base camp and the foot of Broad Peak lie two miles of glacier, crevassed and forested with a maze of ice towers, or *penitentes*. As Pete and I pick our path across suspect snow patches, moving from one rubbly island to another, we probe the snow with our ice axes to check for crevasses. We talk of the route ahead and check off items to ensure that nothing has been forgotten. As we make our way we talk about Lobsang. Yes—it had been perfection, and there would be more. We spoke of more climbs—he'd come to Yosemite and we'd climb El Capitan; I'd visit the Alps in winter; and maybe, just maybe, if Broad Peak went well, we'd find ourselves together on K2. A great warmth radiated from Pete onto me, like the alpenglow clinging to the mountains. His small kindnesses and carefully chosen words told me that I was at last breaking through the carefully guarded barrier with which he surrounded himself.

At a snow patch I probe forward, poking my ice axe shaft into the snow ahead. The snow feels firm. Nothing thuds or tinkles to imply a hollow surface. I deem it safe, but the very moment I assure Pete it is so and move forward, the surface gives way with a crash and I drop into a slot.

"Crevasse," I understate in the sudden quiet that follows smashed mirrors and glassware. I had the foolish surprise one would feel standing on a glass-topped table that had suddenly shattered. More surprising was that the crevasse had a false floor and I had stopped just a bodylength down. Beneath me I could see cracks in the floor that dropped into a black emptiness.

"Thought I'd lost you already," Pete said, seating himself on his pack as I extricated myself. Scalpel-sharp fins of ice had sliced hairline cuts into my arms and face. I looked as if I'd had a tussle with a wildcat.

Pete points over his shoulder. "You'll be pleased to know you've got an audience. Some trekkers watched the whole display from their camp a few hundred feet away."

"How embarrassing."

"Don't worry," Pete added impishly, "no one from our camp saw it."

As we enter the forest of *penitentes* the sun drops, leaving the air breathless and the summit rocks of K2 burning orange. The gurgle and rush of streams fall suddenly silent, choked by night's freeze. As we emerge from the icemaze, Broad Peak stands suddenly before us, its silhouette well defined as the Baltoro grows quickly black with night. On a bed of scree beneath the mountain we pause for a drink and a bite to eat. On the scree lies a cluster of old wooden wedges and hemp slings. We fiddle with these artifacts left by some predecessor, perhaps the Austrians Hermann Buhl, Kurt Diemberger, Fritz Winterstellar, and Marcus Schmuck, who pioneered the first ascent of Broad Peak in 1957 or, perhaps, they belonged to the tragic Polish expedition who'd made the first ascent of the 26,247-foot high Central Peak.

In late July 1975, six Poles set off up the face above us, climbing a more direct variation of the Austrian Route to the 25,591-foot col between the Main and Central summits. That variation has become the voie normal, but from the col they planned to climb the South Ridge of the Central Summit. Snow conditions were poor, the going slow. Beneath the col, as night and storm approached, one man, Roman Bebak, descended, leaving five to complete the climb. As the storm grew stronger and the five rushed to complete the route, three men—Bohdan Nowaczyk, Marek Kesicki, and Andrej Sikorski—took shelter from the wind on the final rock step below the summit, while Kazimierz Glazek and Janusz Kulis persevered to the top. At 7:30 pm Glazek and Kulis reached the summit, then descended to the others. The storm was now upon them. As the last man, Nowaczyk, made the final abseil to the col, the anchor pulled and he fell to his death, taking the vital ropes with him. Trapped in a raging storm and with no way to descend the steep, avalanche-prone chute beneath the col, the climbers bivouacked out, wearing only the clothes on their backs.

At first light they resumed their search for Nowaczyk and the ropes. Nothing was found. In desperation, they tied all their slings and harnesses together to construct a makeshift rope. In the afternoon Glazek descended the gully to the snow-fields and 300 feet down found a site for a bivouac. But behind him the weakened Sikorski slipped, knocking Kesicki and Kulis from the face. Sikorski fell 600 feet; Kesicki slid down the snow-fields and plummeted thousands of feet over the huge seracs; Kulis, the only one of the three to survive the fall, stopped 150 feet below Glazek. Glazek and Kulis endured a second terrible night in a snowhole, then continued down next morning, their fingers and feet frostbitten. Kulis would subsequently lose most of his fingers and toes. On the descent, they found Sikorski, partially buried in snow. Attempts to revive him proved fruitless: He was dead. The only traces of Kesicki were a few tufts of hair and some bloodstains on the snow.

As we enter the first couloirs of Broad Peak the full moon rounds the mountain and douses the West Face in a silvery light that bounces bright as daylight off the snow. We crampon our way quickly over the firm, crystalline surface until a rocky promontory appears, at 18,543 feet. Here sits a small tent—Camp One, established by the Polish women. Anna and Krystyna were climbing the mountain in siege style, placing fixed camps along the route, each stocked with bivvy gear, food, and fuel. We rest here an hour, make tea, then continue into the moonlight.

Step after step, breath after breath, every hour the atmosphere just a little thinner. Behind us, the first hint of dawn turns the Karakoram every shade of blue and gold imaginable, while the moon sits fixed in the sky, great and white, refusing to evaporate. The mountains glow, changing colour by the minute, like a horizon of chameleons. With this view over our shoulders, we zigzag through the gullies and towers of yellow limestone. As we reach the crest of a rocky spur at about 20,000 feet, blinding daylight and heat flood the mountain. Day reveals further relics of past expeditions: shredded tents, bits of fixed rope, and an old oxygen cylinder poking out of the snow. I pick up the steel cylinder to feel what it would be like to hump its weight up a mountain. Weighing at least 20 pounds, it feels like an unexploded bomb, but my lungs wish they could have a taste of the cylinder's juicy contents.

The half-melted tracks of our four members above pit the slope. As I slot my feet into their footsteps I play a brief game of pretend that I am following Buhl's tracks, back in 1957, the year of my birth, and the year too that he died, on Chogolisa. Heat dries our throats so we keep chewing handfuls of snow. Tiny black gnats, blown in from the plains, dot the surface of the snow. At first they look dead, but as the sun warms them they spring to life and crawl around.

At about 20,500 feet on the morning of 26 June we meet Alan, Andy, Roger, and Jean, returning from their successful ascent of the previous day. They look tired, almost aged.

"Well done," Pete says to Andy and Alan, who reach us first and describe their windless summit day.

"It's no punter's peak up there," Alan says. "The summit ridge is at 26,000 feet and is bloody long. Technical too. Andy felt sick all the way along the ridge. And Roger nearly bought it on the descent—he tried to glissade down from the col, got out of control, lost his ice-axe, and went sliding down. By a miracle he stopped in some soft snow."

Andy considers us wearily. "Now I know what they mean when people say '8,000 metres.'" And down they go, sucking at the atmosphere that grew thicker with each step.

From our position on the spur, we can see the jet-black Central and Main summits far above. To the north is K2. To our left, the 300-foot-tall ice cliffs at the foot of the West Face's great snow terrace, above which our route will skirt, appear to threaten our path. This is, however, an optical illusion, for the cliffs are far to the side. Even so, whenever there is a crack and rumble of falling ice we look up in alarm.

At about 21,600 feet Pete stops and points ahead. "Hey—I see numbers!"

"What? You're hallucinating!"

"No. Look—on the side of the Central Peak—three numbers—666."

I scan the wall and just as I feel certain that Pete is succumbing to hypoxia I too see a chance play of sunlight on white snow and black rock that bears a perfect resemblance to three sixes.

"Looks as though Crowley left his mark here too," says Pete, referring to Aleister Crowley, the Irish mountaineer and Satanist who'd been on the flanks of K2 in 1902.

Crowley believed the number 666 had magical powers. On K2's Northeast Ridge his party had reached 20,000 feet with a contingent of Balti porters but steep ice had halted them. Disappointed at the decision to retreat Crowley, who referred to himself as "The Great Beast," got into a violent quarrel with his partner, Guy Knowles, and threatened him with a revolver that he pulled from his pack. A fight ensued that almost dragged the two men over the precipice until Knowles wrested the weapon from Crowley. Seventy-six years later, a strong American expedition climbed the Northeast Ridge, shortly after a Polish team had pioneered the route to over 8,000 metres.

We reach Camp Two at 21,998 feet, late that morning, just as the heat becomes stifling and the snow turns to mush. Here stands another tent left in place by the Polish women. We slip into it and begin to melt snow to fend off dehydration. Doug and Steve reach us in the early afternoon and pitch a tent nearby while we begin to sleep off our long night-shift.

The next morning, 27 June, is again clear. We climb a long, low-angled spur of snow and ice until noon, when at 22,802 feet we find a third ragged and fluttering Polish tent. Here, we all rest and brew up for an hour. Wind cuts fiercely across the slope and rams into the tent's nylon walls. As we set off again Don and Gohar arrive. Don moves in spritely fashion for all his 50 years. These two decide to bivvy here, while Doug, Steve, Pete, and I set off to camp higher. We agree that while we go to the summit the next day, Don and Gohar will move up and occupy our high camp for their own summit bid the following day.

"Better keep climbing if we're going to make it up this hill," Doug says, and we set off.

As we gain elevation K2 disappears behind Broad Peak's squarish Central Summit. Occasional clouds now wander across our path, engulfing us and creating eerie contrasts of diffuse light over the stark neutrals of white snow and black rock. We spread out over the slope, carving a diagonal route upwards, Doug striding powerfully in front, then Steve, me, and finally Pete. At 3:00 pm, at the site of Alan's and Andy's bivouac, we pause for another brew. Their snow cave resembles less a cave than a rabbit hole. Steve checks the altimeter.

"24,300 feet," he announces. It is the highest Steve and I have ever been, short of flying.

We set off again, trudging and gasping at the altitude until twilight begins to darken the mountain. At 24,500 feet, near a jumble of 100-foot-tall seracs, I clear a platform to place our tent, light the stove to melt a pan of snow, and await Pete. Doug and Steve climb through the serac and bivvy 300 feet above. Twenty minutes pass. Pete approaches slowly, coughing raucously.

"Hurry up Pete—you've got the tent!" I call, feeling the cold night bite into my fingers and toes. He staggers up to me, panting at the unsubstantial air, then dumps his pack, and sits on it. I hand him a hot brew. He guzzles it and quickly revives.

"How are you feeling?" I ask.

"Just tired. I'll be better with a rest."

It is late into the night before we finish melting snow for drink. Even then we feel we could have consumed a gallon more.

Our stomachs feel queasy with altitude. Out of the sweets, chocolate, Grain Bars and tinned fish we carry, it is a salty can of sardines that sates us most; with the huge fluid loss through breathing and exertion at altitude our body salts are dropping low. Pete's cough disappears as he rehydrates, then sleep descends on us. I begin to realize the deficit in sleep we have amassed by climbing around the clock for so many hours and by pushing ourselves up the mountain so late into the day.

During that night the altitude creeps into our heads. By morning it is bashing away from inside our skulls. Waking is a long and difficult process, cloudy and drug-like. The crack of wind on the tent walls and the crinkle of our frost-covered Gore-Tex sleeping bags are soon accompanied by the hiss of the stove. While I melt snow I hear Pete mumbling in his sleep, in between the sporadic gasping of Cheynes-Stokes breathing.

"What about this rope then?" he asks.

"Rope? Our rope is in the pack."

"Noooo, not that rope," he chides.

"Then what rope?"

"The rope we're all tied into."

"We're not tied in Pete, we're in the tent, Camp Four, Broad Peak."

"Noooo, you don't understand," and I began to feel like a thick-headed schoolboy giving all the wrong answers. I plied him for more clues to his sleepy riddle and got this:

"It's the rope that all of us are tied to."

"Fixed rope?"

"Noooo," he whined.

"Umbilical cord?" Any wild guess now.

"Noooo!"

"Then you must be speaking of a metaphysical rope eh, one that everyone is tied to but no one is tied to?" But before I can get an answer the smell of sweet tea wakes him. "How is your head?" I ask, as I try to force some hot oatmeal down my throat.

"Terrible." Both of us squint from the pounding pain in our temples.

"Mine too. Maybe we should go down."

"No. Mornings are always the worst. We're nearly there. Give me some aspirin. We'll be OK."

We quaff down three aspirin each and set off, carrying nothing in our packs but a stove. The steep ice of the serac gets our blood flowing and clears our heads. As I pull onto the slope above the serac I see Doug and Steve stomping out the last few feet of the final chute to the col. Following their tracks I enter the steep chute two hours later, wade through soft snow, and arrive at the 25,591-foot col. Here, on Broad Peak's first ascent in 1957, Buhl had almost given up, slumping in the snow until his doggedness and Diemberger's enthusiasm had urged him onto his feet and on to the summit. A strong wind gusts from the north, splashing spindrift over the summit ridge. Ahead, the prow-like summit just toward Sinkiang China. Beneath me, in Sinkiang, lie the North Gasherbrum Glacier, and deep within a fold of valley, the Shaksgam River. China's rust-coloured landscape contrasts sharply with the blinding white of the Godwin-Austen Glacier and the peaks of the Karakoram.

Pete labours up to me via the chute the Austrians in '57 had found to be verglassed, the Poles in '75 a bed of ice, and we in '83 a ribbon of steep snow. While awaiting Pete I'd fallen asleep long enough for the lump of ice I'd dumped in the pan to melt and boil. As I make a brew, Doug and Steve wave from their position on the ridge a few hundred feet away. We signal back. All is well, the summit a few hours away, and within sight. The sky is intensely clear all across Baltistan. Nanga Parbat, 150 miles away, stands on the southwest horizon. Straddling the border of Pakistan and China, as Broad Peak itself does, lies the pyramidal Gasherbrum IV, immediately to our south, and visible to the left of Broad Peak's Main Summit. Gasherbrum IV is an impressive sight, with its unclimbed Northwest Ridge directly before us and the Northeast Ridge of the first ascent on the left. I recall that an American team is working on the Northwest Ridge and wonder if they are gasping away somewhere on the final rocky headwall capping the mountain.

"That's a beautiful mountain down there," Pete remarks of Gasherbrum IV. "We ought to give that Northwest Ridge a shot next season, if it isn't climbed this year."

I agree and we set off along Broad Peak's mile-long summit ridge at ten o'clock.

Along the summit ridge lies the most technical climbing yet, short steps of compact snow interspersed with rock outcrops. We rope up and move together, pausing to belay over tricky sections. The first difficulties of the ridge lie in skirting a large limestone block, across which an old piece of bleached rope is strung, knotted to a rusting piton. As I lead across, in crampons, mitts, and down suit, I squint at the rock and check my eyes to be sure I'm not hallucinating, for the rock over which I climb is pitted with the fossils of sea-shells. Eons ago, this piece of the earth lay on the ocean floor; now it stands at 8,000 metres.

As we near the summit the strain of altitude grows. Each step becomes increasingly harsh. When we pass through the door of 8,000 metres and enter the region climbers call the "death zone," disorientation and fatigue take an exponential leap. At perhaps one o'clock Doug and Steve pass us on their return from the summit.

"We summited at 11:30 am. It's even windier and colder up there," Doug says, shouting above the wind. Plumes of spindrift curl over the ridge ahead.

"How far away?" I ask.

"An hour."

"Doug, let's go. I can't feel my feet," shouts Steve.

Doug yells into my ear: "We'll get as far down the mountain tonight as we can. Good luck, kid." They move off, their steps jerky and tired. Pete and I are now as alone as we will ever be.

Moving at 8,000 metres is like wading through treacle. I gradually become aware of a peculiar sense of disassociation with myself, as if a part of me is external to my body, yet is looking on. I feel this most when setting up boot-axe belays or making difficult moves, a strong feeling as if someone is peering over my shoulder keeping an eye on me, or even as if I have a second invisible head on my shoulders.

We traverse for another half-hour to the False Summit, an icy, corniced dome at 26,382 feet. There we sit, looking toward the tantalizingly close Main Summit. By now those sensations of disassociation are punctuated by feelings of total absence: momentary blackouts, when neither I nor the guy over my shoulder seem to be around. I emerge from these absences a few paces from where they struck me, leading to a concern over stepping off the narrow ridge. "Like a dream," I mutter to Pete, but the wind snatches my words away before he hears them.

I look ahead: The corniced ridge dips down and curves left in a final long, easy slope to the summit, only 18 feet higher than our position. We are nearly there, 30 minutes away. But my fears about what is happening to me double. A vicious headache rings in my ears and pounds at my temples, and a tingling in my arms grows so intense that my fingers curl into a tight fist, making it hard to grip my ice axe. My last shred of rational consciousness raises a cry of concern over the possibility of a stroke, or cerebral edema. But to articulate this to Pete is difficult, as speech and thought seem to have no link in my mind. Exhaustion I can understand, and given that alone I might have crawled to the summit, but something alien is going on within me and I am not prepared to push my luck with it. I get it out that I want down. Pete kneels beside me and gazes at the summit, so near yet so far.

"Go down? But we're so close! Just half an hour!"

The idea of turning away from success when it is so close is maddening to me too, and Pete's ever present determination nearly gets me going. I try to ascertain whether the sensations I feel are imaginary, or are really the beginning of some short circuiting of my body chemistry. There is a state of mind that sometimes infests climbers in which the end result achieves a significance beyond anything that the future may hold. For a few minutes or hours one casts aside all that has been previously held as worth living for, and focuses on one risky move or a stretch of ground that becomes the only thing that has ever mattered. This state of mind is what is both fantastic and reckless about the game. Since everything is at stake in these moments, one had better be sure to recognize them and have no illusions about what lies on the other side of luck. It is one of those times. I have to weigh up what is important and what is most important.

"It'd be nice to reach the top, you and I," Pete says. And so it would, to stand up there with this man who had become such a strong friend in such a short time.

"Didn't you say that summits are important?" he adds. Those are my words he is throwing back at me, shouting above the wind and his own breathlessness, harking back to my determination of a few weeks before that we should succeed on Lobsang Spire. I struggle to compose an intelligible sentence.

"Only important when you're in control . . . Lost control . . . Too high, too fast. You go on. I'll wait below."

"No—we stay together," he replies.

Strain is written on Pete's face as much as mine. In 60 hours we'd climbed from 15,500 feet to over 26,000 feet. We had found our limits. The decision to descend comes without a word. We just get up and begin the long path down, seeing that those red hills in China are now covered in cotton wool clouds, encircling K2 and lapping at Broad Peak's East Face.

A few hundred feet from our high point I feel a sensation like a light blank out in my brain. I have just enough time to kneel down before I slump backwards onto a patch of snow, then black out into a half-world of semi-consciousness and inaction. . . .

"So this is it," I think with a strangely detached curiosity as the day turns pitch; "this is where the plunge into senselessness and apathy begins, where the shades of death descend." Yet at the same time I am conscious of my swaying head and my incoherent mumbling. I think of Salley, whom I have no right to inflict such folly upon. "Get up you idiot, get up," I keep telling myself, until vision gradually returns. How long had I been out? I cannot tell.

Next to me sits Pete, observing my state as a good doctor should. He wears a white lab coat with a stethoscope draped around his neck; I double-check; nonsense. He is wearing his red high-altitude suit. I am beginning to imagine things. A minute later I regain control of myself, as suddenly as I'd lost it. Pete puts a brew of hot grape drink in my hands. As soon as I drink the liquid I throw it up.

"See . . . told you I was sick." The purple stain in the snow forms intricate arabesque designs that grow onto the snow crystals glinting in the afternoon light. I could have watched these hallucinations all day, but Pete urges us onto our feet. Rapidly I begin to improve. My strength and mental faculties return. I'd made it back through the 8,000-metre door before it slammed shut and locked me in. But I'd cut it close.

In the warm glow of evening I take Pete's photo as we reach the col: The summit stands behind him. Had we made the right decision? Should we go on? Would we have the strength to return later? I feel remorse at having let Pete down, but then the tables suddenly turn: Pete appears over a crest on the col, lagging on the end of the rope. He takes short steps and looks stressed.

"I can't breathe properly," he says in a whisper. "It feels as if my diaphragm has collapsed."

A bolt of fear runs up my spine.

"Are my lips blue?" he asks.

"Yes," I say, noting the indication of oxygen starvation.

We stare at each other.

"We'll get down," I blurt out, and we turn and crunch tracks to the end of the wind-blown col. Things were wrong, very wrong. We had to shed altitude, and fast, but a snail's pace was the best Pete could manage in this thin soup of air. We reach the steep chute that we'd climbed to reach the col. The hour is late, about 7:00 pm, but we seem outside of time: we are simply there. I wrap a sling around a spike, double our short rope, and I abseil 60 feet to the start of the snowfield. Pete follows.

On the snowfield wind and driving snow had covered all sign of our tracks. "I'll go ahead and break trail. Follow as fast as you can," I say and Pete nods in response. Dragging the rope behind me I begin loping down the slope. After 300 feet I turn to see that Pete has barely moved.

"Pete!"

No answer.

By the time I fight my way back through the soft snow the last gleam of twilight peters out in the sky and night is upon us. Where had the hours gone? Pete has his headlamp on. It shines out to the windy night. He doesn't speak. When I turn toward the glacier I see a pinpoint of light shining up from base camp, 11,000 feet below. It's Beth, his girlfriend far below, giving the eight o'clock signal as arranged, and Pete is returning it.

Conversation is superfluous. We know we're going to be on the move all night, very high, and in rising wind and storm. Already, clouds are blocking out the stars. I tie the rope to Pete's harness and begin belaying him down, length after length, till his strength begins to ebb. Then I talk him down, ordering and cajoling every step out of him. At about 10:00 pm he collapses in the snow and whispers he can no longer see. So I guide him by direction, telling him to traverse 45-degrees right, or straight down. Even on the easiest ground he has to face in. Without tracks it's all instinct anyway. And all the time wind and spindrift swirl across the slope, and the bastard moon shines everywhere but on the upper slopes of Broad Peak. There is no time to think of what might happen to us, but only that we must move down, move down, move down.

The hours melt into a pastiche of endless, dreamlike movement. Pete becomes too weak to walk, so somehow I support him, dragging him, lowering him, whatever it takes to move. The sensation of being outside of myself is more prevalent than ever. My watcher checks my every move and decision. I keep turning around, expecting to see someone. As I mechanically work toward getting us down, part of my mind begins to wander. I find myself thinking of that first ascent of the Central Summit, by the Poles. The account I'd read called their stormy descent a "struggle for survival." Accompanying the story was a photo of Broad Peak, littered with crosses where climbers had perished. Those crosses were now underfoot, and the ghosts of history were hiding in the shadows. I find that agnostics also pray.

The slope steepens, indicating that somewhere nearby is the band of ice cliffs we'd climbed that morning. We need to find the low spot in them by which we'd ascended, but where that was was anyone's guess. We link arms and shuffle towards what I hope was our earlier position. The wind howls and Pete inches around uncertainly.

"If only I could see . . ."

"I'm your eyes, Pete—move right ten steps!"

And he does.

It soon becomes too steep to blunder about as we are, so I begin making 20-foot leads, shoving my axe into the soft snow and belaying Pete in to me. At the last belay he lets go of everything and swings down to the edge of the ice cliff. The shaft of my axe droops alarmingly. I lose my cool and yell a mouthful of curses at him as I haul him back up.

"Sorry," he whispers calmly. Throughout the ordeal he had remained composed, conserving his energy for matters of survival, rather than letting fear take hold. I clip him to his axe and wrap his arms around it.

"Just don't lose it now, brother. Please."

The wind attacks with unprecedented malice. Waves of spindrift hiss down around us, burning our faces. If my back-tracking is correct, then somewhere in the darkness at the bottom of the ice cliff is our tent, and if things have gone as planned, Don and Gohar are in it. I call till my throat is raw, then shove my ice-axe in to the hilt, from which to lower Pete. Confusion reigns in the seconds it takes to lower him, he is so disoriented that he cannot tell whether he is at the bottom of the cliff or not, I am blinded by spindrift, and feel the axe shifting out of the snow. I wrap the rope around my arm to distribute some of the weight while holding the axe in with my knee. Pete gasps in distress as the rope pinches his waist.

"Are you down?"

"Can't . . . tell."

"For God's sake, you gotta be down!"

He comes to a stop and digs his hands into the snow. I abseil off my second short tool, moving quickly before it slides out. At the bottom of the serac we again link arms to negotiate some broken ground. I glance about, searching with my headlamp for a familiar lump of ice to tell me that we have descended the ice cliffs in the right spot. Then, suddenly, a light appears, illuminating the form of a tent.

"We've got a sick man here, Don," I call to the light. Pete crawls a few feet along a crest of snow then stops completely. A bobbing headlamp approaches. It is Gohar, himself groggy, woken from a deep sleep. I lie on my back, sit with Pete on my shoulders, and slide us down the last 60 feet to the tent, while Gohar belays us. As Don drags Pete into the tent it comes around to 2:00 am. We have been moving for 22 hours.

In the quiet of the tent we lie, all crammed in together, rubbing each other's limbs and melting snow to get vital fluids back into us. Feeling takes a long time to return to my hands and feet, and Pete's are ice cold, yet remarkably, not frostbitten. Warm liquid perks him up.

"How are you Gregor?" Pete asks with a hopeful spark in his voice.

"Done in. Rest a couple of hours till dawn, then we'll head on down."

"I'll watch him, lad," Don says.

I stagger out to repitch our tent, the tent that Pete and I had collapsed and weighted with snow blocks that morning so it wouldn't blow away. It is filled with snow and the foam pads are gone. I throw the rope down for insulation and crawl into my sleeping bag. It seems that a million years have passed since we set out. We've gone beyond mental and physical barriers that we didn't even know existed within us. We'd become a single entity, fighting to survive. Nothing could stop us from getting down now. In a couple of days this would be just an experience we would have shared to become closer. All the bullshit of ethics, ego, competition, and the glamour of big summits have been scraped aside to reveal that in the end everything boils down to one thing—life! My eyelids close under the weight of exhaustion and I dream of grassy places.

But those words of Pete's were the last we ever shared. Two hours later, at dawn on 29 June, he awoke to ask Gohar for water. Gohar pressed a cup of warm liquid to Pete's lips, but Pete didn't drink from it. Don and Gohar looked at each other for a few seconds then called me. I awoke with a throbbing headache. "Dead," they were saying. But that was impossible! We'd made it through that hellish descent! We were going to make it down! Then sense prevailed like a sledge-hammer. I rushed into the tent and tried to force life into him, through his mouth, with mine, forcing my own thin, tired air into him. His lungs gurgled loudly, saturated with the fluid of pulmonary edema. I tore his jacket open and rhythmically pounded my palms against his chest to squeeze a beat from his heart, but he would have none of it. He would only lie there with an expression of sublime rest on his face, as if dreaming the same grassy dream I had dreamed.

Cadillac Desert

by Marc Reisner
from *Cadillac Desert*

The story of one-armed John Wesley Powell and the first exploration of the Colorado River is one of the great stories of the American West.

On the 24th of May, 1869, the Powell Geographic Expedition set out on the Green River from the town of Green River, Wyoming, in four wooden dories: the *Maid of the Canyon,* the *Kitty Clyde's Sister,* the *Emma Dean,* and the *No Name.* For a scientific expedition, it was an odd group. Powell, the leader, was the closest thing to a scientist. He had brought along his brother Walter—moody, sarcastic, morose, one of the thousands of psychiatric casualties of the Civil War. The rest of the party was made up mostly of mountain men: O. G. Howland, his brother Seneca, Bill Dunn, Billy Hawkins, and Jack Sumner, all of whom had been collected by Powell en route to Green River. He had also invited a beet-faced Englishman named Frank

Goodman, who had been patrolling the frontier towns looking for adventure, and Andy Hall, an eighteen-year-old roustabout whose casual skill as an oarsman had impressed Powell when he saw him playing with a boat on the Green River. There was also George Bradley, a tough guy whom Powell had met by accident at Fort Bridger and who had agreed to come along in exchange for a discharge from the army, which Powell managed to obtain for him.

For sixty miles out of the town of Green River, the river was sandy-bottomed and amiable. There were riffles, but nothing that could legitimately be called a rapid. The boatmen played in the currents, acquiring a feel for moving water; the others admired the scenery. As they neared the Uinta Mountains, they went into a sandstone canyon colored in marvelous hues, which Powell, who had a knack for naming things, called Flaming Gorge. The river bore southward until it came up against the flanks of the range, then turned eastward and entered Red Canyon.

In Red Canyon, the expedition got its first lesson in how a few feet of drop per mile can turn a quiet river into something startling. Several of the rapids frightened them into racing for shore and lining or portaging, an awful strain with several thousand pounds of boats, supplies, and gear. After a while, however, even the bigger rapids were not so menacing anymore—if, compared to what was about to come, one could call them big.

Beyond Flaming Gorge the landscape opened up into Brown's Park, but soon the river gathered imperceptible momentum and the canyon ramparts closed around them like a pair of jaws. A maelstrom followed. Huge scissoring waves leaped between naked boulders; the river plunged into devouring holes. The awestruck Andy Hall recited an alliterative verse he had learned as a Scottish schoolboy, "The Cataract of Lodore," by the English Romantic poet Robert Southey.

Over Powell's objection—he did not like using a European name—
the stretch became the Canyon of Lodore.

As they approached the first big rapid in the canyon, the *No
Name* was sucked in by the accelerating current before anyone had a
chance to scout. "I pass around a great crag just in time to see the
boat strike a rock and rebounding from the shock careen and fill the
open compartment with water," wrote Powell in his serialized journal of the trip. "Two of the men lost their oars, she swings around,
and is carried down at a rapid rate broadside on for quite a few yards
and strikes amidships on another rock with great force, is broken
quite in two, and then men are thrown into the river, the larger part
of the boat floating buoyantly. They soon seize it and down the river
they drift for a few hundred yards to a second rapid filled with huge
boulders where the boat strikes again and is dashed to pieces and the
men and fragments are soon carried beyond my sight."

The three crew members survived, but most of the extra
clothes, the barometers, and several weeks' worth of food were
gone. The next day the party found the stern of the boat intact, still
holding the barometers, some flour, and a barrel of whiskey that
Powell, who was something of a prig, did not realize had been
smuggled aboard. When they finally floated out of Lodore Canyon
into the sunlit beauty of Echo Park, Powell wrote in his journal
that despite "a chapter of disaster and toil . . . the canyon of Lodore
was not devoid of scenic interest, even beyond the power of the pen
to tell." And O. G. Howland, who nearly lost his life in Disaster
Falls, wrote haughtily that "a calm, smooth stream is a horror we all
detest now."

Desolation Canyon. Gray Canyon. They were now in territory
even Indians hadn't seen. The landscape closed in and opened up.
Labyrinth Canyon. Stillwater Canyon. They shot a buck and scared

a bighorn lamb off a cliff, their first fresh meat in weeks. Powell, climbing a cliff with his one arm, got himself rimmed and required rescue by Bradley, who got above him, dangled his long johns, and pulled Powell up.

The country grew drier and more desolate. Fantastic mesas loomed in the distance, banded like shells. The Grand Mesa, to the east, the largest mesa in the world, rose to eleven thousand feet from desert badlands into an alpine landscape of forests and lakes. Wind-eroded shiprocks loomed over the rubblized beds of prehistoric seas. Battlements of sandstone rose in the distance like ruins of empire. Deep in uncharted territory the Colorado River, then known as the Grand, rushed in quietly from the northeast, carrying the snowmelt of Longs Peak and most of western Colorado. The river's volume had now doubled, but still it remained quite placid. Was it conceivable that they were near the end of its run? Powell was tempted to believe so, but knew better. There were four thousand feet of elevation loss ahead.

On the 21st, after a short stop to rest and reseal the boats, they were on the water again, which was high, roiled, and the color of cocoa. In a few miles they came to a canyon, frothing with rapids. They lined or portaged wherever they could, ran if they had no alternative. Soon they were between vertical walls and the river was roaring mud. Cataracts launched them downriver before they had time to think; waves like mud huts threw them eight feet into the air. The scouts would venture ahead if there was room enough to walk, and return ashen-faced. They canyon relented a little at times, so they could portage, but the river did not. In one day, they made three-quarters of a mile in Cataract Canyon, portaging everything they saw.

During the daytime, the temperature would reach 106 degrees; at night the men shivered in their dank drawers. Some became edgy, prone to violent outbursts. Bradley's incendiary moods lasted through most of a day, and he would run almost anything rather than portage. Powell's instinctive caution infuriated Bradley, as did his indefatigable specimen gathering, surveying, and consignment of everything to notes. The pace was maddeningly uneven: they would do eight miles in a day, then a mere mile or two. Two months' worth of food remained, most of it musty bread, dried apples, spoiled bacon, and coffee. Once, Billy Hawkins got up in the middle of dinner, walked to the boats, and pulled out the sextant. He said he was trying to find the latitude and longitude of the nearest pie.

On the 23rd of July they passed a foul-smelling little stream coming in from the west; they called it the Dirty Devil. The big river quieted. The hunters took off up the cliffsides and returned with a couple of desert bighorn sheep, which were devoured with sybaritic abandon. The sheep were an omen. For the next several days, they floated on a brisk but serene river through a canyon such as no one had seen. Instead of the pitiless angular black-burned walls of Cataract Canyon, they were now enveloped by rounded pink-and-salmon-colored sandstone, undulating ahead of them in soft contours. There were huge arched chasms, arcadian glens hung with maidenhair ferns, zebra-striped walls, opalescent green fractures irrigated by secret springs. Groping for a name that would properly convey their sense of both awe and relief, Powell decided on Glen Canyon. On August 1 and 2, the party camped in Music Temple.

By the 5th of August, they were down to fifteen pounds of rancid bacon, several bags of matted flour, a small store of dried apples, and a large quantity of coffee. Other than that they would have to try to live off the land, but the land was mostly vertical and the game, which had never been plentiful, had all but disappeared. They met the Escalante River, draining unknown territory in Utah, then the San Juan, carrying in snowmelt from southwestern Colorado.

The river on which they were floating was made up now of most of the mentionable runoff of the far Southwest. They were in country that no white person had seen, riding the runoff of a region the size of Iraq, and they approached each blind bend in the river with a mixture of anticipation and terror. Soon the soft sandstone of Glen Canyon was replaced by the fabulous coloration of Marble Canyon. Then, on August 14, the hard black rock of Cataract Canyon reemerged from the crust of the earth. "The river enters the gneiss!" wrote Powell. Downriver, they heard what sounded like an avalanche.

Soap Creek Rapids, Badger Creek Rapids, Crystal Creek Rapids, Lava Falls. Nearly all of the time, the creeks that plunge down the ravines of the Grand Canyon will barely float a walnut shell, but the flash floods resulting from a desert downpour can dislodge boulders as big as a jitney bus. Tumbled by gravity, the boulders carom into the main river and sit there, creating a dam, which doesn't so much stop the river as make it mad. Except for the rapids of the Susitna, the Niagara, and perhaps a couple of rivers in Canada, the modern Colorado's rapids are the biggest on the continent. Before the dams were built, however, the Colorado's rapids were *really* big. At Lava Falls, where huge chunks of basalt dumped in the main river create a thirty-foot drop, waves at flood stage were as high as three-story houses. There was a cycling wave at the bottom that, every few seconds, would burst apart with the retort of a sixteen-inch gun, drenching anyone on either bank of the river—two hundred feet apart. To run Lava Falls today, in a thirty-foot Hypalon raft, wrapped in a Mae West life jacket, vaguely secure in the knowledge that a rescue helicopter sits on the canyon rim, is a lesson in panic. The Powell expedition was running most of the canyon's rapids in a fifteen-foot pilot boat made of pine and a couple of twenty-one-foot dories made of oak—with the rudest of life jackets, without hope of rescue, without a single human being within hundreds of miles. And Powell himself was running them strapped to a captain's chair, gesticulating wildly with his one arm.

The river twisted madly. It swung north, then headed south, then back north, then east—east!—then back south. Even Powell, constantly consulting sextant and compass, felt flummoxed. The rapids, meanwhile, had grown so powerful that the boats received a terrible battering from the force of the waves alone, and had to be recaulked every day. As they ran out of food and out of caulk, Powell realized that the men were also beginning to run out of will. There was mutiny in their whisperings.

August 25. They had come thirty-five miles, including a portage around a spellbinding rapid where a boulder dam of hardened lava turned the river into the aftermath of Vesuvius. (That, as it turned out, had been Lava Falls.) There were still no Grand Wash Cliffs, which would signal the confluence with the Virgin River and the end of their ordeal. They saw, for the first time in weeks, some traces of Indian habitation, but obviously no one had lived there in years. Occasionally they caught a glimpse of trees on the canyon rim, five thousand feet above. They were in the deepest canyon any of them had ever seen.

August 26. They came on an Indian garden full of fresh squash. With starvation imminent, they stole a dozen gourds and ate them ravenously. "We are three-quarters of a mile in the depths of the earth," wrote Powell. "And the great river shrinks into insignificance, as it dashes its angry waves against the walls and cliffs, that rise to the world above; they are but puny ripples and we but pigmies, running up and down the sands or lost among the boulders. . . . But," he added hopefully, "a few more days like this and we are out of prison."

August 27. The river, which had been tending toward the west, veered again toward the south. The hated Precambrian granite, which had dropped below the riverbed, surfaced again. Immediately came a rapid which they decided to portage. At eleven o'clock in the morning, they came to the worst rapids yet.

"The billows are huge," wrote Bradley. "The spectacle is appalling." It was, Jack Sumner wrote, a "hell of foam." The rapids was bookended by cliffs; there was no way to portage and no way to line. There wasn't even a decent way to scout.

After the party had had a meal of fried flour patties and coffee, O. G. Howland asked Powell to go for a walk with him. The major knew what was coming. It saddened him that if there was to be mutiny, the leader would be Howland. He was a mountain man by nature and experience, but after Powell, still the most literate and scientific-minded of the group. Nonetheless, Howland had been plagued by bad luck; it was he who had steered the *No Name* to its destruction in Lodore Canyon; he who had twice lost maps and notes in swampings. He had tested fate enough. In the morning, Howland told Powell, he and his brother Seneca, together with Bill Dunn, were going to abandon the boats and climb out of the canyon.

Powell did not sleep that night. He took reading after reading with his sextant until he was as positive as he dared be that they were within fifty miles of Grand Wash Cliffs. At the most, they ought to be four days from civilization, with the only remaining obstacle in view a wild twenty-second ride through a terrific rapid. Powell woke Howland in the middle of the night and poured out his conviction, but it was too late. His immediate reaction was two laconic sentences in his journal, but later he offered this version of what took place:

> We have another short talk about the morrow, but for
> me there is no sleep. All night long, I pace up and
> down a little path, of a few yards of sand and beach,

along by the river. Is it wise to go on? I go to the boats again, to look at our rations. I feel satisfied that we can get over the danger immediately before us; what there may be below I know not. From our outlook yesterday, on the cliffs, the cañon seemed to make another great bend to the south, and this, from our experience heretofore, means more and higher granite walls. I am not sure that we can climb out of the cañon here, and, when at the top of the wall, I know enough of the country to be certain that it is a desert of rock and sand, between this and the nearest Mormon town, which on the most direct line, must be seventy-five miles away. True, the last rains have been favorable to us, should we go out, for the probabilities are that we shall find water still standing in holes, and, at one time, I almost conclude to leave the river. But for years I have been contemplating this trip. To leave the exploration unfinished, to say that there is a part of the cañon which I cannot explore, having already almost accomplished it, is more than I am willing to acknowledge, and I determine to go on.

August 28. Breakfast was as "solemn as a funeral." Afterward, Powell asked all of the men, for the last time, whether they planned to go ahead or climb out. The Howlands and Bill Dunn still intended to walk out; the rest would remain. The party gave the three some guns and offered them their equal share of the remaining rations. They accepted the guns. "Some tears are shed," Powell wrote. "It is rather a solemn parting; each party thinks the other is taking the dangerous course." Billy Hawkins stole away and laid some biscuits on a rock the mutineers would pass on their way up the cliffs. "They are as fine fellows as I ever had the good fortune to meet," declared taciturn George Bradley, blinking away a tear.

As the others rowed cautiously toward the monster rapids in their two boats, the Howland brothers and Bill Dunn had already begun climbing up one of the canyon arroyos. Powell felt himself torn between watching them and the approaching rapids. They plunged down the first drop. The hydraulic wave at the bottom inundated them, but the water was so swift that they were out of it before the boat could fill. They were launched atop a pillow of water covering a rock, slid off, then rode out a landscape of haystacks. As the *Maid of the Canyon* circulated quietly in the whirlpool at rapids' end, *Kitty Clyde's Sister* wallowed up alongside. The roar of the rapids was almost submerged by the men's ecstatic shouts. They grabbed rifles and fired volley after volley into the air to show their erstwhile companions that it could be done. Unable to see around the bend in the river or to walk back up, they waited in the eddy for nearly two hours, hoping the others would rejoin them, but they never did.

A few miles below Separation Rapid, the party came to another rapid, Lava Cliffs, which, were it not now under the waters of Lake Mead, would perhaps be the biggest on the river. In a style so much like the man himself—exact and fastidious, yet felicitous and engaging—Powell wrote down what happened there:

[O]n [the] northern side of the canyon [is] a bold escarpment that seems to be a hundred feet high. We can climb it and walk along its summit to a point where we are just at the head of the fall. Here the basalt is broken down again, so it seems to us, and I direct the men to take a line to the top of the cliff and let the boats down along the wall. One man remains in the boat to keep her clear of the rocks and prevent her line from being caught on the projecting angles. I climb the cliff and pass along to a point just over the fall and descend by broken rocks, and find that the break of the fall is above the break of the wall, so that we cannot land, and that still below the river is very bad, and that there is no possibility of a portage. Without waiting further to examine and determine what shall be done, I hasten back to the top of the cliff to stop the boats from coming down. When I arrive I find the men have let one of them down to the head of the fall. She is in swift water and they are not able to pull her back; nor are they able to go on with the line, as it is not long enough to reach the higher part of the cliff which is just before them; so they take a bight around a crag. I send two men back for the other line. The boat is in very swift water, and Bradley is standing in the open compartment, holding out his oar to prevent her from striking against the foot of the cliff. Now she shoots out into the stream and up as far as the line will permit, and then, wheeling, drives headlong against the rock, and then out and back again, now straining on the line, now striking against the rock. As soon as the second line is brought, we pass it down to him; but his attention is all taken up with his own situation, and he does not see that we are passing him the line. I stand on a projecting rock, waving my hat to gain his attention, for my voice is drowned by the roaring of the falls. Just at this moment I see him take his knife from its sheath and step forward to cut the line. He has evidently decided that it is better to go over with the boat as it is than to wait for her to be broken to pieces. As he leans over, the boat sheers again into the stream, the stem-post breaks away and she is loose. With perfect composure Bradley seizes the great scull oar, places it in the stern rowlock, and pulls with all his power (and he is an athlete) to turn the bow of the boat down stream, for he wishes to go bow down, rather than to drift broad-side on. One, two strokes he makes, and a third just as she goes over, and the boat is fairly turned, and she goes down almost beyond our sight, though we are more than a hundred feet above the river. Then she comes up again on a great wave, and down and up, then around behind some great rocks, and is lost in the mad, white foam below. We stand frozen with fear, for we see no boat. Bradley is gone! so it seems. But now, away below, we see something coming out of the waves. It is evidently a boat. A moment more, and we see Bradley standing on deck, swinging his hat to show that he is all right. But he is in a whirlpool. We have the stempost of his boat attached to the line. How badly she may be disabled we know not. I direct Sumner and [Walter] Powell to pass along the cliff and see if they can reach him from below. Hawkins, Hall, and myself run to the other boat, jump aboard, push out, and away we go over the falls. A wave rolls over us and our boat is unmanageable. Another great wave strikes us, and the boat rolls over, and tumbles and tosses, I know not how. All I know is that Bradley is picking us up. We soon have all right again, and row to the cliff and wait until Sumner and Powell can come. After a difficult climb they reach us. We run two or three miles farther and turn again to the northwest, continuing until night, when we have run out of the granite once more.

August 30. At the confluence of the Colorado and Virgin River, three Mormons and an Indian helper are seine-netting fish. They have been there for weeks, under orders from Brigham Young to watch for the Powell expedition. Since the members of the expedition have already been reported dead several times in the newspapers, the Mormons are really on the lookout for corpses and wreckage; they hope to salvage whatever journals and maps have survived in order that they might learn something about the unexplored portion of the region where they have banished themselves. Late in the morning, one of them flings a glance upriver and freezes. There are two boats coming down, and, unless they are ghosts, the people inside them seem to be alive.

The Seventh Man

by Haruki Murakami

"A huge wave nearly swept me away," said the seventh man, almost whispering. "It happened one September afternoon when I was ten years old."

The man was the last one to tell his story that night. The hands of the clock had moved past ten. The small group that huddled in a circle could hear the wind tearing through the darkness outside, heading west. It shook the trees, set the windows to rattling, and moved past the house with one final whistle.

"It was the biggest wave I had even seen in my life," he said. "A strange wave. An absolute giant."

He paused.

"It just barely missed me, but in my place it swallowed everything that mattered most to me and swept it off to another world. I took years to find it again and to recover from the experience—precious years that can never be replaced."

The seventh man appeared to be in his mid-fifties. He was a thin man, tall, with a moustache, and next to his right eye he had a short but deep-looking scar that could have been made by the stab of a small blade. Stiff, bristly patches of white marked his short hair. His face had the look you see on people when they can't quite find the words they need. In his case, though, the expression seemed to have been there from long before, as though it were part of him. The man wore a simple blue shirt under a grey tweed coat, and every now and then he would bring his hand to his collar. None of those assembled there knew his name or what he did for a living.

He cleared his throat, and for a moment or two his words were lost in silence. The others waited for him to go on.

"In my case, it was a wave," he said. "There's no way for me to tell, of course, what it will be for each of you. But in my case it just happened to take the form of a gigantic wave. It presented itself to me all of a sudden one day, without warning. And it was devastating."

I grew up in a seaside town in the Province of S. It was such a small town, I doubt that any of you would recognize the name if I were to mention it. My father was the local doctor, and so I led a rather comfortable childhood. Ever since I could remember, my best friend was a boy I'll call K. His house was close to ours, and he was a grade behind me in school. We were like brothers, walking to and from school together, and always playing together when we got home. We never once fought during our long friendship. I did have a brother, six years older, but what with the age difference and differences in our personalities, we were never very close. My real brotherly affection went to my friend K.

K. was a frail, skinny little thing, with a pale complexion and a face almost pretty enough to be a girl's. He had some kind of speech impediment, though, which might have made him seem retarded to anyone who didn't know him. And because he was so frail, I always played his protector, whether at school or at home. I was kind of big and athletic, and the other kids all looked up to me. But the main reason I enjoyed spending time with K. was that he was such a sweet, pure-hearted boy. He was not the least bit retarded, but because of his impediment, he didn't do too well at school. In most subjects, he could barely keep up. In art class, though, he was great. Just give him a pencil or paints and he would make pictures that were so full of life that even the teacher was amazed. He won prizes in one contest after another, and I'm sure he would have become a famous painter if he had continued with his art into adulthood. He liked to do seascapes. He'd go out to the shore for hours, painting. I would often sit beside him, watching the swift, precise movements of his brush, wondering how, in a few seconds, he could possibly create such lively shapes and colours where, until then, there had been only blank white paper. I realize now that it was a matter of pure talent.

One year, in September, a huge typhoon hit our area. The radio said it was going to be the worst in ten years. The schools were closed, and all the shops in town lowered their shutters in preparation for the storm. Starting early in the morning, my father and brother went around the house nailing shut all the storm-doors, while my mother spent the day in the kitchen cooking emergency provisions. We filled bottles and canteens with water, and packed our most important possessions in rucksacks for possible evacuation. To the adults, typhoons were an annoyance and a threat they had to face almost annually, but to the kids, removed as we were from such practical concerns, it was just a great big circus, a wonderful source of excitement.

Just after noon the colour of the sky began to change all of a sudden. There was something strange and unreal about it. I stayed outside on the porch, watching the sky, until the wind began to howl and the rain began to beat against the house with a weird dry sound, like handfuls of sand. Then we closed the last storm-door and gathered together in one room of the darkened house, listening to the radio. This particular storm did not have a great deal of rain, it said, but the winds were doing a lot of damage, blowing roofs off houses and capsizing ships. Many people had been killed or injured by flying debris. Over and over again, they warned people against leaving their homes. Every once in a while, the house would creak and shudder as if a huge hand were shaking it, and sometimes there would be a great crash of some heavy-sounding object against a storm-door. My father guessed that these were tiles blowing off the neighbours' houses. For lunch we ate the rice and omelettes my mother had cooked, waiting for the typhoon to blow past.

But the typhoon gave no sign of blowing past. The radio said it had lost momentum almost as soon as it came ashore at S. Province, and now it was moving north-east at the pace of a slow runner. The wind kept up its savage howling as it tried to uproot everything that stood on land.

Perhaps an hour had gone by with the wind at its worst like this when a hush fell over everything. All of a sudden it was so quiet, we could hear a bird crying in the distance. My father opened the storm-door a crack and looked outside. The wind had stopped, and the rain had ceased to fall. Thick, grey clouds edged across the sky, and patches of blue showed here and there. The trees in the yard were still dripping their heavy burden of rainwater.

"We're in the eye of the storm," my father told me. "It'll stay quiet like this for a while, maybe fifteen, twenty minutes, kind of like an intermission. Then the wind'll come back the way it was before."

I asked him if I could go outside. He said I could walk around a little if I didn't go far. "But I want you to come right back here at the first sign of wind."

I went out and started to explore. It was hard to believe that a wild storm had been blowing there until a few minutes before. I looked up at the sky. The storm's great "eye" seemed to be up there, fixing its cold stare on all of us below. No such "eye" existed, of course: we were just in that momentary quiet spot at the centre of the pool of whirling air.

While the grown-ups checked for damage to the house, I went down to the beach. The road was littered with broken tree branches, some of them thick pine boughs that would have been too heavy for an adult to lift alone. There were shattered roof tiles everywhere, cars with cracked windshields, and even a doghouse that had tumbled into the middle of the street. A big hand might have swung down from the sky and flattened everything in its path.

K. saw me walking down the road and came outside.

"Where are you going?" he asked.

"Just down to look at the beach," I said.

Without a word, he came along with me. He had a little white dog that followed after us.

"The minute we get any wind, though, we're going straight back home," I said, and K. gave me a silent nod.

The shore was a 200-yard walk from my house. It was lined with a concrete breakwater—a big dyke that stood as high as I was tall in those days. We had to climb a short flight of steps to reach the water's edge. This was where we came to play almost every day, so there was no part of it we didn't know well. In the eye of the typhoon, though, it all looked different: the colour of the sky and of the sea, the sound of the waves, the smell of the tide, the whole expanse of the shore. We sat atop the breakwater for a time, taking in the view without a word to each other. We were supposedly in the middle of a great typhoon, and yet the waves were strangely hushed. And the point where they washed against the beach was much farther away than usual, even at low tide. The white sand stretched out before us as far as we could see. The whole, huge space felt like a room without furniture, except for the band of flotsam that lined the beach.

We stepped down to the other side of the breakwater and walked along the broad beach, examining the things that had come to rest there. Plastic toys, sandals, chunks of wood that had probably once been parts of furniture, pieces of clothing, unusual bottles, broken crates with foreign writing on them, and other, less recognizable items: it was like a big candy store. The storm must have carried these things from very far away. Whenever something unusual caught our attention, we would pick it up and look at it every which way, and when we were done, K.'s dog would come over and give it a good sniff.

We couldn't have been doing this more than five minutes when I realized that the waves had come up right next to me. Without any sound or other warning, the sea had suddenly stretched its long, smooth tongue out to where I stood on the beach. I had never seen anything like it before. Child though I was, I had grown up on the shore and knew how frightening the ocean could be—the savagery with which it could strike unannounced.

And so I had taken care to keep well back from the waterline. In spite of that, the waves had slid up to within inches of where I stood. And then, just as soundlessly, the water drew back—and stayed back. The waves that had approached me were as unthreatening as waves can be—a gentle washing of the sandy beach. But something ominous about them—something like the touch of a reptile's skin—had sent a chill down my spine. My fear was totally groundless—and totally real. I knew instinctively that they were alive. They knew I was here and they were planning to grab me. I felt as if some huge, man-eating beast were lying somewhere on a grassy plain, dreaming of the moment it would pounce and tear me to pieces with its sharp teeth. I had to run away.

"I'm getting out of here!" I yelled to K. He was maybe ten yards down the beach, squatting with his back to me, and looking at something. I was sure I had yelled loud enough, but my voice did not seem to have reached him. He might have been so absorbed in whatever it was he had found that my call made no impression on him. K. was like that. He would get involved with things to the point of forgetting everything else. Or possibly I had not yelled as loudly as I had thought. I do recall that my voice sounded strange to me, as though it belonged to someone else.

Then I heard a deep rumbling sound. It seemed to shake the earth. Actually, before I heard the rumble I heard another sound, a weird gurgling as though a lot of water was surging up through a hole in the ground. It continued for a while, then stopped, after which I heard the strange rumbling. Even that was not enough to make K. look up. He was still squatting, looking down at something at his feet, in deep concentration. He probably did not hear the rumbling. How he could have missed such an earth-shaking sound, I don't know. This may seem odd, but it might have been a sound that only I could hear—some special kind of sound. Not even K.'s dog seemed to notice it, and you know how sensitive dogs are to sound.

I told myself to run over to K., grab hold of him, and get out of there. It was the only thing to do. I *knew* that the wave was coming, and K. didn't know. As clearly as I knew what I ought to be doing, I found myself running the other way—running full speed toward the dyke, alone. What made me do this, I'm sure, was fear, a fear so over-powering it took my voice away and set my legs to running on their own. I ran stumbling along the soft sand beach to the breakwater, where I turned and shouted to K.

"Hurry, K.! Get out of there! The wave is coming!" This time my voice worked fine. The rumbling had stopped, I realized, and now, finally, K. heard my shouting and looked up. But it was too late. A wave like a huge snake with its head held high, poised to strike, was racing towards the shore. I had never seen anything like it in my life. It had to be as tall as a three-storey building. Soundlessly (in my memory, at least, the image is soundless), it rose up behind K. to block out the sky. K. looked at me for a few seconds, uncomprehending. Then, as if sensing something, he turned towards the wave. He tried to run, but now there was no time to run. In the next instant, the wave had swallowed him.

The wave crashed on to the beach, shattering into a million leaping waves that flew through the air and plunged over the dyke where I stood. I was able to dodge its impact by ducking behind the breakwater. The spray wet my clothes, nothing more. I scrambled back up on to the wall and scanned the shore. By then the wave had turned and, with a wild cry, it was rushing back out to sea. It looked like part of a gigantic rug that had been yanked by someone at the other end of the earth. Nowhere on the shore could I find any trace of K., or of his dog. There was only the empty beach. The receding wave had now pulled so much water out from the shore that it seemed to expose the entire ocean bottom. I stood alone on the breakwater, frozen in place.

The silence came over everything again—a desperate silence, as though sound itself had been ripped from the earth. The wave had swallowed K. and disappeared into the far distance. I stood there, wondering what to do. Should I go down to the beach? K. might be down there somewhere, buried in the sand . . . But I decided not to leave the dyke. I knew from experience that big waves often came in twos and threes.

I'm not sure how much time went by—maybe ten or twenty seconds of eerie emptiness—when, just as I had guessed, the next wave came. Another gigantic roar shook the beach, and again, after the sound had faded, another huge wave raised its head to strike. It towered before me, blocking out the sky, like a deadly cliff. This time, though, I didn't run. I stood rooted to the sea wall, entranced, waiting for it to attack. What good would it do to run, I thought, now that K. had been taken? Or perhaps I simply froze, overcome with fear. I can't be sure what it was that kept me standing there.

The second wave was just as big as the first—maybe even bigger. From far above my head it began to fall, losing its shape, like a brick wall slowly crumbling. It was so huge that it no longer looked like a real wave. It was like something from another, far-off world, that just happened to assume the shape of a wave. I readied myself for the moment the darkness would take me. I didn't even close my eyes. I remember hearing my heart pound with incredible clarity.

The moment the wave came before me, however, it stopped. All at once it seemed to run out of energy, to lose its forward motion and simply hover there, in space, crumbling in stillness. And in its crest, inside its cruel, transparent tongue, what I saw was K.

Some of you may find this impossible to believe, and if so, I don't blame you. I myself have trouble accepting it even now. I can't explain what I saw any better than you can, but I know it was no illusion, no hallucination. I am telling you as honestly as I can what happened at that moment—what really happened. In the tip of the wave, as if enclosed in some kind of transparent capsule, floated K.'s body, reclining on its side. But that is not all. K. was looking straight at me, smiling. There, right in front of me, so close that I could have reached out and touched him, was my friend, my friend K. who, only moments before, had been swallowed by the wave. And he was smiling at me. Not with an ordinary smile—it was a big, wide-open grin that literally stretched from ear to ear. His cold, frozen eyes were locked on mine. He was no longer the K. I knew. And his right arm was stretched out in my direction, as if he were trying to grab my hand and pull me into that other world where he was now. A little closer, and his hand would have caught mine. But, having missed, K. then smiled at me one more time, his grin wider than ever.

I seem to have lost consciousness at that point. The next thing I knew, I was in bed in my father's clinic. As soon as I awoke the nurse went to call my father, who came running. He took my pulse, studied my pupils, and put his hand on my forehead. I tried to move my arm, but I couldn't lift it. I was burning with fever, and my mind was clouded. I had been wrestling with a high fever for some time, apparently. "You've been asleep for three days," my father said to me. A neighbour who had seen the whole thing had picked me up and carried me home. They had not been able to find K. I wanted to say something to my father. I *had* to say something to him. But my numb and swollen tongue could not form words. I felt as if some kind of creature had taken up residence in my mouth. My father asked me to tell him my name, but before I could remember what it was, I lost consciousness again, sinking into darkness.

Altogether, I stayed in bed for a week on a liquid diet. I vomited several times, and had bouts of delirium. My father told me afterwards that I was so bad that he had been afraid I might suffer permanent neurological damage from the shock and high fever. One way or another, though, I managed to recover—physically, at least. But my life would never be the same again.

They never found K.'s body. They never found his dog, either. Usually when someone drowned in that area, the body would wash up a few days later on the shore of a small inlet to the east. K.'s body never did. The big waves probably carried it far out to sea—too far for it to reach the shore. It must have sunk to the ocean bottom to be eaten by the fish. The search went on for a very long time, thanks to the cooperation of the local fishermen, but eventually it petered out. Without a body, there was never any funeral. Half crazed, K.'s parents would wander up and down the beach every day, or they would shut themselves up at home, chanting sutras.

As great a blow as this had been for them, though, K.'s parents never chided me for having taken their son down to the shore in the midst of a typhoon. They knew how I had always loved and protected K. as if he had been my own little brother. My parents, too, made a point of never mentioning the incident in my presence. But I knew the truth. I knew that I could have saved K. if I had tried. I probably could have run over and dragged him out of the reach of the wave. It would have been close, but as I went over the timing of the events in my memory, it always seemed to me that I could have made it. As I said before, though, overcome with fear, I abandoned him there and saved only myself. It pained me all the more that K.'s parents failed to blame me and that everyone else was so careful never to say anything to me about what had happened. It took me a long time to recover from the emotional shock. I stayed away from school for weeks. I hardly ate a thing, and spent each day in bed, staring at the ceiling.

K. was always there, lying in the wave tip, grinning at me, his hand outstretched, beckoning. I couldn't get that picture out of my mind. And when I managed to sleep, it was there in my dreams—except that, in my dreams, K. would hop out of his capsule in the wave and grab my wrist to drag me back inside with him.

And then there was another dream I had. I'm swimming in the ocean. It's a beautiful summer afternoon, and I'm doing an easy breaststroke far from shore. The sun is beating down on my back, and the water feels good. Then, all of a sudden, someone grabs my right leg. I feel an ice-cold grip on my ankle. It's strong, too strong to shake off. I'm being dragged down under the surface. I see K.'s face there. He has the same huge grin, split from ear to ear, his eyes locked on mine. I try to scream, but my voice will not come. I swallow water, and my lungs start to fill.

I wake up in the darkness, screaming, breathless, drenched in sweat.

At the end of the year I pleaded with my parents to let me move to another town. I couldn't go on living in sight of the beach where K. had been swept away, and my nightmares wouldn't stop. If I didn't get out of there, I'd go crazy. My parents understood and made arrangements for me to live elsewhere. I moved to Nagano Province in January to live with my father's family in a mountain village near Komoro. I finished elementary school in Nagano and stayed on through junior and senior high school there. I never went home, even for holidays. My parents came to visit me now and then.

I live in Nagano to this day. I graduated from a college of engineering in the City of Nagano and went to work for a precision toolmaker in the area. I still work for them. I live like anybody else. As you can see, there's nothing unusual about me. I'm not very sociable, but I have a few friends I go mountain climbing with. Once I got away from my home town, I stopped having nightmares all the time. They remained a part of my life, though. They would come to me now and then, like debt collectors at the door. It happened whenever I was on the verge of forgetting. And it was always the same dream, down to the smallest detail. I would wake up screaming, my sheets soaked with sweat.

That is probably why I never married. I didn't want to wake someone sleeping next to me with my screams in the middle of the night. I've been in love with several women over the years, but I never spent a night with any of them. The terror was in my bones. It was something I could never share with another person.

I stayed away from my home town for over forty years. I never went near that seashore—or any other. I was afraid that if I did, my dream might happen in reality. I had always enjoyed swimming, but after that day I never even went to swim in a pool. I wouldn't go near deep rivers or lakes. I avoided boats and wouldn't take a plane to go abroad. Despite all these precautions, I couldn't get rid of the image of myself drowning. Like K.'s cold hand, this dark premonition caught hold of my mind and refused to let go.

Then, last spring, I finally revisited the beach where K. had been taken by the wave.

My father had died of cancer the year before, and my brother had sold the old house. In going through the storage shed, he had found a cardboard carton crammed with childhood things of mine, which he sent to me in Nagano. Most of it was useless junk, but there was one bundle of pictures that K. had painted and given to me. My parents had probably put them away for me as a keepsake of K., but the pictures did nothing but reawaken the old terror. They made me feel as if K.'s spirit would spring back to life from them, and so I quickly returned them to their paper wrapping, intending to throw them away. I couldn't make myself do it, though. After several days of indecision, I opened the bundle again and forced myself to take a long, hard look at K.'s watercolours.

Most of them were landscapes, pictures of the familiar stretch of ocean and sand beach and pine woods and the town, and all done with that special clarity and coloration I knew so well from K.'s hand. They were still amazingly vivid despite the years, and had been executed with even greater skill than I recalled. As I leafed through the bundle, I found myself steeped in warm memories. The deep feelings of the boy K. were there in his pictures—the way his eyes were opened on the world. The things we did together, the places we went together began to come back to me with great intensity. And I realized that his eyes were my eyes, that I myself had looked upon the world back then with the same lively, unclouded vision as the boy who had walked by my side.

I made a habit after that of studying one of K.'s pictures at my desk each day when I got home from work. I could sit there for hours with one painting. In each I found another of those soft landscapes of childhood that I had shut out of my memory for so long. I had a sense, whenever I looked at one of K.'s works, that something was permeating my very flesh.

Perhaps a week had gone by like this when the thought suddenly struck me one evening: I might have been making a terrible mistake all those years. As he lay there in the tip of the wave, surely K. had not been looking at me with hatred or resentment; he had not been trying to take me away with him. And that terrible grin he had fixed me with: that, too, could have been an accident of angle or light and shadow, not a conscious act on K.'s part. He had probably already lost consciousness, or perhaps he had been giving me a gentle smile of eternal parting. The intense look of hatred I thought I saw on his face had been nothing but a reflection of the profound terror that had taken control of me for the moment.

The more I studied K.'s watercolour that evening, the greater the conviction with which I began to believe these new thoughts of mine. For no matter how long I continued to look at the picture, I could find nothing in it but a boy's gentle, innocent spirit.

I went on sitting at my desk for a very long time. There was nothing else I could do. The sun went down, and the pale darkness of evening began to envelop the room. Then came the deep silence of night, which seemed to go on for ever. At last, the scales tipped, and dark gave way to dawn. The new day's sun tinged the sky with pink.

It was then I knew I must go back.

I threw a few things in a bag, called the company to say I would not be in, and boarded a train for my old home town.

I did not find the same quiet, little seaside town that I remembered. An industrial city had sprung up nearby during the rapid development of the Sixties, bringing great changes to the landscape. The one little gift shop by the station had grown into a mall, and the town's only movie theatre had been turned into a supermarket. My house was no longer there. It had been demolished some months before, leaving only a scrape on the earth. The trees in the yard had all been cut down, and patches of weeds dotted the black stretch of ground. K.'s old house had disappeared as well, having been replaced by a concrete parking lot full of commuters' cars and vans. Not that I was overcome by sentiment. The town had ceased to be mine long before.

I walked down to the shore and climbed the steps of the break-water. On the other side, as always, the ocean stretched off into the distance, unobstructed, huge, the horizon a single straight line. The shoreline, too, looked the same as it had before: the long beach, the lapping waves, people strolling at the water's edge. The time was after four o'clock, and the soft sun of late afternoon embraced everything below as it began its long, almost meditative descent to the west. I lowered my bag to the sand and sat down next to it in silent appreciation of the gentle seascape. Looking at this scene, it was impossible to imagine that a great typhoon had once raged here, that a massive wave had swallowed my best friend in all the world. There was almost no one left now, surely, who remembered those terrible events. It began to seem as if the whole thing were an illusion that I had dreamed up in vivid detail.

And then I realized that the deep darkness inside me had vanished. Suddenly. As suddenly as it had come. I raised myself from the sand and, without bothering to take off my shoes or roll up my cuffs, walked into the surf and let the waves lap at my ankles.

Almost in reconciliation, it seemed, the same waves that had washed up on the beach when I was a boy were now fondly washing my feet, soaking black my shoes and pant cuffs. There would be one slow-moving wave, then a long pause, and then another wave would come and go. The people passing by gave me odd looks, but I didn't care.

I looked up at the sky. A few grey cotton chunks of cloud hung there, motionless. They seemed to be there for me, though I'm not sure why I felt that way. I remembered having looked up at the sky like this in search of the "eye" of the typhoon. And then, inside me, the axis of time gave one great heave. Forty long years collapsed like a dilapidated house, mixing old time and new time together in a single swirling mass. All sounds faded, and the light around me shuddered. I lost my balance and fell into the waves. My heart throbbed at the back of my throat, and my arms and legs lost all sensation. I lay that way for a long time, face in the water, unable to stand. But I was not afraid. No, not at all. There was no longer anything for me to fear. Those days were gone.

I stopped having my terrible nightmares. I no longer wake up screaming in the middle of the night. And I am trying now to start life over again. No, I know it's probably too late to start again. I may not have much time left to live. But even if it comes too late, I am grateful that, in the end, I was able to attain a kind of salvation, to effect some sort of recovery. Yes, grateful: I could have come to the end of my life unsaved, still screaming in the dark, afraid.

The seventh man fell silent and turned his gaze upon each of the others. No one spoke or moved or even seemed to breathe. All were waiting for the rest of his story. Outside, the wind had fallen, and nothing stirred. The seventh man brought his hand to his collar once again, as if in search of words.

"They tell us that the only thing we have to fear is fear itself; but I don't believe that," he said. Then, a moment later, he added: "Oh, the fear is there, all right. It comes to us in many different forms, at different times, and overwhelms us. But the most frightening thing we can do at such times is to turn our backs on it, to close our eyes. For then we take the most precious thing inside us and surrender it to something else. In my case, that something was the wave."

—Translation by Jay Rubin

To Build a Fire

by Jack London

Day had broken cold and gray, exceedingly cold and gray, when the young man turned aside from the main Yukon trail and climbed the high earth-bank, where a dim and little-travelled trail led eastward through the fat spruce timberland. It was a steep bank, and he paused for breath at the top, excusing the act to himself by looking at his watch. It was nine o'clock. There was no sun nor hint of sun, though there was not a cloud in the sky. It was a clear day, and yet there seemed an intangible pall over the face of things, a subtle gloom that made the day dark, and that was due to the absence of sun. This fact did not worry the man. He was used to the lack of sun. It had been days since he had seen the sun, and he knew that a few more days must pass before that cheerful orb, due south, would just peep above the sky-line and dip immediately from view.

The man flung a look back along the way he had come. The Yukon lay a mile wide and hidden under three feet of ice. On top of this ice were as many feet of snow. It was all pure white, rolling in gentle undulations where the ice-jams of the freeze-up had formed. North and south, as far as his eye could see, it was unbroken white, save for a dark hair-line that curved and twisted from around the spruce-covered island to the south, and that curved and twisted away into the north, where it disappeared behind another spruce-covered island. This dark hair-line was the trail—the main trail—that led south five hundred miles to the Chilcoot Pass, Dyea, and salt water; and that led north seventy miles to Dawson, and still on to the north a thousand miles to Nulato, and finally to St. Michael on Bering Sea, a thousand miles and half a thousand more.

But all this—the mysterious, far-reaching hair-line trail, the absence of sun from the sky, the tremendous cold, and the strangeness and weirdness of it all—made no impression on the man. It was not because he was long used to it. He was a newcomer in the land, a *chechaquo,* and this was his first winter. The trouble with him was that he was without imagination. He was quick and alert in the things of life, but only in the things, and not in the significances. Fifty degrees below zero meant eighty-odd degrees of frost. Such fact impressed him as being cold and uncomfortable, and that was all. It did not lead him to meditate upon his frailty as a creature of temperature, and upon man's frailty in general, able only to live within certain narrow limits of heat and cold; and from there on it did not lead him to the conjectural field of immortality and man's place in the universe. Fifty degrees below zero stood for a bite of frost that hurt and that must be guarded against by the use of mittens, ear-flaps, warm moccasins, and thick socks. Fifty degrees below zero was to him just precisely fifty degrees below zero. That there should be anything more to it than that was a thought that never entered his head.

As he turned to go on, he spat speculatively. There was a sharp explosive crackle that startled him. He spat again. And again, in the air, before it could fall to the snow, the spittle crackled. He knew that at fifty below spittle crackled on the snow, but this spittle had crackled in the air. Undoubtedly it was colder than fifty below—how much colder he did not know. But the temperature did not matter. He was bound for the old claim on the left fork of Henderson Creek, where the boys were already. They had come over across the divide from the Indian Creek country, while he had come the roundabout way to take a look at the possibilities of getting out logs in the spring from the islands in the Yukon. He would be in to camp by six o'clock; a bit after dark, it was true, but the boys would be there, a fire would be going, and a hot supper would be ready. As for lunch, he pressed his hand against the protruding bundle under his jacket. It was also under his shirt, wrapped up in a handkerchief and lying against the naked skin. It was the only way to keep the biscuits from freezing. He smiled agreeably to himself as he thought of those biscuits, each cut open and sopped in bacon grease, and each enclosing a generous slice of fried bacon.

He plunged in among the big spruce trees. The trail was faint. A foot of snow had fallen since the last sled had passed over, and he was glad he was without a sled, travelling light. In fact, he carried nothing but the lunch wrapped in the handkerchief. He was surprised, however, at the cold. It certainly was cold, he concluded, as he rubbed his numb nose and cheek-bones with his mittened hand. He was a warm-whiskered man, but the hair on his face did not protect the high cheek-bones and the eager nose that thrust itself aggressively into the frosty air.

At the man's heels trotted a dog, a big native husky, the proper wolf-dog, gray-coated and without any visible or temperamental difference from its brother, the wild wolf. The animal was depressed by the tremendous cold. It knew that it was no time for travelling. Its instinct told it a truer tale than was told to the man by the man's judgment. In reality, it was not merely colder than fifty below zero; it was colder than sixty below, than seventy below. It was seventy-five degrees below zero. Since the freezing-point is thirty-two above zero, it meant that one hundred and seven degrees of frost obtained. The dog did not know anything about thermometers. Possibly in its brain there was no sharp consciousness of a condition of very cold such as was in the man's brain. But the brute had its instinct. It experienced a vague but menacing apprehension that subdued it and made it slink along at the man's heels, and that made it question eagerly every unwonted movement of the man as if expecting him to go into camp or to seek shelter somewhere and build a fire. The dog had learned fire, and it wanted fire, or else to burrow under the snow and cuddle its warmth away from the air.

The frozen moisture of its breathing had settled on its fur in a fine powder of frost, and especially were its jowls, muzzle, and eyelashes whitened by its crystalled breath. The man's red beard and mustache were likewise frosted, but more solidly, the deposit taking the form of ice and increasing with every warm, moist breath he exhaled. Also, the man was chewing tobacco, and the muzzle of ice held his lips so rigidly that he was unable to clear his chin when he expelled the juice. The result was that a crystal beard of the color and solidity of amber was increasing its length on his chin. If he fell down it would shatter itself, like glass, into brittle fragments. But he did not mind the appendage. It was the penalty all tobacco-chewers paid in that country, and he had been out before in two cold snaps. They had not been so cold as this, he knew, but by the spirit thermometer at Sixty Mile he knew they had been registered at fifty below and at fifty-five.

He held on through the level stretch of woods for several miles, crossed a wide flat of niggerheads, and dropped down a bank to the frozen bed of a small stream. This was Henderson Creek, and he knew he was ten miles from the forks. He looked at his watch. It was ten o'clock. He was making four miles an hour, and he calculated that he would arrive at the forks at half-past twelve. He decided to celebrate that event by eating his lunch there.

The dog dropped in again at his heels, with a tail drooping discouragement, as the man swung along the creek-bed. The furrow of the old sled-trail was plainly visible, but a dozen inches of snow covered the marks of the last runners. In a month no man had come up or down that silent creek. The man held steadily on. He was not much given to thinking, and just then particularly he had nothing to think about save that he would eat lunch at the forks and that at six o'clock he would be in camp with the boys. There was nobody to talk to; and, had there been, speech would have been impossible because of the ice-muzzle on his mouth. So he continued monotonously to chew tobacco and to increase the length of his amber beard.

Once in a while the thought reiterated itself that it was very cold and that he had never experienced such cold. As he walked along he rubbed his cheek-bones and nose with the back of his mittened hand. He did this automatically, now and again changing hands. But rub as he would, the instant he stopped, his cheek-bones went numb, and the following instant the end of his nose went numb. He was sure to frost his cheeks; he knew that, and experienced a pang of regret that he had not devised a nose-strap of the sort Bud wore in cold snaps. Such a strap passed across the cheeks, as well, and saved them. But it didn't matter much, after all. What were frosted cheeks? A bit painful, that was all; they were never serious.

Empty as the man's mind was of thoughts, he was keenly observant, and he noticed the changes in the creek, the curves and bends and timber-jams, and always he sharply noted where he placed his feet. Once, coming around a bend, he shied abruptly, like a startled horse, curved away from the place where he had been walking, and retreated several paces back along the trail. The creek he knew was frozen clear to the bottom—no creek could contain water in that arctic winter—but he knew also that there were springs that bubbled out from the hillsides and ran along under the snow and on top the ice of the creek. He knew that the coldest snaps never froze these springs, and he knew likewise their danger. They were traps. They hid pools of water under the snow that might be three inches deep, or three feet. Sometimes a skin of ice half an inch thick covered them, and in turn was covered by the snow. Sometimes there were alternate layers of water and ice-skin, so that when one broke through he kept on breaking through for a while, sometimes wetting himself to the waist.

That was why he had shied in such panic. He had felt the give under his feet and heard the crackle of a snow-hidden ice-skin. And to get his feet wet in such a temperature meant trouble and danger. At the very least it meant delay, for he would be forced to stop and build a fire, and under its protection to bare his feet while he dried his socks and moccasins. He stood and studied the creek-bed and its banks, and decided that the flow of water came from the right. He reflected awhile, rubbing his nose and cheeks, then skirted to the left stepping gingerly and testing the footing for each step. Once clear of the danger, he took a fresh chew of tobacco and swung along at his four-mile gait.

In the course of the next two hours he came upon several similar traps. Usually the snow above the hidden pools had a sunken, candied appearance that advertised the danger. Once again, however, he had a close call; and once, suspecting danger, he compelled the dog to go on in front. The dog did not want to go. It hung back until the man shoved it forward, and then it went quickly across the white, unbroken surface. Suddenly it broke through, floundered to one side, and got away to firmer footing. It had wet its fore-feet and legs, and almost immediately the water that clung to it turned to ice. It made quick efforts to lick the ice of its legs, then dropped down in the snow and began to bite out the ice that had formed between the toes. This was a matter of instinct. To permit the ice to remain would mean sore feet. It did not know this. It merely obeyed the mysterious prompting that arose from the deep crypts of its being. But the man knew, having achieved a judgment on the subject, and he removed the mitten from his right hand and helped tear out the ice-particles. He did not expose his fingers more than a minute, and was astonished at the swift numbness that smote them. It certainly was cold. He pulled on the mitten hastily, and beat the hand savagely across his chest.

At twelve o'clock the day was at its brightest. Yet the sun was too far south on its winter journey to clear the horizon. The bulge of the earth intervened between it and Henderson Creek, where the man walked under a clear sky at noon and cast no shadow. At half-past twelve, to the minute, he arrived at the forks of the creek. He was pleased at the speed he had made. If he kept it up, he would certainly be with the boys by six. He unbuttoned his jacket and shirt and drew forth his lunch. The action consumed no more than a quarter of a minute, yet in that brief moment the numbness laid hold of the exposed fingers. He did not put the mitten on, but, instead, struck the fingers a dozen sharp smashes against his leg. Then he sat down on a snow-covered log to eat. The sting that followed upon the striking of his fingers against his leg ceased so quickly that he was startled. He had had no chance to take a bite of biscuit. He struck the fingers repeatedly and returned them to the mitten, baring the other hand for the purpose of eating. He tried to take a mouthful, but the ice muzzle prevented. He had forgotten to build a fire and thaw out. He chuckled at his foolishness, and as he chuckled he noted the numbness creeping into the exposed fingers. Also, he noted that the stinging which had first come to his toes when he sat down was already passing away. He wondered whether the toes were warm or numb. He moved them inside the moccasins and decided that they were numb.

He pulled the mitten on hurriedly and stood up. He was a bit frightened. He stamped up and down until the stinging returned to his feet. It certainly was cold, was his thought. That man from Sulphur Creek had spoken the truth when telling how cold it sometimes got in the country. And he had laughed at him at the time! That showed one must not be too sure of things. There was no mistake about it, it *was* cold. He strode up and down, stamping his feet and threshing his arms, until reassured by the returning warmth. Then he got out matches and proceeded to make a fire. From the undergrowth, where high water of the previous spring had lodged a supply of seasoned twigs, he got his fire-wood. Working carefully from a small beginning, he soon had a roaring fire, over which he thawed the ice from his face and in the protection of which he ate his biscuits. For the moment the cold of space was outwitted. The dog took satisfaction in the fire, stretching out close enough for warmth and far enough away to escape being singed.

When the man had finished, he filled his pipe and took his comfortable time over a smoke. Then he pulled on his mittens, settled the ear-flaps of his cap firmly about his ears, and took the creek trail up the left fork. The dog was disappointed and yearned back toward the fire. This man did not know cold. Possibly all the generations of his ancestry had been ignorant of cold, of real cold, of cold one hundred and seven degrees below freezing-point. But the dog knew; all its ancestry knew, and it had inherited the knowledge. And it knew that it was not good to walk abroad in such fearful cold. It was the time to lie snug in a hole in the snow and wait for a curtain of cloud to be drawn across the face of outer space whence this cold came. On the other hand, there was no keen intimacy between the dog and the man. The one was the toil-slave of the other, and the only caresses it had ever received were the caresses of the whip-lash and of harsh and menacing throat-sounds that threatened the whip-lash. So the dog made no effort to communicate its apprehension to the man. It was not concerned with the welfare of the man; it was for its own sake that it yearned back toward the fire. But the man whistled, and spoke to it with the sound of whip-lashes, and the dog swung in at the man's heels and followed after.

The man took a chew of tobacco and proceeded to start a new amber beard. Also, his moist breath quickly powdered with white his mustache, eyebrows, and lashes. There did not seem to be so many springs on the left fork of the Henderson, and for half an hour the man saw no signs of any. And then it happened. At a place where there were no signs, where the soft, unbroken snow seemed to advertise solidity beneath, the man broke through. It was not deep. He wet himself halfway to the knees before he floundered out to the firm crust.

He was angry, and cursed his luck aloud. He had hoped to get into camp with the boys at six o'clock, and this would delay him an hour, for he would have to build a fire and dry out his foot-gear. This was imperative at that low temperature—he knew that much; and he turned aside to the bank, which he climbed. On top, tangled in the underbrush about the trunks of several small spruce trees, was a high-water deposit of dry fire-wood—sticks and twigs, principally, but also larger portions of seasoned branches and fine, dry, last-year's grasses. He threw down several large pieces on top of the snow. This served for a foundation and prevented the young flame from drowning itself in the snow it otherwise would melt. The flame he got by touching a match to a small shred of birch-bark that he took from his pocket. This burned even more readily than paper. Placing it on the foundation, he fed the young flame with wisps of dry grass and with the tiniest dry twigs.

He worked slowly and carefully, keenly aware of his danger. Gradually, as the flame grew stronger, he increased the size of the twigs with which he fed it. He squatted in the snow, pulling the twigs out from their entanglement in the brush and feeding directly to the flame. He knew there must be no failure. When it is seventy-five below zero, a man must not fail in his first attempt to build a fire—that is, if his feet are wet. If his feet are dry, and he fails, he can run along the trail for half a mile and restore his circulation. But the circulation of wet and freezing feet cannot be restored by running when it is seventy-five below. No matter how fast he runs, the wet feet will freeze the harder.

All this the man knew. The old-timer on Sulphur Creek had told him about it the previous fall, and now he was appreciating the advice. Already all sensation had gone out of his feet. To build the fire he had been forced to remove his mittens, and the fingers had quickly gone numb. His pace of four miles an hour had kept his heart pumping blood to the surface of his body and to all the extremities. But the instant he stopped, the action of the pump eased down. The cold of space smote the unprotected tip of the planet, and he, being on that unprotected tip, received the full force of the blow. The blood of his body recoiled before it. The blood was alive, like the dog, and like the dog it wanted to hide away and cover itself up from the fearful cold. So long as he walked four miles an hour, he pumped that blood, willy-nilly, to the surface; but now it ebbed away and sank down into the recesses of his body. The extremities were the first to feel its absence. His wet feet froze the faster, and his exposed fingers numbed the faster, though they had not yet begun to freeze. Nose and cheeks were already freezing, while the skin of all his body chilled as it lost its blood.

But he was safe. Toes and nose and cheeks would be only touched by the frost, for the fire was beginning to burn with strength. He was feeding it with twigs the size of his finger. In another minute he would be able to feed it with branches the size of his wrist, and then he could remove his wet foot-gear, and, while it dried, he could keep his naked feet warm by the fire, rubbing them at first, of course, with snow. The fire was a success. He was safe. He remembered the advice of the old-timer on Sulphur Creek, and smiled. The old-timer had been very serious in laying down the law that no man must travel alone in the Klondike after fifty below. Well, here he was; he had had the accident; he was alone; and he had saved himself. Those old-timers were rather womanish, some of them, he thought. All a man had to do was to keep his head, and he was all right. Any man who was a man could travel alone. But it was surprising, the rapidity with which his cheeks and nose were freezing. And he had not thought his fingers could go lifeless in so short a time. Lifeless they were, for he could scarcely make them move together to grip a twig, and they seemed remote from his body and from him. When he touched a twig, he had to look and see whether or not he had hold of it. The wires were pretty well down between him and his finger-ends.

All of which counted for little. There was the fire, snapping and crackling and promising life with every dancing flame. He started to untie his moccasins. They were coated with ice; the thick German socks were like sheaths of iron halfway to the knees; and the moccasin strings were like rods of steel all twisted and knotted as by some conflagration. For a moment he tugged with his numb fingers, then, realizing the folly of it, he drew his sheath-knife.

But before he could cut the strings, it happened. It was his own fault or, rather, his mistake. He should not have built the fire under the spruce tree. He should have built it in the open. But it had been easier to pull the twigs from the brush and drop them directly on the fire. Now the tree under which he had done this carried a weight of snow on its boughs. No wind had blown for weeks, and each bough was fully freighted. Each time he had pulled a twig he had communicated a slight agitation to the tree—an imperceptible agitation, so far as he was concerned, but an agitation sufficient to bring about the disaster. High up in the tree one bough capsized its load of snow. This fell on the boughs beneath, capsizing them. This process continued, spreading out and involving the whole tree. It grew like an avalanche, and it descended without warning upon the man and the fire, and the fire was blotted out! Where it had burned was a mantle of fresh and disordered snow.

The man was shocked. It was as though he had just heard his own sentence of death. For a moment he sat and stared at the spot where the fire had been. Then he grew very calm. Perhaps the old-timer on Sulphur Creek was right. If he had only had a trail-mate he would have been in no danger now. The trail-mate could have built the fire. Well, it was up to him to build the fire over again, and this second time there must be no failure. Even if he succeeded, he would most likely lose some toes. His feet must be badly frozen by now, and there would be some time before the second fire was ready.

Such were his thoughts, but he did not sit and think them. He was busy all the time they were passing through his mind. He made a new foundation for a fire, this time in the open, where no treacherous tree could blot it out. Next, he gathered dry grasses and tiny twigs from the high-water flotsam. He could not bring his fingers together to pull them out, but he was able to gather them by the handful. In this way he got many rotten twigs and bits of green moss that were undesirable, but it was the best he could do. He worked methodically, even collecting an armful of the larger branches to be used later when the fire gathered strength. And all the while the dog sat and watched him, a certain yearning wistfulness in its eyes, for it looked upon him as the fire provider, and the fire was slow in coming.

When all was ready, the man reached in his pocket for a second piece of birch-bark. He knew the bark was there, and, though he could not feel it with his fingers, he could hear its crisp rustling as he fumbled for it. Try as he would, he could not clutch hold of it. And all the time, in his consciousness, was the knowledge that each instant his feet were freezing. This thought tended to put him in a panic, but he fought against it and kept calm. He pulled on his mittens with his teeth, and threshed his arms back and forth, beating his hands with all his might against his sides. He did this sitting down, and he stood up to do it; and all the while the dog sat in the snow, its wolf-brush of a tail curled around warmly over its forefeet, its sharp wolf-ears pricked forward intently as it watched the man. And the man, as he beat and threshed with his arms and hands, felt a great surge of envy as he regarded the creature that was warm and secure in its natural covering.

After a time he was aware of the first faraway signals of sensation in his beaten fingers. The faint tingling grew stronger till it evolved into a stinging ache that was excruciating, but which the man hailed with satisfaction. He stripped the mitten from his right hand and fetched forth the birch-bark. The exposed fingers were quickly going numb again. Next he brought out his bunch of sulphur matches. But the tremendous cold had already driven the life out of his fingers. In his effort to separate one match from the others, the whole bunch fell in the snow. He tried to pick it out of the snow, but failed. The dead fingers could neither touch nor clutch. He was very careful. He drove the thought of his freezing feet, and nose, and cheeks, out of his mind, devoting his whole soul to the matches. He watched, using the sense of vision in place of that of touch, and when he saw his fingers on each side of the bunch, he closed them—that is, he willed to close them, for the wires were down, and the fingers did not obey. He pulled the mitten on the right hand, and beat it fiercely against his knee. Then, with both mittened hands, he scooped the bunch of matches, along with much snow, into his lap. Yet he was no better off.

After some manipulation he managed to get the bunch between the heels of his mittened hands. In this fashion he carried it to his mouth. The ice crackled and snapped when by a violent effort he opened his mouth. He drew the lower jaw in, curled the upper lip out of the way and scraped the bunch with his upper teeth in order to separate a match. He succeeded in getting one, which he dropped on his lap. He was no better off. He could not pick it up. Then he devised a way. He picked it up in his teeth and scratched it on his leg. Twenty times he scratched before he succeeded in lighting it. As it flamed he held it with his teeth to the birch bark. But the burning brimstone went up his nostrils and into his lungs, causing him to cough spasmodically. The match fell into the snow and went out.

The old-timer on Sulphur Creek was right, he thought in the moment of controlled despair that ensued: after fifty below, a man should travel with a partner. He beat his hands, but failed in exciting any sensation. Suddenly he bared both hands, removing the mittens with his teeth. He caught the whole bunch between the heels of his hands. His arm-muscles not being frozen enabled him to press the hand-heels tightly against the matches. Then he scratched the bunch along his leg. It flared into flame, seventy sulphur matches all at once! There was no wind to blow them out. He kept his head to one side to escape the strangling fumes, and held the blazing bunch to the birch-bark. As he so held it, he became aware of sensation in his hand. His flesh was burning. He could smell it. Deep down below the surface he could feel it. The sensation developed into pain that grew acute. And still he endured it, holding the flame of the matches clumsily to the bark that would not light readily because his own burning hands were in the way, absorbing most of the flame.

At last, when he could endure no more, he jerked his hands apart. The blazing matches fell sizzling into the snow, but the birch-bark was alight. He began laying dry grasses and the tiniest twigs on the flame. He could not pick and choose, for he had to lift the fuel between the heels of his hands. Small pieces of rotten wood and green moss clung to the twigs, and he bit them off as well as he could with his teeth. He cherished the flame carefully and awkwardly. It meant life, and it must not perish. The withdrawal of blood from the surface of his body now made him begin to shiver, and he grew more awkward. A large piece of green moss fell squarely on the little fire. He tried to poke it out with his fingers, but his shivering frame made him poke too far, and he disrupted the nucleus of the little fire, the burning grasses and tiny twigs separating and scattering. He tried to poke them together again, but in spite of the tenseness of the effort, his shivering got away with him, and the twigs were hopelessly scattered. Each twig gushed a puff of smoke and went out. The fire-provider had failed. As he looked apathetically about him, his eyes chanced on the dog, sitting across the ruins of the fire from him, in the snow, making restless, hunching movements, slightly lifting one forefoot and then the other, shifting its weight back and forth on them with wistful eagerness.

The sight of the dog put a wild idea into his head. He remembered the tale of the man, caught in a blizzard, who killed a steer and crawled inside the carcass, and so was saved. He would kill the dog and bury his hands in the warm body until the numbness went out of them. Then he could build another fire. He spoke to the dog, calling it to him; but in his voice was a strange note of fear that frightened the animal, who had never known the man to speak in such a way before. Something was the matter, and its suspicious nature sensed danger—it knew not what danger, but somewhere, somehow, in its brain arose an apprehension of the man. It flattened its ears down at the sound of the man's voice, and its restless, hunching movements and the liftings and shiftings of its forefeet became more pronounced; but it would not come to the man. He got on his hands and knees and crawled toward the dog. This unusual posture again excited suspicion, and the animal sidled mincingly away.

The man sat up in the snow for a moment and struggled for calmness. Then he pulled on his mittens, by means of his teeth, and got upon his feet. He glanced down at first in order to assure himself that he was really standing up, for the absence of sensation in his feet left him unrelated to the earth. His erect position in itself started to drive the webs of suspicion from the dog's mind; and when he spoke peremptorily, with the sound of whip-lashes in his voice, the dog rendered its customary allegiance and came to him. As it came within reaching distance, the man lost his control. His arms flashed out to the dog, and he experienced genuine surprise when he discovered that his hands could not clutch, that there was neither bend nor feeling in the fingers. He had forgotten for the moment that they were frozen and that they were freezing more and more. All this happened quickly, and before the animal could get away, he encircled its body with his arms. He sat down in the snow, and in this fashion held the dog, while it snarled and whined and struggled.

But it was all he could do, hold its body encircled in his arms and sit there. He realized that he could not kill the dog. There was no way to do it. With his helpless hands he could neither draw nor hold his sheath-knife nor throttle the animal. He released it, and it plunged wildly away, with tail between its legs, and still snarling. It halted forty feet away and surveyed him curiously, with ears sharply pricked forward. The man looked down at his hands in order to locate them, and found them hanging on the ends of his arms. It struck him as curious that one should have to use his eyes in order to find out where his hands were. He began threshing his arms back and forth, beating the mittened hands against his sides. He did this for five minutes, violently, and his heart pumped enough blood up to the surface to put a stop to his shivering. But no sensation was aroused in the hands. He had an impression that they hung like weights on the ends of his arms, but when he tried to run the impression down, he could not find it.

A certain fear of death, dull and oppressive, came to him. This fear quickly became poignant as he realized that is was no longer a mere matter of freezing his fingers and toes, or of losing his hands and feet, but that it was a matter of life and death with the chances against him. This threw him into a panic, and he turned and ran up the creek-bed along the old, dim trail. The dog joined in behind and kept up with him. He ran blindly, without intention, in fear such as he had never known in his life. Slowly as he ploughed and floundered through the snow, he began to see things again,—the banks of the creek, the old timber-jams, the leafless aspens, and the sky. The running made him feel better. He did not shiver. Maybe, if he ran on, his feet would thaw out; and, anyway, if he ran far enough, he would reach camp and the boys. Without doubt he would lose some fingers and toes and some of his face; but the boys would take care of him, and save the rest of him when he got there. And at the same time there was another thought in his mind that said he would never get to the camp and the boys; that it was too many miles away, that the freezing had too great a start on him, and that he would soon be stiff and dead. This thought he kept in the background and refused to consider. Sometimes it pushed itself forward and demanded to be heard, but he thrust it back and strove to think of other things.

It struck him as curious that he could run at all on feet so frozen that he could not feel them when they struck the earth and took the weight of his body. He seemed to himself to skim along above the surface, and to have no connection with the earth. Somewhere he had once seen a winged Mercury, and he wondered if Mercury felt as he felt when skimming over the earth.

His theory of running until he reached camp and the boys had one flaw in it: he lacked the endurance. Several times he stumbled, and finally he tottered, crumpled up, and fell. When he tried to rise, he failed. He must sit and rest, he decided, and next time he would merely walk and keep on going. As he sat and regained his breath, he noted that he was feeling quite warm and comfortable. He was not shivering, and it even seemed that a warm glow had come to his chest and trunk. And yet, when he touched his nose or cheeks, there was no sensation. Running would not thaw them out. Nor would it thaw out his hands and feet. Then the thought came to him that the frozen portions of his body must be extending. He tried to keep this thought down, to forget it, to think of something else; he was aware of the panicky feeling that it caused, and he was afraid of the panic.

But the thought asserted itself, and persisted, until it produced a vision of his body totally frozen. This was too much, and he made another wild run along the trail. Once he slowed down to a walk, but the thought of the freezing extending itself made him run again.

And all the time the dog ran with him, at his heels. When he fell down a second time, it curled its tail over its forefeet and sat in front of him, facing him, curiously eager and intent. The warmth and security of the animal angered him, and he cursed it till it flattened down its ears appeasingly. This time the shivering came more quickly upon the man. He was losing in his battle with the frost. It was creeping into his body from all sides. The thought of it drove him on, but he ran no more than a hundred feet, when he staggered and pitched headlong. It was his last panic. When he had recovered his breath and control, he sat up and entertained in his mind the conception of meeting death with dignity. However, the conception did not come to him in such terms. His idea of it was that he had been making a fool of himself, running around like a chicken with its head cut off—such was the simile that occurred to him. Well, he was bound to freeze anyway, and he might as well take it decently. With this newfound peace of mind came the first glimmerings of drowsiness. A good idea, he thought, to sleep off to death. It was like taking an anæsthetic. Freezing was not so bad as people thought. There were lots worse ways to die.

He pictured the boys finding his body next day. Suddenly he found himself with them, coming along the trails and looking for himself. And, still with them, he came around a turn in the trail and found himself lying in the snow. He did not belong with himself any more, for even then he was out of himself, standing with the boys and looking at himself in the snow. It certainly was cold, was his thought. When he got back to the States he could tell the folks what real cold was. He drifted on from this to a vision of the old-timer on Sulphur Creek. He could see him quite clearly, warm and comfortable, and smoking a pipe.

"You were right, old hoss; you were right," the man mumbled to the old-timer of Sulphur Creek.

Then the man drowsed off into what seemed to him the most comfortable and satisfying sleep he had ever known. The dog sat facing him and waiting. The brief day drew to a close in a long, slow twilight. There were no signs of a fire to be made, and, besides, never in the dog's experience had it known a man to sit like that in the snow and make no fire. As the twilight drew on, its eager yearning for the fire mastered it, and with a great lifting and shifting of forefeet, it whined softly, then flattened its ears down in anticipation of being chidden by the man. But the man remained silent. Later the dog whined loudly. And still later it crept close to the man and caught the scent of death. This made the animal bristle and back away. A little longer it delayed, howling under the stars that leaped and danced and shone brightly in the cold sky. Then it turned and trotted up the trail in the direction of the camp it knew, where were the other food-providers and fire-providers.

A Descent into the Maelström

by Edgar Allan Poe

The ways of God in Nature, as in Providence, are not as our *ways;
nor are the models that we frame any way commensurate to the vastness,
profundity, and unsearchableness of His works,* which have a depth in
them greater than the well of Democritus.

—*Joseph Glanville*

We had now reached the summit of the loftiest crag. For some
minutes the old man seemed too much exhausted to speak.

"Not long ago," said he at length, "and I could have guided you
on this route as well as the youngest of my sons; but, about three years
past, there happened to me an event such as never happened before to
mortal man—or at least such as no man ever survived to tell of—and
the six hours of deadly terror which I then endured have broken me
up body and soul. You suppose me a *very* old man—but I am not. It
took less than a single day to change these hairs from a jetty black to

white, to weaken my limbs, and to unstring my nerves, so that I tremble at the least exertion, and am frightened at a shadow. Do you know I can scarcely look over this little cliff without getting giddy?"

The "little cliff," upon whose edge he had so carelessly thrown himself down to rest that the weightier portion of his body hung over it, while he was only kept from falling by the tenure of his elbow on its extreme and slippery edge—this "little cliff" arose, a sheer unobstructed precipice of black shining rock, some fifteen or sixteen hundred feet from the world of crags beneath us. Nothing would have tempted me to within half a dozen yards of its brink. In truth so deeply was I excited by the perilous position of my companion, that I fell at full length upon the ground, clung to the shrubs around me, and dared not even glance upward at the sky—while I struggled in vain to divest myself of the idea that the very foundations of the mountain were in danger from the fury of the winds. It was long before I could reason myself into sufficient courage to sit up and look out into the distance.

"You must get over these fancies," said the guide, "for I have brought you here that you might have the best possible view of the scene of that event I mentioned—and to tell you the whole story with the spot just under your eye."

"We are now," he continued, in that particularizing manner which distinguished him—"we are now close upon the Norwegian coast—in the sixty-eighth degree of latitude—in the great province of Nordland—and in the dreary district of Lofoden. The mountain upon whose top we sit is Helseggen, the Cloudy. Now raise yourself up a little higher—hold on to the grass if you feel giddy—so—and look out, beyond the belt of vapor beneath us, into the sea."

I looked dizzily, and beheld a wide expanse of ocean, whose waters wore so inky a hue as to bring at once to my mind the Nubian geographer's account of the *Mare Tenebrarum*. A panorama more deplorably desolate no human imagination can conceive. To the right and left, as far as the eye could reach, there lay outstretched, like ramparts of the world, lines of horridly black and beetling cliff, whose character of gloom was but the more forcibly illustrated by the surf which reared high up against it its white and ghastly crest, howling and shrieking for ever. Just opposite the promontory upon whose apex we were placed, and at a distance of some five or six miles out at sea, there was visible a small, bleak-looking island; or, more properly, its position was discernible through the wilderness of surge in which it was enveloped. About two miles nearer the land, arose another of smaller size, hideously craggy and barren, and encompassed at various intervals by a cluster of dark rocks.

The appearance of the ocean, in the space between the more distant island and the shore, had something very unusual about it. Although, at the time, so strong a gale was blowing landward that a brig in the remote offing lay to under a double-reefed trysail, and constantly plunged her whole hull out of sight, still there was here nothing like a regular swell, but only a short, quick, angry cross dashing of water in every direction—as well in the teeth of the wind as otherwise. Of foam there was little except in the immediate vicinity of the rocks.

"The island in the distance," resumed the old man, "is called by the Norwegians Vurrgh. The one midway is Moskoe. That a mile to the northward is Ambaaren. Yonder are Iflesen, Hoeyholm, Kieldholm, Suarven, and Buckholm. Farther off—between Moskoe and Vurrgh—are Otterholm, Flimen, Sandflesen, and Skarholm. These are the true names of the places—but why it has been thought necessary to name them at all, is more than either you or I can understand. Do you hear any thing? Do you see any change in the water?"

We had now been about ten minutes upon the top of Helseggen, to which we had ascended from the interior of Lofoden, so that we had caught no glimpse of the sea until it had burst upon us from the summit. As the old man spoke, I became aware of a loud and gradually increasing sound, like the moaning of a vast herd of buffaloes upon an American prairie; and at the same moment I perceived that what seamen term the *chopping* character of the ocean beneath us was rapidly changing into a current which was set to the eastward. Even while I gazed, this current acquired a monstrous velocity. Each moment added to its speed—to its headlong impetuosity. In five minutes the whole sea, as far as Vurrgh, was lashed into ungovernable fury; but it was between Moskoe and the coast that the main uproar held its sway. Here the vast bed of the waters, seamed and scarred into a thousand conflicting channels, burst suddenly into phrensied convulsion—heaving, boiling, hissing—gyrating in gigantic and innumerable vortices, and all whirling and plunging on to the eastward with a rapidity which water never elsewhere assumes except in precipitous descents.

In a few minutes more, there came over the scene another radical alternation. The general surface grew somewhat more smooth, and the whirlpools, one by one, disappeared, while prodigious streaks of foam became apparent where none had been seen before. These streaks, at length, spreading out to a great distance, and entering into combination, took unto themselves the gyratory motion of the subsided vortices, and seemed to form the germ of another more vast. Suddenly—very suddenly—this assumed a distinct and definite existence, in a circle of more than half a mile in diameter. The edge of the whirl was represented by a broad belt of gleaming spray; but no particle of this slipped into the mouth of the terrific funnel, whose interior, as far as the eye could fathom it, was a smooth, shining, and jet-black wall of water, inclined to the horizon at an angle of some forty-five degrees, speeding dizzily round and round with a swaying and sweltering motion, and sending forth to the winds an appalling voice, half shriek, half roar, such as not even the mighty cataract of Niagara ever lifts up in its agony to Heaven.

The mountain trembled to its very base, and the rock rocked. I threw myself upon my face, and clung to the scant herbage in an excess of nervous agitation.

"This," said I at length, to the old man—"this *can* be nothing else than the great whirlpool of the Maelström."

"So it is sometimes termed," said he. "We Norwegians call it the Moskoe-ström, from the island of Moskoe in the midway."

The ordinary accounts of this vortex had by no means prepared me for what I saw. That of Jonas Ramus, which is perhaps the most circumstantial of any, cannot impart the faintest conception either of the magnificence, or of the horror of the scene—or of the wild bewildering sense of *the novel* which confounds the beholder. I am not sure from what point of view the writer in question surveyed it, nor at what time; but it could neither have been from the summit of Helseggen, nor during a storm. There are some passages of his description, nevertheless, which may be quoted for their details, although their effect is exceedingly feeble in conveying an impression of the spectacle.

"Between Lofoden and Moskoe," he says, "the depth of the water is between thirty-six and forty fathoms; but on the other side, toward Ver (Vurrgh) this depth decreases so as not to afford a convenient passage for a vessel, without the risk of splitting on the rocks, which happens even in the calmest weather. When it is flood, the stream runs up the country between Lofoden and Moskoe with a boisterous rapidity; but the roar of its impetuous ebb to the sea is scarce equaled by the loudest and most dreadful cataracts; the noise being heard several leagues off, and the vortices or pits are of such an extent and depth, that if a ship comes within its attraction, it is inevitably absorbed and carried down to the bottom, and there beat to pieces against the rocks; and when the water relaxes, the fragments thereof are thrown up again. But these intervals of tranquility are only at the turn of the ebb and flood, and in calm weather, and last but a quarter of an hour, its violence gradually returning. When the stream is most boisterous, and its fury heightened by a storm, it is dangerous to come within a Norway mile of it. Boats, yachts, and ships have been carried away by not guarding against it before they were within its reach. It likewise happens frequently, that whales come too near the stream, and are overpowered by its violence; and then it is impossible to describe their howlings and bellowings in their fruitless struggles to disengage themselves. A bear once, attempting to swim from Lofoden to Moskoe, was caught by the stream and borne down, while he roared terribly, so as to be heard on shore. Large stocks of firs and pine trees, after being absorbed by the current, rise again broken and torn to such a degree as if bristles grew upon them. This plainly shows the bottom to consist of craggy rocks, among which they are whirled to and fro. This stream is regulated by the flux and reflux of the sea—it being constantly high and low water every six hours. In the year 1645, early in the morning of Sexagesima Sunday, it raged with such noise and impetuosity that the very stones of the houses on the coast fell to the ground."

In regard to the depth of the water, I could not see how this could have been ascertained at all in the immediate vicinity of the vortex. The "forty fathoms" must have reference only to portions of the channel close upon the shore either of Moskoe or Lofoden. The depth in the centre of the Moskoe-ström must be immeasurably greater; and no better proof of this fact is necessary than can be obtained from even the sidelong glance into the abyss of the whirl which may be had from the highest crag of Helseggen. Looking down from this pinnacle upon the howling Phlegethon below, I could not help smiling at the simplicity with which the honest Jonas Ramus records, as a matter difficult of belief, the anecdotes of the whales and the bears; for it appeared to me, in fact, a self-evident thing, that the largest ship of the line in existence, coming within the influence of that deadly attraction, could resist it as little as a feather the hurricane, and must disappear bodily and at once.

The attempts to account for the phenomenon—some of which, I remember, seemed to me sufficiently plausible in perusal—now wore a very different and unsatisfactory aspect. The idea generally received is that this, as well as three smaller vortices among the Ferroe islands, "have no other cause than the collision of waves rising and falling, at flux and reflux, against a ridge of rocks and shelves, which confines the water so that it precipitates itself like a cataract; and thus the higher the flood rises, the deeper must the fall be, and the natural result of all is a whirlpool or vortex, the prodigious suction of which is sufficiently known by lesser experiments."—These are the words of the Encyclopædia Britannica. Kircher and others imagine that in the centre of the channel of the Maelström is an abyss penetrating the globe, and issuing in some very remote part—the Gulf of Bothnia being somewhat decidedly named in one instance. This opinion, idle in itself, was the one to which, as I gazed, my imagination most readily assented; and, mentioning it to the guide, I was rather surprised to hear him say that, although it was the view almost universally entertained of the subject by the Norwegians, it nevertheless was not his own. As to the former notion he confessed his inability to comprehend it; and here I agreed with him—for, however conclusive on paper, it becomes altogether unintelligible, and even absurd, amid the thunder of the abyss.

"You have had a good look at the whirl now," said the old man, "and if you will creep round this crag, so as to get in its lee, and deaden the roar of the water, I will tell you a story that will convince you I ought to know something of the Moskoe-ström."

I placed myself as desired, and he proceeded.

"Myself and my two brothers once owned a schooner-rigged smack of about seventy tons burthen, with which we were in the habit of fishing among the islands beyond Moskoe, nearly to Vurrgh. In all violent eddies at sea there is good fishing, at proper opportunities, if one has only the courage to attempt it; but among the whole of the Lofoden coastmen, we three were the only ones who made a regular business of going out to the islands, as I tell you. The usual grounds are a great way lower down to the southward. There fish can be got at all hours, without much risk, and therefore these places are preferred. The choice spots over here among the rocks, however, not only yield the finest variety, but in far greater abundance; so that we often got in a single day, what the more timid of the craft could not scrape together in a week. In fact, we made it a matter of desperate speculation—the risk of life standing instead of labor, and courage answering for capital.

"We kept the smack in a cover about five miles higher up the coast than this; and it was our practice, in fine weather, to take advantage of the fifteen minutes' slack to push across the main channel of the Moskoe-ström, far above the pool, and then drop down upon anchorage somewhere near Otterholm, or Sandflesen, where the eddies are not so violent as elsewhere. Here we used to remain until nearly time for slackwater again, when we weighed and made for home. We never set out upon this expedition without a steady side wind for going and coming—one that we felt sure would not fail us before our return—and we seldom made a mis-calculation upon this point. Twice, during six years, we were forced to stay all night at anchor on account of a dead calm, which is a rare thing indeed just about here; and once we had to remain on the grounds nearly a week, starving to death, owing to a gale which blew up shortly after our arrival, and made the channel too boisterous to be thought of. Upon this occasion we should have been driven out to sea in spite of everything, (for the whirlpools threw us round and round so violently, that, at length, we fouled our anchor and dragged it) if it had not been that we drifted into one of the innumerable cross currents—here to-day and gone to-morrow—which drove us under the lee of Flimen, where, by good luck, we brought up.

"I could not tell you the twentieth part of the difficulties we encountered 'on the grounds'—it is a bad spot to be in, even in good weather—but we made shift always to run the gauntlet of the Moskoe-ström itself without accident; although at times my heart has been in my mouth when we happened to be a minute or so behind or before the slack. The wind sometimes was not as strong as we thought it at starting, and then we made rather less way than we could wish, while the current rendered the smack unmanageable. My eldest brother had a son eighteen years old, and I had two stout boys of my own. These would have been of great assistance at such times, in using the sweeps, as well as afterward in fishing—but, somehow, although we ran the risk ourselves, we had not the heart to let the young ones get into the danger—for, after all is said and done, it *was* a horrible danger, and that is the truth.

"It is now within a few days of three years since what I am going to tell you occurred. It was on the tenth day of July, 18—, a day which the people of this part of the world will never forget—for it was one in which blew the most terrible hurricane that ever came out of the heavens. And yet all the morning, and indeed until late in the afternoon, there was a gentle and steady breeze from the southwest, while the sun shone brightly, so that the oldest seaman among us could not have foreseen what was to follow.

"The three of us—my two brothers and myself—had crossed over to the islands about two o'clock p.m., and had soon nearly loaded the smack with fine fish, which, we all remarked, were more plenty that day than we had ever known them. It was just seven, *by my watch,* when we weighed and started for home, so as to make the worst of the Ström at slack water, which we knew would be at eight.

"We set out with a fresh wind on our starboard quarter, and for some time spanked along at a great rate, never dreaming of danger, for indeed we saw not the slightest reason to apprehend it. All at once we were taken aback by a breeze from over Helseggen. This was most unusual—something that had never happened to us before—and I began to feel a little uneasy, without exactly knowing why. We put the boat on the wind, but could make no headway at all for the eddies, and I was upon the point of proposing to return to the anchorage, when, looking astern, we saw the whole horizon covered with a singular copper-colored cloud that rose with the most amazing velocity.

"In the meantime the breeze that had headed us off fell away, and we were dead becalmed, drifting about in every direction. This state of things, however, did not last long enough to give us time to think about it. In less than a minute the storm was upon us—in less than two the sky was entirely overcast—and what with this and the driving spray, it became suddenly so dark that we could not see each other in the smack.

"Such a hurricane as then blew it is folly to attempt describing. The oldest seaman in Norway never experienced anything like it. We had let our sails go by the run before it cleverly took us; but, at the first puff, both our masts went by the board as if they had been sawed off—the mainmast taking with it my youngest brother, who had lashed himself to it for safety.

"Our boat was the lightest feather of a thing that ever sat upon water. It had a complete flush deck, with only a small hatch near the bow, and this hatch it had always been our custom to batten down when about to cross the Ström, by way of precaution against the chopping seas. But for this circumstance we should have foundered at once—for we lay entirely buried for some moments. How my elder brother escaped destruction I cannot say, for I never had an opportunity of ascertaining. For my part, as soon as I had let the foresail run, I threw myself flat on deck, with my feet against the narrow gunwale of the bow, and with my hands grasping a ring-bolt near the foot of the foremast. It was mere instinct that prompted me to do this—which was undoubtedly the very best thing I could have done—for I was too much flurried to think.

"For some moments we were completely deluged, as I say, and all this time I held my breath, and clung to the bolt. When I could stand it no longer I raised myself upon my knees, still keeping hold with my hands, and thus got my head clear. Presently our little boat gave herself a shake, just as a dog does in coming out of the water, and thus rid herself, in some measure, of the seas. I was now trying to get the better of the stupor that had come over me, and to collect my senses so as to see what was to be done, when I felt somebody grasp my arm. It was my elder brother, and my heart leaped for joy, for I had made sure that he was overboard—but the next moment all this joy was turned into horror—for he put his mouth close to my ear, and screamed out the word 'Moskoe-ström!'

"No one ever will know what my feelings were at that moment. I shook from head to foot as if I had had the most violent fit of the ague. I knew what he meant by that one word well enough—I knew what he wished to make me understand. With the wind that now drove us on, we were bound for the whirl of the Ström, and nothing could save us!

"You perceive that in crossing the Ström *channel,* we always went a long way up above the whirl, even in the calmest weather, and then had to wait and watch carefully for the slack—but now we were driving right upon the pool itself, and in such a hurricane as this! 'To be sure,' I thought, 'we shall get there just about the slack— there is some little hope in that'—but in the next moment I cursed myself for being so great a fool as to dream of hope at all. I knew very well that we were doomed, had we been ten times a ninety-gun ship.

"By this time the first fury of the tempest had spent itself, or perhaps we did not feel it so much, as we scudded before it, but at all events the seas, which at first had been kept down by the wind, and lay flat and frothing, now got up into absolute mountains. A singular change, too, had come over the heavens. Around in every direction it was still as black as pitch, but nearly overhead there burst out, all at once, a circular rift of clear sky—as clear as I ever saw—and of a deep bright blue—and through it there blazed forth the full moon with a lustre that I never before knew her to wear. She lit up every thing about us with the greatest distinctness—but, oh God, what a scene it was to light up!

"I now made one or two attempts to speak to my brother—but, in some manner which I could not understand, the din had so increased that I could not make him hear a single word, although I screamed at the top of my voice in his ear. Presently he shook his head, looking as pale as death, and held up one of his fingers, as if to say *'listen!'*

"At first I could not make out what he meant—but soon a hideous thought flashed upon me. I dragged my watch from its fob. It was not going. I glanced at its face by the moonlight, and then burst into tears as I flung it far away into the ocean. *It had run down at seven o'clock! We were behind the time of the slack, and the whirl of the Ström was in full fury!*

"When a boat is well built, properly trimmed, and not deep laden, the waves in a strong gale, when she is going large, seem always to slip from beneath her—which appears very strange to a landsman—and this is what is called *riding,* in sea phrase. Well, so far we had ridden the swells very cleverly; but presently a gigantic sea happened to take us right under the counter, and bore us with it as it rose—up—up—as if into the sky. I would not have believed that any wave could rise so high. And then down we came with a sweep, a slide, and a plunge, that made me feel sick and dizzy, as if I was falling from some lofty mountain-top in a dream. But while we were up I had thrown a quick glance around—and that one glance was sufficient. I saw our exact position in an instant. The Moskoe-ström whirlpool was about a quarter of a mile dead ahead—but no more like the every-day Moskoe-ström, than the whirl as you now see it is like a mill-race. If I had not known where we were, and what we had to expect, I should not have recognised the place at all. As it was, I involuntarily closed my eyes in horror. The lids clenched themselves together as if in a spasm.

"It could not have been more than two minutes afterward until we suddenly felt the waves subside, and were enveloped in foam. The boat made a sharp half turn to larboard, and then shot off in its new direction like a thunderbolt. At the same moment the roaring noise of the water was completely drowned in a kind of shrill shriek—such a sound as you might imagine given out by the waste-pipes of many thousand steam-vessels, letting off their steam all together. We were now in the belt of surf that always surrounds the whirl; and I thought, of course, that another moment would plunge us into the abyss—down which we could only see indistinctly on account of the amazing velocity with which we were borne along. The boat did not seem to sink into the water at all, but to skim like an air-bubble upon the surface of the surge. Her starboard side was next the whirl, and on the larboard arose the world of ocean we had left. It stood like a huge writhing wall between us and the horizon.

"It may appear strange, but now, when we were in the very jaws of the gulf, I felt more composed than when we were only approaching it. Having made up my mind to hope no more, I got rid of a great deal of that terror which unmanned me at first. I suppose it was despair that strung my nerves.

"It may look like boasting—but what I tell you is truth—I began to reflect how magnificent a thing it was to die in such a manner, and how foolish it was in me to think of so paltry a consideration as my own individual life, in view of so wonderful a manifestation of God's power. I do believe that I blushed with shame when this idea crossed my mind. After a little while I became possessed with the keenest curiosity about the whirl itself. I positively felt a *wish* to explore its depths, even at the sacrifice I was going to make; and my principal grief was that I should never be able to tell my old companions on shore about the mysteries I should see. These, no doubt, were singular fancies to occupy a man's mind in such extremity— and I have often thought since, that the revolutions of the boat around the pool might have rendered me a little light-headed.

"There was another circumstance which tended to restore my self-possession; and this was the cessation of the wind, which could not reach us in our present situation—for, as you saw yourself, the belt of surf is considerably lower than the general bed of the ocean, and this latter now towered above us, a high, black, mountainous ridge. If you have never been at sea in a heavy gale, you can form no idea of the confusion of mind occasioned by the wind and spray together. They blind, deafen, and strangle you, and take away all power of action or reflection. But we were now, in a great measure, rid of these annoyances—just as death-condemned felons in prison are allowed petty indulgences, forbidden them while their doom is yet uncertain.

"How often we made the circuit of the belt it is impossible to say. We careened round and round for perhaps an hour, flying rather than floating, getting gradually more and more into the middle of the surge, and then nearer and nearer to its horrible inner edge. All this time I had never let go of the ring-bolt. My brother was at the stern, holding on to a large empty water cask which had been securely lashed under the coop of the counter, and was the only thing on deck that had not been swept overboard when the gale first took us. As we approached the brink of the pit he let go his hold upon this, and made for the ring, from which, in the agony of his terror, he endeavored to force my hands, as it was not large enough to afford us both a secure grasp. I never felt a deeper grief than when I saw him attempt this act—although I knew he was a madman when he did it—a raving maniac through sheer fright. I did not care, however, to contest the point with him. I thought it could make no difference whether either of us held on at all; so I let him have the bolt, and went astern to the cask. This there was no great difficulty in doing; for the smack flew round steadily enough, and upon an even keel— only swaying to and fro, with the immense sweeps and swelters of the whirl. Scarcely had I secured myself in my new position, when we gave a wild lurch to starboard, and rushed headlong into the abyss. I muttered a hurried prayer to God, and thought all was over.

"As I felt the sickening sweep of the descent, I had instinctively tightened my hold upon the barrel, and closed my eyes. For some seconds I dared not open them—while I expected instant destruction, and wondered that I was not already in my death-struggles with the water. But moment after moment elapsed. I still lived. The sense of falling had ceased; and the motion of the vessel seemed much as it had been before while in the belt of foam, with the exception that she now lay more along. I took courage, and looked once again upon the scene.

"Never shall I forget the sensations of awe, horror, and admiration with which I gazed about me. The boat appeared to be hanging, as if by magic, midway down, upon the interior surface of a funnel vast in circumference, prodigious in depth, and whose perfectly smooth sides might have been mistaken for ebony, but for the bewildering rapidity with which they spun around, and for the gleaming and ghastly radiance they shot forth, as the rays of the full moon, from that circular rift amid the clouds which I have already described, streamed in a flood of golden glory along the black walls, and far away down into the inmost recesses of the abyss.

"At first I was too much confused to observe anything accurately. The general burst of terrific grandeur was all that I beheld. When I recovered myself a little, however, my gaze fell instinctively downward. In this direction I was able to obtain an unobstructed view, from the manner in which the smack hung on the inclined surface of the pool. She was quite upon an even keel— that is to say, her deck lay in a plane parallel with that of the water— but this latter sloped at an angle of more than forty-five degrees, so that we seemed to be lying upon our beam-ends. I could not help observing, nevertheless, that I had scarcely more difficulty in maintaining my hold and footing in this situation, than if we had been upon a dead level; and this, I suppose, was owing to the speed at which we revolved.

"The rays of the moon seemed to search the very bottom of the profound gulf; but still I could make out nothing distinctly, on account of a thick mist in which everything there was enveloped, and over which there hung a magnificent rainbow, like that narrow and tottering bridge which Mussulmen say is the only pathway between

Time and Eternity. This mist, or spray, was no doubt occasioned by the clashing of the great walls of the funnel, as they all met together at the bottom—but the yell that went up to the Heavens from out of that mist, I dare not attempt to describe.

"Our first slide into the abyss itself, from the belt of foam above, had carried us a great distance down the slope; but our farther descent was by no means proportionate. Round and round we swept—not with any uniform movement—but in dizzying swings and jerks, that sent us sometimes only a few hundred feet—sometimes nearly the complete circuit of the whirl. Our progress downward, at each revolution, was slow, but very perceptible.

"Looking about me upon the wide waste of liquid ebony on which we were thus borne, I perceived that our boat was not the only object in the embrace of the whirl. Both above and below us were visible fragments of vessels, large masses of building timber and trunks of trees, with many smaller articles, such as pieces of house furniture, broken boxes, barrels and staves. I have already described the unnatural curiosity which had taken the place of my original terrors. It appeared to grow upon me as I drew nearer and nearer to my dreadful doom. I now began to watch, with a strange interest, the numerous things that floated in our company. I *must* have been delirious—for I even sought *amusement* in speculating upon the relative velocities of their several descents toward the foam below. 'This fir tree,' I found myself at one time saying, 'will certainly be the next thing that takes the awful plunge and disappears,'—and then I was disappointed to find that the wreck of a Dutch merchant ship overtook it and went down before. At length, after making several guesses of this nature, and being deceived in all—this fact—the fact of my invariable miscalculation—set me upon a train of reflection that made my limbs again tremble, and my heart beat heavily once more.

"It was not a new terror that thus affected me, but the dawn of a more exciting *hope*. This hope arose partly from memory, and partly from present observation. I called to mind the great variety of buoyant matter that strewed the coast of Lofoden, having been absorbed and then thrown forth by the Moskoe-ström. By far the greater number of the articles were shattered in the most extraordinary way—so chafed and roughened as to have the appearance of being stuck full of splinters—but then I distinctly recollected that there were *some* of them which were not disfigured at all. Now I could not account for this difference except by supposing that the roughened fragments were the only ones which had been *completely absorbed*—that the others had entered the whirl at so late a period of the tide, or, for some reason, had descended so slowly after entering, that they did not reach the bottom before the turn of the flood came, or of the ebb, as the case might be. I conceived it possible, in either instance, that they might thus be whirled up again to the level of the ocean, without undergoing the fate of those which had been drawn in more early, or absorbed more rapidly. I made, also, three important observations. The first was, that, as a general rule, the larger the bodies were, the more rapid their descent;—the second, that, between two masses of equal extent, the one spherical, and the other *of any other shape,* the superiority in speed of the descent was with the sphere;—the third, that, between two masses of equal size, the one cylindrical, and the other of any other shape, the cylinder was absorbed the more slowly. Since my escape, I have had several conversations on this subject with an old school-master of the district; and it was from him that I learned the use of the words 'cylinder' and 'sphere.' He explained to me—although I have forgotten the explanation—how what I observed was, in fact, the natural consequence of the forms of the floating fragments—and showed me how it happened that a cylinder, swimming in a vortex, offered more resistance to its suction, and was drawn in with greater difficulty than an equally bulky body, of any form whatever.*

"There was one startling circumstance which went a great way in enforcing these observations, and rendering me anxious to turn them to account, and this was that, at every revolution, we passed something like a barrel, or else the broken yard or the mast of a vessel, while many of these things, which had been on our level when I first opened my eyes upon the wonders of the whirlpool, were now high up above us, and seemed to have moved but little from their original station.

"I no longer hesitated what to do. I resolved to lash myself securely to the water cask upon which I now held, to cut it loose from the counter, and to throw myself with it into the water. I attracted my brother's attention by signs, pointed to the floating barrels that came near us, and did everything in my power to make him understand what I was about to do. I thought at length that he comprehended my design—but, whether this was the case or not, he shook his head despairingly, and refused to move from his station by the ring-bolt. It was impossible to force him; the emergency admitted no delay; and so, with a bitter struggle, I resigned him to his fate, fastened myself to the cask by means of the lashings which secured it to the counter, and precipitated myself with it into the sea, without another moment's hesitation.

"The result was precisely what I had hoped it might be. As it is myself who now tells you this tale—as you see that I *did* escape—and as you are already in possession of the mode in which this escape was effected, and must therefore anticipate all that I have farther to say—I will bring my story quickly to conclusion. It might have been an hour, or

*See Archimedes, "De Incidentibus in Fluido."— lib. 2.

thereabout, after my quitting the smack, when, having descended to a vast distance beneath me, it made three or four wild gyrations in rapid succession, and bearing my loved brother with it, plunged headlong, at once and forever, into the chaos of foam below. The cask to which I was attached sank very little farther than half the distance between the bottom of the gulf and the spot at which I leaped overboard, before a great change took place in the character of the whirlpool. The slope of the sides of the vast funnel became momently less and less steep. The gyrations of the whirl grew, gradually, less and less violent. By degrees, the froth and the rainbow disappeared, and the bottom of the gulf seemed slowly to uprise. The sky was clear, the winds had gone down, and full moon was setting radiantly in the west, when I found myself on the surface of the ocean, in full view of the shores of Lofoden, and above the spot where the pool of the Moskoe-ström *had been.* It was the hour of the slack—but the sea still heaved in mountainous waves from the effects of the hurricane. I was borne violently into the channel of the Ström, and in a few minutes was hurried down the coast into the 'grounds' of the fishermen. A boat picked me up—exhausted from fatigue—and (now that the danger was removed) speechless from the memory of its horror. Those who drew me on board were my old mates and daily companions—but they knew me no more than they would have known a traveller from the spirit-land. My hair which had been raven-black the day before, was as white as you see it now. They say too that the whole expression of my countenance had changed. I told them my story. They did not believe it. I now tell it to *you*—and I can scarcely expect you to put more faith in it than did the merry fishermen of Lofoden."

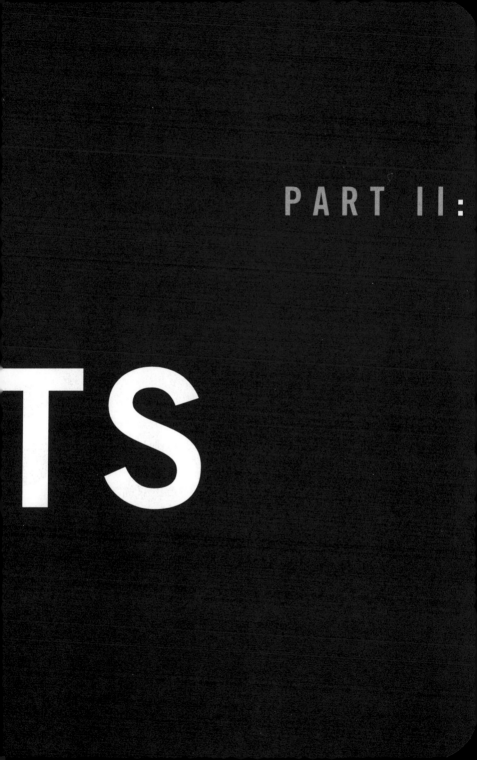

PART II:

TS

The Hyena

by Paul Bowles

A stork was passing over desert country on his way north. He was thirsty, and he began to look for water. When he came to the mountains of Khang el Ghar, he saw a pool at the bottom of a ravine. He flew down between the rocks and lighted at the edge of the water. Then he walked in and drank.

At that moment a hyena limped up and, seeing the stork standing in the water, said: "Have you come a long way?" The stork had never seen a hyena before. "So this is what a hyena is like," he thought. And he stood looking at the hyena because he had been told that if the hyena can put a little of his urine on someone, that one will have to walk after the hyena to whatever place the hyena wants him to go.

"It will be summer soon," said the stork. "I am on my way north." At the same time, he walked further out into the pool, so as not to be so near the hyena. The water here was deeper, and he almost lost his balance and had to flap his wings to keep upright. The hyena walked to the other side of the pool and looked at him from there.

"I know what is in your head," said the hyena. "You believe the story about me. You think I have that power? Perhaps long ago hyenas were like that. But now they are the same as everyone else. I could wet you from here with my urine if I wanted to. But what for? If you want to be unfriendly, go to the middle of the pool and stay there."

The stork looked around at the pool and saw that there was no spot in it where he could stand and be out of reach of the hyena.

"I have finished drinking," said the stork. He spread his wings and flapped out of the pool. At the edge he ran quickly ahead and rose into the air. He circled above the pool, looking down at the hyena.

"So you are the one they call the ogre," he said. "The world is full of strange things."

The hyena looked up. His eyes were narrow and crooked. "Allah brought us all here," he said. "You know that. You are the one who knows about Allah."

The stork flew a little lower. "That is true," he said. "But I am surprised to hear you say it. You have a very bad name, as you yourself just said. Magic is against the will of Allah."

The hyena tilted his head. "So you still believe the lies!" he cried.

"I have not seen the inside of your bladder," said the stork. "But why does everyone say you can make magic with it?"

"Why did Allah give you a head, I wonder? You have not learned how to use it." But the hyena spoke in so low a voice that the stork could not hear him.

"Your words got lost," said the stork, and he let himself drop lower.

The hyena looked up again. "I said: 'Don't come too near me. I might lift my leg and cover you with magic!'" He laughed, and the stork was near enough to see that his teeth were brown.

"Still, there must be some reason," the stork began. Then he looked for a rock high above the hyena, and settled himself on it. The hyena sat and stared up at him. "Why do they call you an ogre? What have you done?"

The hyena squinted. "You are lucky," he told the stork. "Men never try to kill you, because they think you are holy. They call you a saint and a sage. And yet you seem like neither a saint nor a sage."

"What do you mean?" said the stork quickly.

"If you really understood, you would know that magic is a grain of dust in the wind, and that Allah has power over everything. You would not be afraid."

The stork stood for a long time, thinking. He lifted one leg and held it bent in front of him. The ravine grew red as the sun went lower. And the hyena sat quietly looking up at the stork, waiting for him to speak.

Finally the stork put his leg down, opened his bill, and said: "You mean that if there is not magic, the one who sins is the one who believes there is."

The hyena laughed. "I said nothing about sin. But you did, and you are the sage. I am not in the world to tell anyone what is right or wrong. Living from night to night is enough. Everyone hopes to see me dead."

The stork lifted his leg again and stood thinking. The last daylight rose into the sky and was gone. The cliffs at the sides of the ravine were lost in the darkness.

At length the stork said: "You have given me something to think about. That is good. But now night has come. I must go on my way." He raised his wings and started to fly straight out from the boulder where he had stood. The hyena listened. He heard the stork's wings beating the air slowly, and then he heard the sound of the stork's body as it hit the cliff on the other side of the ravine. He climbed up over the rocks and found the stork. "Your wing is broken," he said. "It would have been better for you to go while there was still daylight."

"Yes," said the stork. He was unhappy and afraid.

"Come home with me," the hyena told him. "Can you walk?"

"Yes," said the stork. Together they made their way down the valley. Soon they came to a cave in the side of the mountain. The hyena went in first and called out: "Bend your head." When they were well inside, he said: "Now you can put your head up. The cave is high here."

There was only darkness inside. The stork stood still. "Where are you?" he said.

"I am here," the hyena answered, and he laughed.

"Why are you laughing?" asked the stork.

"I was thinking that the world is strange," the hyena told him. "The saint has come into my cave because he believed in magic."

"I don't understand," said the stork.

"You are confused. But at least now you can believe that I have no magic. I am like anyone else in the world."

The stork did not answer right away. He smelled the stench of the hyena very near him. Then he said, with a sigh: "You are right, of course. There is no power beyond the power of Allah."

"I am happy," said the hyena, breathing into his face. "At last you understand." Quickly he seized the stork's neck and tore it open. The stork flapped and fell on his side.

"Allah gave me something better than magic," the hyena said under his breath. "He gave me a brain."

The stork lay still. He tried to say once more: "There is no power beyond the power of Allah." But his bill merely opened very wide in the dark.

The hyena turned away. "You will be dead in a minute," he said over his shoulder. "In ten days I shall come back. By then you will be ready."

Ten days later the hyena went to the cave and found the stork where he had left him. The ants had not been there. "Good," he said. He devoured what he wanted and went outside to a large flat rock above the entrance to the cave. There in the moonlight he stood a while, vomiting.

He ate some of his vomit and rolled for a long time in the rest of it, rubbing it deep into his coat. Then he thanked Allah for eyes that could see the valley in the moonlight, and for a nose that could smell carrion on the wind. He rolled some more and licked the rock under him. For a while he lay there panting. Soon he got up and limped on his way.

Tangier, 1960

"Come Quick! I'm Being Eaten by a Bear!"

by Larry Kanuit

"Bears usually will kill humans only when surprised or super hungry."
(Captain Robert Penman, Alaska Department of Public Safety, personal interview, Anchorage, February 1977)

I first heard about Cynthia Dusel-Bacon over a local radio newscast August 13, 1977. She had been frightfully mauled by a bear while working for the United States Geological Survey somewhere up north, around Fairbanks. My interest in her experience led me to write her at the University of Stanford Medical Center.

This courageous lady sent me a tape with her story. She was more than eager to offer her experience in hopes of helping others avoid a similar situation, and she wrote in her letter (typed while holding a stylus between her jaws), "I couldn't be more pleased about your efforts to amass all available information about bear maulings in Alaska. I can't think of a greater contribution one could make to educate people about the potential danger of a bear encounter. I believe very strongly in what you are doing."

A short time later I received her tape and her story.

"The summer of 1977 was my third summer in the Yukon-Tanana Upland of Alaska, doing geologic field mapping for the Alaskan Geology Branch of the U.S. Geological Survey. I began working for the survey in the summer of 1975, making helicopter-assisted traverses in the highest terrain of the 6,000-square-mile Big Delta quadrangle. The second summer, as our budget did not provide for helicopter expenses, the project chief and I found it necessary to map the geology by backpacking, usually a week at a time. Last summer we were again funded for helicopter transport after an initial month of backpacking. All five geologists in our group, after being transported by air to the field area, usually mapped alone. I personally felt quite comfortable.

"Every summer in the upland area we saw bears. The first one I saw was walking slowly along on the far side of a small mountain meadow, and I froze. It didn't see me and disappeared into the forest. Another time I was walking through a spruce forest and saw a black bear moving through the trees some distance away. Again I was apparently not noticed. The second summer while I was backpacking, I encountered a small black bear coming along the trail toward me. I had been busy looking down at the ground for chips of rock, when I heard a slight rustling sound. I looked up to see the bear about 40 feet in front of me. Startled, it turned around and ran off in the other direction, crashing through the brush as it left the trail. This particular experience reassured me that what I had heard about black bears being afraid of people was, in fact, true.

I See My First Grizzly

"During my third summer, I saw my first grizzly, but only from the air while traveling in the helicopter. Although other members of our field party had seen them on the ground, I felt myself fortunate to have encountered only black bears. Grizzlies were generally considered to be more unpredictable and dangerous.

"All three summers I had hiked through the bush unarmed, as it was the belief of our project chief that guns added more danger to an encounter than they might prevent. A wounded, angry bear would probably be more dangerous than a frightened one. She had therefore strongly discouraged us from carrying any kind of firearm. We all carried walkie-talkie radios so as to keep in constant touch with one another and with our base camp. And we were warned against surprising bears or getting between a mother and her cubs. Whenever I was doing field mapping, I always attempted to make noise as I walked so that I would alert any bears within hearing and give them time to run away from me. For two summers this system worked perfectly.

"Last summer we were scheduled to complete the reconnaissance mapping of the Big Delta quadrangle. Since it covers such a vast area, we needed helicopter transportation in order to finish traversing all the ridges by mid-September.

"At about 8:00 a.m. of August 13, 1977, Ed Spencer, our helicopter pilot, dropped me off near the top of a rocky, brush-covered ridge approximately 60 miles southeast of Fairbanks. I was dressed in khaki work pants and a cotton shirt, wore sturdy hiking boots, and carried a rucksack. In the right-hand outside pocket of my pack I carried a light lunch of baked beans, canned fruit, fruit juice, and a few pilot crackers. My walkie-talkie radio was stashed in the left-hand outside pocket, complete with covering flap, strap and buckle. I was to take notes on the geology and collect samples by means of the geologist's hammer I carried on my belt, record my location on the map, and stow the samples in my rucksack.

"Standard safety procedure involved my making radio contact with the other geologists and with our base camp several times during the day, at regular intervals. The radio in camp, about 80 miles south of the mapping area, was being monitored by the wife of the helicopter pilot. Plans called for me to be picked up by helicopter at the base of the eight-mile-long ridge on a designated gravel bar of the river at the end of the day.

A Nice Narrow Trail

"After noticing, with unexpected pleasure, that I was going to be able to use a narrow trail that had been bulldozed along the crest of the ridge, I started off downhill easily, on the trail that passed through tangles of birch brush and over rough, rocky slides. The ridge was in one of the more populated parts of the quadrangle, as there are a few small cabins about 15 or 20 miles downstream along the Salcha River, and a short landing strip for airplanes about 10 miles from the ridge. Fisherman occasionally come this far up the river, too, so the bears in the area have probably seen human beings occasionally. This particular morning I wasn't expecting to see bears at all; the hillside was so rocky, so dry looking and tangled with brush, it just didn't seem like bear country. If I were to see a bear that day, it would more likely be at the end of the day, down along the river bar and adjoining woods.

"I descended the ridge slowly for several hundred yards, moving from one outcrop of rock to another, chipping off samples and stowing them in my pack. I stopped at one large outcrop to break off an interesting piece and examined it intently. A sudden loud crash in the undergrowth below startled me and I looked around just in time to see a black bear rise up out of the brush about 10 feet away. My first thought was 'Oh no! a bear. I'd better do the right thing.' My next thought was one of relief: 'It's only a black bear, and a rather small one at that.' Nevertheless, I decided to get the upper hand immediately and scare it away. I shouted at it, face-to-face, in my most commanding tone of voice: 'Shoo! Get out here, bear! Go on! Get away!' The bear remained motionless and glared back. I clapped my hands and yelled even louder. Even this had no effect on the bear.

"Instead of turning and running away into the brush, it began slowly walking, climbing toward my level, watching me stealthily. I waved my arms, clapped, yelled even more wildly. I began banging on the outcrop with my hammer, making all the noise I could to intimidate this bear that was just not acting like a black bear is supposed to. I took a step back, managing to elevate myself another foot or so in an attempt to reach a more dominant position. But as I did this, the bear darted suddenly around behind the outcrop, behind me.

"My sensation was that of being struck a staggering blow from behind. I felt myself being thrown forward and landed face down on the ground, with my arms outstretched. I froze, not instinctively but deliberately, remembering that playing dead was supposed to cause an attacking bear to lose interest and go away.

"Instead of hearing the bear crashing off through the brush though, I felt the sudden piercing pain of the bear's teeth biting deep into my right shoulder. I felt myself being shaken with tremendous, irresistible power by my shoulder, by teeth deep in my shoulder. Then it stopped, and seemed to be waiting to see if I were still alive.

I Tried For My Radio

"I tried to lie perfectly still, hoping it was satisfied. 'I've got to get at my radio in the pack, I've got to get a call out,' I thought. My left arm was free so I tried to reach behind myself to the left outside pocket of my rucksack to get at the walkie-talkie. The strap was buckled so tightly I realized I couldn't get the pocket open without taking off my pack. My movement caused the bear to start a new flurry of biting and tearing at the flesh of my upper right arm again. I was completely conscious of feeling my flesh torn, teeth against bone, but the sensation was more of numb horror at what was happening to me than of specific reaction to each bite. I remember thinking, 'Now I'm never going to be able to call for help. I'm dead unless this bear decides to leave me alone.'

"The bear had no intention of leaving me alone. After chewing on my right shoulder, arm, and side repeatedly, the bear began to bite my head and tear at my scalp. As I heard the horrible crunching sound of the bear's teeth biting into my skull, I realized it was all too hopeless. I remember thinking, 'This has got to be the worst way to go.' I knew it would be a slow death because my vital signs were all still strong. My fate was to bleed to death. I thought, 'Maybe I should just shake my head and get the bear to do me in quickly.'

"All of a sudden, the bear clamped its jaws into me and began dragging me by the right arm down the slope through the brush. I was dragged about 20 feet or so before the bear stopped as if to rest, panting in my ear. It began licking at the blood that was by now running out of a large wound under my right arm. Again the bear pulled me along the ground, over rocks and through brush, stopping frequently to rest, and chewing at my arm. Finally it stopped, panting heavily. It had been dragging me and my 20-pound pack—a combined weight of about 150 pounds—for almost a half-hour. Now it walked about four feet away and sat down to rest, still watching me intently.

"Here, I thought, might be a chance to save myself yet—if only I could get at that radio. Slowly I moved my left arm, which was on the side away from the bear, and which was still undamaged, behind me to get at that pack buckle. But this time the pocket, instead of being latched tight, was wide open—the buckle probably tore off from the bear's clawing or the dragging over the rocks. I managed to reach down into the pocket and pull out the radio.

Come Quick! I'm Being Eaten By A Bear

"Since my right arm was now completely numb and useless, I used my left hand to stealthily snap on the radio switch, pull up two of the three segments of the antenna, and push in the button activating the transmitter. Holding the radio close to my mouth, I said as loudly as I dared, 'Ed, this is Cynthia. Come quick, I'm being eaten by a bear.' I said 'eaten' because I was convinced that the bear wasn't just mauling me or playing with me, but was planning to consume me. I was its prey and it had no intention of letting the 'catch' escape.

"I repeated my message and then started to call out some more information, hoping that my first calls had been heard. 'Ed, I'm just down the hill from where you left me off this morning . . .' but I got no further. The bear by this time had risen to its feet; it bounded quickly over to me, and savagely attacked my left arm, knocking the radio out of my hand. I screamed in pain as I felt my good arm now being torn and mangled by claws and teeth.

"It was then I realized I had done all I could to save my life. I had no way of knowing whether anyone had even heard my calls. I really doubted it, since no static or answering sound from someone trying to call back had come over the receiver. I knew I hadn't taken time to extend the antenna completely. I knew I was down in a ravine, with many ridges between me and the receiving set. I knew there was really no chance for me. I was doomed. So I screamed and yelled as the bear tore at my arm, figuring that it was going to eat me anyway and there was no longer any reason to try to control my natural reactions.

"I remember that the bear then began sniffing around my body, going down to my calves, up my thighs. I thought 'I wonder if he's going to open up new wounds or continue working on the old ones.' I didn't dare to look around at what was happening—my eyes were fixed upon the dirt and leaves on the ground only inches below my face. Then I felt a tearing at the pack on my back, and heard the bear begin crunching cans in its teeth—cans I had brought for my lunch. This seemed to occupy its attention for a while; at least it let my arms alone and gave me a few moments to focus my mind on my predicament.

"'Is this how I'm going to go?' I remember marveling at how clear my mind was, how keen my senses were. All I could think of as I lay there on my stomach, with my face down in the dry grass and dirt, and that merciless, blood-thirsty thing holding me down, was how much I wanted to live and how much I wanted to return to Charlie, my husband of five months, and how tragic it would be to end it all three days before I turned 31.

"It was about 10 minutes, I think, before I heard the faint sound of a helicopter in the distance. It came closer and then seemed to circle, as if making a pass, but not directly over me. Then I heard the helicopter going away, leaving me. What had gone wrong? Maybe it was just a routine pass to transfer one of the other geologists to a different ridge, or to go to a gas cache to refuel, and not an answer to my call for help. No one heard my call.

"The bear had not been frightened by the sound of the helicopter, for now having finished with the contents of my pack it began to tear again at the flesh under my right arm. Then I heard the helicopter coming back, circling, getting closer. Being flat on my face, with the remains of the pack still on my back, and both arms now completely without feeling, I kicked my legs to show whoever was up above me that I was still alive. This time, however, I was certain that I was to be rescued because the pilot hovered directly over me.

Silence

"But again I heard the helicopter suddenly start away over the ridge. In a few seconds all was silence, agonizing silence. I couldn't believe it. For some completely senseless, heartless, stupid reason they'd left me for a second time.

"Suddenly I felt, or sensed, that the bear was not beside me. The sound of the chopper had undoubtedly frightened it away. Again I waited in silence for some 10 minutes. Then I heard the helicopter coming over the ridge again, fast and right over me. I kicked my legs again, and heard the helicopter move up toward the crest of the ridge for what I was now sure was a landing. Finally I heard the engine shut down, then voices, and people calling out."

The Wolves of Aguila

by Peter Matthiessen

On those rare occasions when a lean gray wolf wandered north across the border from the Espuela Mountains, trotting swiftly and purposefully into the Animas Valley or the Chiricahuas or Red Rock Canyon as so many had in years gone by, describing a half-circle seventy miles or more back into Mexico, and leaving somewhere along its run a mangled sheep or mutilated heifer, then Miller was sent for and Miller would go. He was a wolf hunter, hiring himself out on contract to ranchers and government agencies, and if the killing for which he was paid was confined more and more to coyotes and bobcats, the purpose of his life remained the wolf. He considered the lesser animals unworthy of his experience, deserving no better than the strychnine and the cyanide guns that filled the trunk of his sedan. Even the sedan had been forced upon him, when the wolf runs which once traced the border regions of New Mexico and Arizona had become so few and faded as to no longer justify the maintenance of a saddle pony. The southerly withdrawal of the gray wolf into the brown, dust-misted mountains of Chihuahua and Sonora had come to Will Miller as a loss, a reaction he had never anticipated. He was uneasily aware that persecution of the wolf was no longer justified, that each random kill he now effected contributed to the death of a wild place and a way of life that he knew was all he had.

Nevertheless, with mixed feelings of elation and penitence, he would travel to the scene of the last raid. There he would scout the area for scent posts where the wolf had left fresh sign. Kneeling on a piece of calf hide, he worked his clean steel traps into the earth with ritualistic care, rearranging every stick and pebble when he had finished, and carrying off the displaced dirt on the hide. His hands were gloved and his soles were smeared with the dung of the live-stock using the range, and leaving the scene, he moved away back-ward, scratching out his slightest print with a frayed stick. Nor did he visit his traps until the wolf had time to come again, gauging this according to the freshness of the sign and according to his instinct.

Because of his silence and solitary habits, his glinting eyes and wind-eroded visage, and his wild Navajo blood, Miller was credited with the ability to think like an animal. His success was a border leg-end, and while it was true that he understood its creatures very well, he was successful because he did not take their timeless traits for granted. The dark history of *Canis lupus,* the great gray wolf of the world, he considered an important part of his practical education. Not that Miller accepted the old tales of werewolves and wolf-children, or not, at least, in the forefront of his mind. But the heritage in him of the Old People, the deep-running responses to the natural signs and sacraments, did not discount them. The eerie intelligence of this night animal, its tirelessness and odd ability to vanish, had awed him more than once, and he had even imagined, in his long solitude, that should he ever pursue it into the brown haze to the south, the wolf spirit would revenge itself in that shadowed land. Such knowledge lent his life a mystery and meaning that the church missions could not replace, and his mind asked no more. He was not a modern Indian, and he shunned the modern towns. Like the wolf itself, he abided by older laws.

Night powers were incarnate in the Aguila wolf, which was known to have slaughtered sixty-five sheep in a single night and laid waste the stock in western Arizona for eight long years, fading back into the oblivion of time in 1924. One trapper in pursuit of it had disappeared without a trace, and Miller had always wondered if, at some point in that man's last terrible day beneath the sun, the Aguila wolf had not passed nearby, pausing in its ceaseless round to scent the dry, man-tainted air before padding on about its age-old business. Somewhere its progeny still hunted, and he often thought that the black male that once circled his traps for thirteen months and dragged the one that finally caught it forty miles must have descended from the old Aguila.

Most wolves gave him little trouble. Within a week or ten days of its raid, the usual animal would trot north out of Mexico again and, retracing its hunting route in a counterclockwise direction, investigate the scent posts, pausing at each to void itself and scratch the earth. At one of these, sooner or later, it would place its paw in a slight depression, the dirt would give way, and the steel jaws would snap on its foreleg. If its own bone was too heavy to gnaw through, and the trap well staked, it would finally lie down and wait. It would sense Miller's coming and, if still strong enough, would stand. Though its hair would bristle, it rarely snarled. Invariably, Miller stood respectfully at a distance, as if trying to see in the animal's flat gaze the secret of his own fascination. Then he would dispatch it carefully with a .38 revolver. But when the wolf lay inert at his feet, a hush seemed to fall in the mesquite and paloverde, as if the bright early-morning desert had died with the shot. The red sun, rising up, would whiten, and the faint smell of desert flowers fade, and the cactus wrens would still. In the carcass, already shrunken, lay the death of this land as it once was, and in the vast silence a reproach. The last time, Miller had broken his trap and sworn that he would never kill a wolf again.

Some years passed before two animals, hunting together according to the reports, made kills all along the border, from Hidalgo County in New Mexico to Cochise and Santa Cruz counties in Arizona, with scattered raids as far west at Sonoita, in Sonora. They used the ancient runs and developed new ones, but their wide range and unpredictable behavior had defeated all efforts at trapping them. The ranchers complained to the federal agencies, which in turn sent for Will Miller.

Miller at first refused to go. But he had read of the two wolves, and his restlessness overcame him. A few days later, he turned up in the regional wildlife office, a small, dark, well-made man of forty-eight in sweated khakis, with a green neckerchief and worn boots and a battered black felt hat held in both hands. Beneath a lank hood of ebony hair, his hawk face, hard and creased, was pleasant, and his step and manner quiet, unobtrusive. He had all his possessions with him. These included eight hundred dollars, a change of clothes, and the equipment of his profession in the sedan outside, as well as an indifferent education, a war medal, and the knowledge that, until this moment, he had never done anything in his life that dishonored him. Placing his hat on the game agent's desk, he picked restlessly through the reports. Then he asked questions. Angry with himself for being there, he hardly listened while the agent explained that the two wolves seemed immune to ordinary methods, which was why Will had been sent for. Miller ignored the patronizing use of the Indian's first name as well as the compliment. Unsmiling, he asked if the two wolves were really so destructive that they couldn't be left alone. The agent answered that Miller sounded scared of *Canis lupus* after all these years and, because Miller's expression made him uneasy, laughed too loudly.

"Them wolves was here before we come," Miller said. "I'd like to know they was a few left when we go."

Miller went west to Ajo, where he got drunk and visited a woman and, before the evening was out, got drunk all over again. He was not a habitual drinker, and drank heavily only in the rueful certainty that he would be sick for days to come. Later he drove out into the desert and staggered among the huge shapes of the saguaros, shouting.

"I'm comin after you, goddamn you, I'm comin, you hear that?"

And he shook his fist toward the distant mountains of Mexico. In doing so, he lost his balance and sat down hard, cutting his out-stretched hand on a leaf of yucca. Glaring at the blood, black in the moonlight, he began to laugh. But a little later, awed and sobered by the hostile silhouettes of the desert night, he licked at the black patterns traced upon his hand and shivered. Then he lay down flat upon his back and stared at the eternity of the stars.

Toward dawn, closing his eyes at last, he sighed, and wondered if it could really be that he felt like crying. He jeered at himself instead. Unable to admit to loneliness, he told himself it was time he settled down, had children. He could decide who and how and where first thing in the morning. But a few hours later, getting up, he felt too sick to consider the idea. He cursed himself briefly and sincerely and headed south toward Sonoita, where the wolves had been reported last.

The town of Sonoita lies just across the border from the organ-pipe cactus country of southern Arizona, on the road to Puerto Peñasco and the Gulf of California. Miller arrived there at mid-morning. The heat was searing, even for this land, as menacing in its still might as violent weather elsewhere. The Mexican border guards were apathetic, waving him through from beneath the shelter of their shed.

Miller had a headache from the alcohol and desert glare. Making inquiries, he found no one who understood him. Finally by dint of repeating *"Lobo, lobo"* into the round, rapt faces, he was led ceremonially to the parched remains of a steer outside the town. The carcass had been scavenged by the people, and a moping vulture flopped clumsily into the air. The trail was cold. Since Sonoita lay on the edge of the Gran Desierto, he did not believe that the wolves would wander farther west. From here, he would have to work back east, to New Mexico, if necessary.

Yet the villagers picked insistently at his shoulder—*Sst! Señor, sst!*—and pointed westward. When he stared at them, then shook his head and pointed east, they murmured humbly among themselves, but one old man again extended a bony, implacable arm toward the desert. Like children, mouths slack, hands diffident behind their backs, the rest surrounded Miller, their black eyes bright as those of reptiles. *Sí, amigo. Sí, sí.* Abruptly, he pushed through them and returned into the town.

Clutching a beer glass in the cantina, encircled by his silent following, he knew he had not made a thorough search for wolf sign, and could not do so in his present state of mind. The prospect of long days ahead in the dry canyons, piecing out the faded trail, oppressed him so that he sat stupefied. He felt sick and uneasy and, in some way he could not define, afraid. He wanted to talk to someone, to flee from his forebodings, and he thought of a nice woman he knew in Yuma. But Yuma lay westward a hundred miles or more, via an old road across the mountain deserts to San Luis and Mexicali. He did not know the road, and he had heard tales of the violence of this desert, and he dreaded the journey through an unfamiliar land in his present condition, and in such heat. On the other hand, these people had directed him toward the west. How could they know? Considering this, he felt dizzy and his palms grew damp. Still, by way of San Luis, he could reach Yuma by mid-afternoon and come back, in better spirits, tomorrow morning. Meanwhile, the wolves might kill again in Sonoita, leaving fresh sign. And if he got drunk enough, he thought, he might even come back married.

"To hell with it," he told the nodding Mexicans. "I'll go."

Outside, the heat struck him full in the face, stopping him short. His lungs squeezed the dry air for sustenance, and his nose pinched tight on the fine mist of alkali shrouding the town. In the shade, the natives and their animals squatted mute, awaiting the distant rains of summer. The town was inert, silent, in its dull awareness of Miller's car.

At the garage, Miller checked his oil and water carefully, knowing he should carry spare water with him, for the San Luis Road, stretching away into the Gran Desierto, would be long and barren. But he could not locate a container of any kind, and his growing apprehension irritated him, and on impulse he left without the water, quitting the town in a swirl of dust and gravel. Once on the road, however, he felt foolish, and he was not out of sight of the last adobe hut when he caught himself glancing at the oil pressure and water temperature gauges. He did it again a few minutes later.

The road ran west through low, scorched hills before curving south into the open desert. At one point it ran north to Quitobaquito Springs, the only green place on the San Luis Road. Miller stopped the car. Across the springs, beneath a cottonwood, he saw a hut; a family of Papagos, two dogs, and a wild-maned horse gazed at him, motionless. The dogs were silent. In the treetops, two black, shiny phainopeplas fluttered briefly and were still.

"How do," Miller called. The Indians observed him, unblinking. It occurred to Miller that his was the only voice in this dead land, where people answered him, when they answered at all, with nods and grunts and soft, indecipherable hisses. He stood a moment, unwilling to think, then returned slowly to the sedan.

For a mile or so beyond the springs, a gravel road detoured from a stretch of highway left long ago in half-repair. The detour was rutted and pocked with holes, and he could barely keep the toiling car in motion. He was easing it painfully onto the highway again when he heard a clear, animal cry. The sound was wild and shrill, and startled Miller. Breaking the sedan, he stalled it. In the sudden silence, the cry was repeated, and a moment later he glimpsed a movement at the mouth of a hollow in a road bank. An animal the size of a large dog slipped from the hole. In the glare, he did not recognize it as a child until it stood and approached the car. This creature, a boy of indefinite age, was followed instantly by another, who paused on all fours at the cave entrance before joining the first.

Already the first was at the window, fixing Miller with clear, flat eyes located high and to the side of his narrow face. His brother— for their features were almost identical—had brown hair rather than black, and his eyes were dull, reflecting everything and seeing nothing. Over the other's shoulder, he looked past Miller rather than at him, and after a moment turned his head away, as if scenting the air. Then the first boy smiled, a reflexive smile that traveled straight back along his jaw instead of curling, and pointed his finger toward the west. When he lowered his hand, he placed it on the door handle.

Miller could not make himself speak. He stared at the hole from which the two had crept, unable to believe they had really come out of it, unable to imagine what they were doing here at all. His first thought had been that these boys must belong to the Papago family at the springs, but one look at their faces told him this could not be so. These heads were sharp and clear-featured, reminiscent of something he could not recall, with a certain hardness about the mouth and nostrils. There was none of the blunt impassivity of the Papagos. There was nothing of poverty about them, either, and yet clearly they were homeless, without belongings of any kind. Still, they might be bandit children. He peered once again into the black eyes at the window, but his efforts to remember where he had seen that gaze were unsuccessful, and he shook his head to clear his dizziness.

The boys watched him without expression. After a while, when he did nothing, the older one opened the door and slipped into the car, and the second followed.

Miller felt oddly under duress. Moving the car forward onto the highway, he glanced uneasily at the gauges. It upset him that the Indians had not inquired as to where he was going. On the San Luis Road, one came and one went, but one made certain of a destination. It was as if, were he to drive his car off southward across the hard desert into oblivion, those two would accompany him with foreknowledge and without surprise.

At last he said, in his poor Spanish: *"En donde va? A San Luis? Mexicali?"*

The older boy smiled his curious smile and nodded, hissing briefly between white teeth. Miller took this to mean *"Sí."*

"San Luis?" Miller said.

The boy nodded.

"Mexicali?" Miller said, after a moment.

The boy nodded. Either he did not understand, or the matter was of no importance to him. He raised his hand in a grotesque salute and smiled again. The eyes of the other boy switched back and forth, observing their expressions.

Though the heat had grown, the day had darkened, and odd clouds, wild scudding blots of gray, swept up across the sallow sky from the remote Gulf. A wind came, fitfully at first, fanning sand across the highway. Miller, in a sort of trance, clung to the wheel. His car, which he knew he was driving too fast, was straining in the heat, and he sighed in the intensity of his relief when a large orange truck, the first sign of life in miles of thinning mesquite and saguaro, came at him out of the bleached distances ahead.

He glanced at the two boys. They seemed to have sensed the coming of the truck long before Miller himself, for their eyes were fixed upon it, and the eyebrows of the elder were raised, alert.

As the truck neared, an arm protruded from the cab and flagged Miller to a stop.

The truck driver, lighting a brown cigarette, peered about him at the hostile desert before speaking, as if sharing the desolation with Miller. He then asked in Spanish the distance to Sonoita. Miller, who was now counting every mile of the hundred-odd to San Luis, knew the exact distance, and suspected the truck driver knew it, too. The chance meeting on the highway was, for both of them, a respite, a source of nourishment for the journey which, like the springs at Quitobaquito, was not to be passed up lightly. However, he could not think of the correct Spanish numeral, and when the other repeated the question, inclining his head slightly to peer past Miller at the Indians, Miller turned to them for help. Both boys stared straight ahead through the windshield. The Mexican driver repeated the question in what Miller took to be an Indian dialect, but still the boys sat mute. The older maintained his tense, alert expression, as if on the point of sudden movement.

"*Treinta-cinco*," Miller said at last, choosing an approximate round figure.

The driver thanked him, glancing once again at the two boys. He exchanged a look with Miller, then shrugged, forcing his machine into gear as he did so. The truck moaned away down the empty road, and the outside world it represented became a fleeting speck of orange in the rearview mirror. When Miller could see it no longer, and the solitude closed around him, he inspected his temperature gauge once again. The red needle, which had climbed while the car was idling, returned slowly to a position just over normal, flickered, and was still.

The road ran on among gravel ridges, which mounted endlessly and sloped away to nothing. Only stunted saguaros survived in this country, their ribs protruded with desiccation, and an abandoned hawk's nest testified to the fact that life had somehow been sustained here. Miller, who had seen no sign of wildlife since leaving the springs, wondered why a swift creature like a hawk would linger in such a place when far less formidable terrains awaited it elsewhere. And of course it had not remained. The nest might be many years old, as Miller knew, and the hawk young, mummified, might still be in it. On this sere, stifled valley floor, a crude dwelling, forsaken and untended, would remain intact for decades, with only dry wind to eat at it, grain by grain. Not, he thought, that any man could survive here, or even the Mexican wolf. And he had convinced himself of this when, at a long bend in the road, an outcropping of rock he had seen from some miles away was transformed by the muted glare into a low building of adobe and gray wood.

Removing his foot from the accelerator, he wiped his forehead with the back of a cold hand. The black sedan, still in gear, whined down across a gravel flat of dead saguaros.

The cantina lay fetched up against a ridge just off the highway, as if uprooted elsewhere and set down again, like tumbleweed, by some ill wind. Around it the heat rose and fell in shimmers; he thought it abandoned until he saw the hot glitter of a trash heap to one side. There were no cars or horses. Beside him, the older boy stared straight ahead, but he gave Miller the feeling that his vision encompassed the cantina, on one side, and Miller himself on the other. Both boys were pressed so close to the far window that there was a space between them and Miller on the narrow seat, and a tension as tight as heat filled the small compartment. Miller opened his door abruptly and got out. When the two turned to watch him, he pointed at the cantina and waited. After a moment, the dark boy reached across the younger one to the door handle, and both slipped out on the far side.

By the doorway, Miller paused and touched a hide stretched inside out upon the wall, allowing the Indians to draw near him and trail him into the cantina. He could not put away his dread, and the idea of leaving them alone with the car and equipment made him uneasy. But although they had moved forward, the two boys paused when he paused, like stalking animals. Heads partly averted, squinting in the violent sun of noon, they followed his hand upon the pelt, as if his smallest move might have its meaning for them.

For a moment, indecisive, he inspected the sun-cracked skin, through the old wounds of which the grizzled hair protruded. The wolf had been nailed long ago against the wall, and although most of the nails had fallen away, it maintained its tortured shape on the parched wood. With the tar paper and tin, the hide now served to patch the shack's loose structure. One flank and shoulder shifted in the wind from the Gran Desierto, and the claws of the right forefoot, still intact, stirred restlessly, a small, insistent scratching which Miller stifled by bending the claws into the slats. In doing so, he freed a final nail, and the upper quarter of the hide sagged outward from the wall, revealing the scraggy fur. Miller stooped to retrieve the nail. Half-bent, he stopped, then straightened, glancing back at the mute boys. Their narrow eyes shone flat, unblinking. He turned and moved through the doorless opening, stumbling on the sill.

In a room kept dark against the glare, a man sat in a canvas chair behind the bar. He stared blindly at the sour walls, as if permanently ready to do business but unwilling to solicit it. The only sound was a raw, discordant clanging of a loose tin sheet upon the roof, the only movement dust in the bright doorway. For a moment, Miller imagined him carved of wood, but at the tip of a brown cigarette stub in the center of his mouth was a small glow.

"Buenos días," he said.

The proprietor's answer was a soft tentative whispering, scarcely audible above the clanging of the tin. Asking for a beer, Miller whispered, too. In answer, the man reached behind him into a black vat of water, drawing out a bottle with no label. He held it at arm's length like a trophy, the stale water sliding down his wrist. The vat, roiled by his hand, gave off a fetid odor.

"All right," said Miller. *"Sí."*

He turned to locate the two boys. The older one stood outside the doorway, but the other was not in sight. Miller waved at the first to enter, but the boy did not stir. The proprietor, glimpsing him for the first time, glanced at Miller. Miller took the tepid beer and requested two bottles of soda. The man held up two fingers, raised his eyebrows. "There's another outside," Miller explained. He awaited the warm bottles, then walked quickly to the door.

The younger boy was squatted beneath the pelt, staring away over the desert. Though his head did not move, his eye flickered once or twice, aware of Miller, who sensed that, should he make a sudden motion, this creature would spring sideways and away, coming to rest, still watching him, after a single bound. Wild as they were, however, the two seemed less afraid of him than intent upon him. He could not rid himself of the notion that these wild, strange boys had been awaiting him in their cave near the Quitobaquito Springs.

The dark boy drew near and took the two bottles of soda from Miller's hands. The exchange was ceremonial, without communication. The squatting boy, in turn, received his bottle from the other, clutching it with both hands and sniffing it over before bending his head and sucking the liquid upward.

Miller returned inside to get his beer, and leaned backward heavily against the counter. His headache had grown worse, and the smell of the rancid water on the bottle sickened him. He put it down, seizing the counter as a wave of vertigo shrouded his sight, and the boy in the doorway wavered in black silhouette.

From somewhere near at hand, a soft voice probed for his attention. He recovered himself, sweating unnaturally, heart pounding.

"*Lobo . . .*"

"Yes," he heard his own voice say, "that's a fine wolf hide . . ."

"*. . . el lobo de Aguila . . .*"

"No," Miller murmured. "*No es posible.*"

"*Sí, sí,*" hissed the proprietor. "*Sí, sí.*"

"No," Miller repeated. He made his way to a crate against the wall and sagged down upon it, clasping his damp hands in a violent effort to squeeze out thought.

"*Sí, amigo. El lobo de Aguila . . .*"

Wind shook the hut, and spurts of sand scraped at the outside wall. Miller heard the crack of stiffened skin as the wolf hide fell. He pitched to his feet in time to see it skitter across the yard toward the open desert, in time to see the squatting boy run it down in one swift bound. He crouched on it, eyeing Miller over his left shoulder, the hair on the back of his head erect in the hot wind. At Miller's approach, he backed away a little distance, not quite cringing. Miller took the hide to the proprietor, who peered at all of them out of the shadows. The dark boy, when Miller glanced at him, smiled his wide, sudden smile.

The water in his radiator was still boiling when he removed the cap. He refilled the radiator with liquid from the beer vat inside, aware of the tremor in his hand. Paying the man, he dropped the money to the ground and had to grope for it. The two boys moved toward the car in response to some signal between them, and the man in the doorway, clutching the hide, hissed for Miller's attention.

"*Señor . . .*"

He did not continue, and would not meet Miller's eyes.

"*Adiós,*" Miller said, after a moment, and the man's lips moved, but no whisper came.

The motor, still hot, was hard to start, and the car, once moving, handled sluggishly. Miller rolled the windows up to close out the gusts of heat, but after a moment he could not catch his breath. Gasping, he rolled them down again. The two boys watched him.

According to his reckoning they were now halfway to San Luis. In early afternoon, the temperature had risen and the glare, oddly bright beneath an intermittent sun, was painful to his eyes. He saw with difficulty. His passengers seemed not to mind the heat, absorbed as they were with his expressions, the movements of his hands.

Miller's intuitions ran headlong through his mind, but a curious despair, a resignation, muted them. He would reach San Luis or he would not, and that was all.

The sedan was passing south of the Cabeza Prieta Mountains, great tumbled barrens looming up out of the foothills to the northward.

Somewhere up there, Miller had heard, lay the still body of a flier, who only last week had left a note in his grounded plane and wandered west in search of help. He had not been found. In this weather, in this desert, a man made a single mistake, a single, small mistake— say, a mislaid hat, a neglected landmark, an unfilled canteen . . . He must have expressed part of this thought aloud, for the dark boy was nodding warily. When Miller squinted at him, he smiled.

"You wouldn't last six hours out there," Miller told him. "Don't matter *who* you are."

The boy nodded, smiling.

Miller laughed harshly, and the second boy sat forward on the edge of his seat, eyes wide. Abruptly, Miller stopped and turned away. He felt lightheaded, a little drunk.

The landscape altered quickly now, and mountains appeared in scattered formations to the south. Their color was burnt black rather than brown, and their outlines looked crusted. Farther on, they crowded toward the road, extending weird shapes in heaps of squat, black boulders. The dull gravel of the desert floor was invaded, then replaced, by sand, and the last stunted saguaros disappeared. With every mile, the sand increased in volume, overflowing the rock and creeping up the dead crevasses. The huge boulders sank down, one by one, beneath bare dunes, until finally the distances were white, scarred here and there with outcroppings of darkness. On the road itself, broad tongues of sand seeped out from the south side, and the sky turned to a sick, whitish pall, like the smoke of subterranean fires.

They had entered the Gran Desierto. He thought about the mountains of the moon.

Miller looked a last time at his gauges. The oil pressure was stable still, but the temperature needle, a streak of bright red in the monotone of his vision, was climbing. He knew he should slow the whining car, but he could not. Huddled together, his passengers sat rigid, eyes narrowed to slits against the sea of white. The younger one was panting audibly.

Miller tried to sing, but no sound came. The dark boy gazed at Miller, then placed his arm about his brother's shoulder.

A tire split before the water went, and the car swerved onto the sand shoulder of the road. He wrenched at the wheel in a spasm of shock, and the sedan lurched free again like a mired animal, stalling and coming to rest as the rear tire settled. Miller fought for breath. He sat a moment blinking, as the sand, in wind-whipped sheets, whitened the pavement. Then he got out, and the two boys followed. Retreating a little distance, they observed him as he opened the trunk and yanked the jack and lug wrench and spare tire from the litter of bags and traps.

The cement was too hot to touch, and the unseen sun too high in the pale sky to afford shade. Miller spread his bedroll and kneeled on it, working feverishly but ineffectually. He felt near to fainting, and the blown sand seared his face, and he burned his hands over and over on the hot shell of the sedan. But he managed at last to free the tire, and was fighting the spare into place when a sound behind him made him whirl. The dark boy stood over him, holding the iron lug wrench.

Miller leapt up, stumbling backward.

"Christ!" his voice croaked. Crouching, he came forward again, stalking the child, who dropped the wrench and moved away. Miller picked it up and followed him. The younger was squatting on the roadside, lifting one scorched foot and then the other, and emitting a queer, mournful whine. His brother took his hand and pulled him away. Unwilling to leave the shelter of the car, they kept just out of reach. When Miller stopped, they stopped also, peering uneasily at the wrench in his clenched hand. Then Miller raised the wrench and went for them, and the younger moaned and ran. The older did not move. Miller, lowering his arm, stopped short. The boy's gaze was bared, implacable. Then he, too, turned and moved after the other, and took his hand. Miller watched until their small shimmering forms disappeared behind black boulders.

Swaying on the road, Miller licked his lips. Something had passed. Maybe the kid was only trying to help, he thought. What the hell's the matter? Didn't you see them children holding hands?

"You ignorant bastard," he murmured, stunned. He repeated it, then cried aloud in pain. He ran to the car and finished the job, leaving the tools and broken tire on the road. The motor started weakly, but in his desperate efforts to turn the car around, he sank it inexorably into the sand of the road shoulder. The engine block cracked and the car died. He got out and stared. Then he started off, half-running, in the direction taken by the children.

Nearing the boulders, he stopped and shouted, *"Niños, niños! I don't mean no harm!"*

But his throat was parched and his tongue dry, and the sound he made was cracked and muted. Somewhere the boys were taking shelter, but if they heard him, they were afraid and silent. Over his head, the sun glowed like a great white coal, dull with the ash of its own burning, without light.

"Niños!"

He knew that if he did not find them, they might die. Tired, he entered the maze of rocks, calling out every little while to the vast silence. The rocks climbed gradually in growing masses toward a far black butte, and as the day burned to its end, the wind died and a pallid sun shone through the haze. It sank away, and its last light crept slowly toward the summit, reddening the stones to fierce magnificence, only to fade at sunset into the towering sky.

Miller toiled up through the shadows. He reached the crest toward evening, on his knees, and his movement ceased. From somewhere below, a little later, he heard a shrill, clear call, and the call was answered, as he awoke, from a point nearer. In the dream, the children had walked toward him hand in hand.

He sat up a little, blinking, and fingered the dry furrows of his throat. To the north, the flier's empty eyes stared up, uncomprehending. But Miller, without thinking, understood. His hand fell, and as his wait began, his still face grew entranced, impassive. The rocks turned cold. About him, in strange shapes of night, the mountains of Mexico gaped, crowded, leapt and stretched away across the moonlit wastes. The nameless range where he now lay stalked south through the Gran Desierto, sinking at last on the dead, salt shores of the Gulf of California.

1958

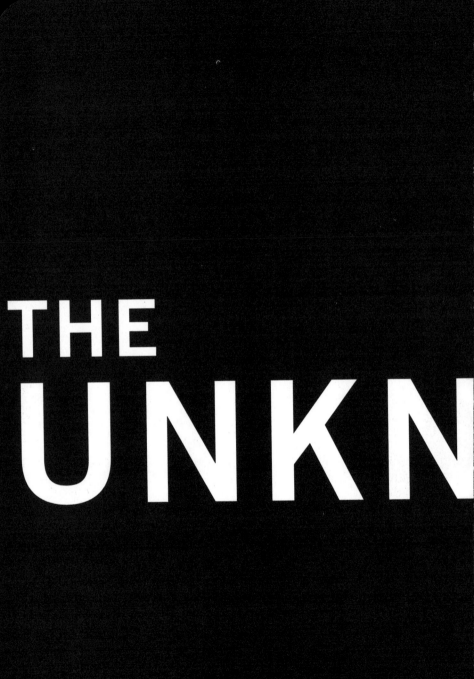

THE
UNKN

PART III:

OWN

The Cremation of Sam McGee

by Robert W. Service

There are strange things done in the midnight sun
    By the men who moil for gold;
The Arctic trails have their secret tales
    That would make your blood run cold;
The Northern Lights have seen queer sights,
    But the queerest they ever did see
Was that night on the marge of Lake Lebarge
    I cremated Sam McGee.

Now Sam McGee was from Tennessee, where
the cotton blooms and blows.
Why he left his home in the South to roam
'round the Pole, God only knows.
He was always cold, but the land of gold seemed
to hold him like a spell;
Though he'd often say in his homely way that
"he'd sooner live in hell."

On a Christmas Day we were mushing our way
over the Dawson trail.
Talk of your cold! through the parka's fold it
stabbed like a driven nail.
If our eyes we'd close, then the lashes froze till
sometimes we couldn't see;
It wasn't much fun, but the only one to whimper
was Sam McGee.

And that very night, as we lay packed tight in
our robes beneath the snow,
And the dogs were fed, and the stars o'erhead
were dancing heel and toe,
He turned to me, and "Cap," says he, "I'll cash
in this trip, I guess;
And if I do, I'm asking that you won't refuse my
last request."

Well, he seemed so low that I couldn't say no;
    then he says with a sort of moan:
"It's the cursed cold, and it's got right hold till
    I'm chilled clean through to the bone.
Yet 'tain't being dead—it's my awful dread of
    the icy grave that pains;
So I want you to swear that, foul or fair, you'll
    cremate my last remains."

A pal's last need is a thing to heed, so I swore
    I would not fail;
And we started on at the streak of dawn; but
    God! he looked ghastly pale.
He crouched on the sleigh, and he raved all day
    of his home in Tennessee;
And before nightfall a corpse was all that was
    left of Sam McGee.

There wasn't a breath in that land of death, and
    I hurried, horror-driven,
With a corpse half hid that I couldn't get rid,
    because of a promise given;
It was lashed to the sleigh, and it seemed to say:
    "You may tax your brawn and brains,
But you promised true, and it's up to you to
    cremate those last remains."

Now a promise made is a debt unpaid, and the
     trail has its own stern code.
In the days to come, though my lips were dumb,
     in my heart how I cursed that load.
In the long, long night, by the lone firelight,
     while the huskies, round in a ring,
Howled out their woes to the homeless snows
     —O God! how I loathed the thing.

And every day that quiet clay seemed to heavy
     and heavier grow;
And on I went, though the dogs were spent and
     the grub was getting low;
The trail was bad, and I felt half mad, but I
     swore I would not give in;
And I'd often sing to the hateful thing, and it
     hearkened with a grin.

Till I came to the marge of Lake Lebarge, and
     a derelict there lay;
It was jammed in the ice, but I saw in a trice it
     was called the "Alice May."
And I looked at it, and I thought a bit, and I
     looked at my frozen chum;
Then "Here," said I, with a sudden cry, "is
     my cre-ma-tor-eum."

Some planks I tore from the cabin floor, and I
    lit the boiler fire;
Some coal I found that was lying around, and I
    heaped the fuel higher;
The flames just soared, and the furnace roared
    —such a blaze you seldom see;
And I burrowed a hole in the glowing coal, and
    I stuffed in Sam McGee.

Then I made a hike, for I didn't like to hear him
    sizzle so;
And the heavens scowled, and the huskies
    howled, and the wind began to blow.
It was icy cold, but the hot sweat rolled down my
    cheeks, and I don't know why;
And the greasy smoke in an inky cloak went
    streaking down the sky.

I do not know how long in the snow I wrestled
    with grisly fear;
But the stars came out and they danced about
    ere again I ventured near;
I was sick with dread, but I bravely said: "I'll
    just take a peep inside.
I guess he's cooked, and it's time I looked"; . . .
    then the door I opened wide.

And there sat Sam, looking cool and calm, in the
      heart of the furnace roar;
And he wore a smile you could see a mile, and
      he said: "Please close that door.
It's fine in here, but I greatly fear you'll let in
      the cold and storm—
Since I left Plumtree, down in Tennessee, it's
      the first time I've been warm."

There are strange things done in the midnight sun
      By the men who moil for gold;
The Arctic trails have their secret tales
      That would make your blood run cold;
The Northern Lights have seen queer sights,
      But the queerest they ever did see
Was that night on the marge of Lake Lebarge
      I cremated Sam McGee.

The Marfa Lights

by Judith M. Brueske
adapted from *The Marfa Lights*

In 1988, Judith Brueske interviewed people with firsthand accounts of "mysterious lights" sightings in West Texas, known commonly as the Marfa Lights. A long history of such sightings inspired Brueske, who has a Ph.D. in Anthropology and is a longtime resident of neighboring Alpine, Texas, to go beyond the secondhand stories and rumors to find witnesses who had actually seen the lights. Her work includes the firsthand testimony of some twenty-five people who have seen the lights one or more times.

There are lights in West Texas. If you sit out at night on the high desert plain, as the wind starts up and the moon begins its slow trip across the large sky, you will see winking beads of headlights, far away, or spot the blinkers of a turbo prop skirting the dark Chinati Mountains to the south. The stationary and familiar dots to the east are ranch houses, trailers, illuminated outposts of civilization in a place where civilization seems small and rare. You get used to darkness in a place like Marfa, Texas. You get to recognize the stars and the shadows in the desert. You notice the lights. You notice where they are and if they belong, and you notice when they start to appear and disappear and move off suddenly in wrong directions.

People who live in Marfa and Alpine and Presidio see strange lights. The Marfa Lights, mystery lights, Chinati lights, ghost lights. It's not important what you call them. They are lights that come from nowhere or divide or merge or change colors, depending on who you talk to. Sometimes they appear singly, and sometimes many at a time. The only sure thing is that they appear, night after night, month after month, year after year.

There were several in the group that Katherine Hollingsworth reported seeing in 1987, but "one light," she said, "was the largest. It would hover about in mid-air. It would seem to flicker like a ball of fire and then shoot up into the sky, and at times it would split and one part would go right as the other part would go left. It seemed to at times have an essence of a soft greenish-blue color quickly changing to a red."

Ophelia Ward saw them fourteen years before that on a drive from Marfa to Alpine. "When I got home," she remembers, "they said, 'What's wrong?' They said I was as white as a sheet. I was still feeling the whole thing." She had seen the lights before that night, but only from a distance. "We've always seen them, you know. You would see them and you would not see them. But I never saw them right there, next to me."

Ophelia remembers where she was. She remembers passing the point on route 90 where many sightings have occurred. "I started getting this weird feeling. It never bothered me [before]. This is something we've lived with . . . I was born and raised here, as was my family before me. [But] I got this weird feeling, like someone was in the van with me. But there was nobody there with me. Because I kept looking."

There was no one else there in the van, but when she looked south, she saw something. "Something that looks like a ball of fire. . . . It's moving but it's coming towards the van. And it was close, and I got scared."

The light she saw was orange-red, about two and a half feet in diameter. It spun and rolled. It grew larger as it approached the van, until it was moving towards her from twenty feet away, just on the other side of the fence that parallels the highway.

"I'm trying not to look at it, because at that hour not one other soul, not another car was on the road. And every hair on my body was sticking up, I could feel it, you know. . . . And I started stepping on the gas, faster, and it started like it was racing with me. So we're having a race. It's [spinning] and I'm just going as fast as I can out of there. I watch it every once in a while, but I'm going ninety."

She reached the big curve in the road at the hill where the sign reads "15 Miles to Alpine." She took the turn, and when she looked again, the light was gone.

"I don't know [what it was]. Something comes out of the wide open spaces, without any warning."

Marilyn Olson and Belle Frahm saw a light they could not explain early in the summer of 1988. Belle tells her story relucantly, as if she thinks she might not be believed. But Marilyn corroborates the details of that night: the white light that followed them and then wandered off the road, into a field. It was not the only time she saw the lights. In the spring of 1987, she and her mother were driving back to Marfa after dark.

"Suddenly a huge red and green light appeared right behind the car," she says. "It seemed like it was right on top of the back window."

Her mother estimates the lights were about thirty feet up off the ground. There was no sound of any kind except for the engine of their car.

They weren't far from the spot where Cara Lee Ridout saw the lights, years before. "I've never told this story before," she says. "I saw three big balls of fire lined up. It was two to three hundred yards to the nearest one. You hear people say the lights are moving, but these were stationary." The balls were red, she says, like a full moon. They lined up equidistantly in the pasture and held their ground. It was the same formation that Jim Sheffield says he saw in 1984, although when he saw them the lights were farther away. "The lights started popping up at the base of the mountains," he says. "They would enlarge, get very bright. One light got real intense and it split, and then those two split and there were four, in a horizontal line. . . . I don't know how anyone could mistake them for car lights."

Most of the people who've seen the lights were in their cars on the desolate roads of Presidio and Brewster County, but Robert Black was not driving a car. He was stuck for the night, and he was a little bit lost. Robert and a friend had started climbing Goat Mountain at eleven o'clock on the Saturday after Thanksgiving, 1985. It was a beautiful day, very warm for that time of year. Robert studied geology as a graduate student at Sul Ross University, and his interest in Goat Mountain was academic.

The morning was clear and dry. There had been no rain for some time. Both men were dressed lightly: cotton pants, T-shirts under long-sleeved shirts. The hike to the top of Goat Mountain was longer than they expected. When they reached the peak, Black collected ten rock samples, made a note of the geology, and mapped the area. They had lunch. The wind had come up a bit, and they settled down against the rocks for a little shelter.

"Look," said Robert's friend.

They looked, squinting into the red-orange glare of the sinking sun.

"It's going down," the friend said.

They did not stay to enjoy it, but finished their sandwiches and started down the mountain. It was later than they thought. The sun set quickly. They were both hiking hard, now, and when they reached the ridge where they could make out Robert's truck sitting far away in the flats, they started to run.

They hit the flats on the west side of Goat Mountain just after dusk.

They could not find the truck.

"Anyone who knows the Marfa flats," Robert says, "knows that it is flat, featureless and boring—no geological marker out in the sea of desert, really no way to find your way around, especially in the dark." They had no flashlight, no extra clothes, and only a few matches. They walked and argued and finally decided to find a place to spend the night. Their eyes adjusted slowly to the onyx all around them, and they stumbled as they gathered creosote bushes to build a fire. They managed to start one, and worked to keep it going. The temperature dropped. They decided they would stay up, and keep the fire burning all night.

A little after midnight, they had stopped talking for a while. There was only a sliver of a moon coming up low in the sky. The two of them sat with their backs against small rocks, looking towards the north and northwest. They were, they realized, right in the flats where Marfa Lights were often seen.

Black saw it first: "a horizontal length of light that had a sort of dancing, vibration movement . . . [There] were little beams of light that would dance up and down in a kind of wave formation, move across, then they'd seem to jump straight up vertically, come back down, then dance horizontally, then disappear."

They saw the lights four or five times that night, for a few seconds each time. The lights appeared about six feet above the horizon, several feet above the tops of the creosote bushes. The colors were yellows and oranges through reds. The third time the lights appeared, the men realized that they always seemed to be in the same location. It was not far away. They kept expecting to hear something, a train whistle, an engine, voices, but the night was quiet. They stayed by their fire and watched. The last light came a little before dawn, the same as the rest, rolling and jumping. They heard nothing.

The sun finally came up and they could see frost on the ground. They left quickly, and found Black's truck. Before they left, they went back towards the spot where they had seen the lights. But there was nothing there, and they did not stay for long.

There are lights in West Texas, and there are reasons too. There are people who believe in the phosphorescence of mineral deposits in the mountains. There is talk about luminous swamp gas, natural gas, or the flickering cold flames of the will-o'-the-wisp. The lights are campfires or mirages reflected hundreds of miles across the Mexican border and onto the dark Texas desert plain. They are static electricity playing sparks off the horns and flanks of cattle as they walk and shift at night. Ball lightning. St. Elmo's fire. Piezoelectricity occurring from pressure deep in the earth along shifting fault lines. Fluorescent guano clinging to the wings of bats as they emerge from their caves for the nighttime hunt. There are reasons, but none of them seem exactly right to the people who have met the lights unexpectedly or to the scientists who have studied them or to the observers who watch for them on moonless nights.

There are reasons, and there are stories, too. Reports of unexplained lights started surfacing in the 1800s, when wagon trains from Ojinaga, Mexico bound for San Antonio passed through the area. A rancher named J.E. Ellison reported a strange light in 1883 as he drove cattle through Paisano Pass on the way to Marfa.

The best known story around Marfa is the story of Alsate, the last Apache leader in the Big Bend region. He was a war chief who had made a peace with the Texans in San Carlos, but was hunted by Mexican Rurales for his raids to the south. Once, he was captured and taken to Mexico City, where he somehow talked his way out of execution. The Mexicans released him, then changed their minds and hunted him down again. This time he was brought to Presidio, Texas and shot. His followers were taken into Mexico and sold as slaves.

Only a few years passed before Alsate's name began to surface again along the old frontier of the Chisos Mountains and the Chinatis. Shepherds and vaqueros, gathering at their campfires in the desert night, spoke of seeing something in the old lands of the Chisos Apaches. One had seen a single man in full Indian dress slowly walking up a steep slope, and another had seen the dead chief standing on a rocky point high above the Rio Grande. He appeared in the Del Carmen Mountains and in the Chinatis. Sometimes the ghost appeared to them as a man, and sometimes as only a feeling, an unsettling and watchful presence. Sometimes, increasingly, he appeared as a fluorescence, or a collection of mysterious lights.

There are stories and reasons, but in the end, there is only the fact of a desert that shines and flashes and winks in the dark, cool nights. It is not a matter of belief. "Something," as Ophelia Ward says, "something comes out of the wide open spaces, without any warning."

They Bite

by Anthony Boucher

There was no path, only the almost vertical ascent. Crumbled rock for a few yards, with the roots of sage finding their scanty life in the dry soil. Then jagged outcroppings of crude crags, sometimes with accidental footholds, sometimes with overhanging and untrustworthy branches of greasewood, sometimes with no aid to climbing but the leverage of your muscles and the ingenuity of your balance.

The sage was as drably green as the rock was drably brown. The only color was the occasional rosy spikes of a barrel cactus.

Hugh Tallant swung himself up on to the last pinnacle. It had a deliberate, shaped look about it—a petrified fortress of Lilliputians, a Gibralter of pygmies. Tallant perched on its battlements and unslung his fieldglasses.

The desert valley spread below him. The tiny cluster of buildings that was Oasis, the exiguous cluster of palms that gave name to the town and shelter to his own tent and to the shack he was building, the dead-ended highway leading straightforwardly to nothing, the oiled roads diagramming the vacant blocks of an optimistic subdivision.

Tallant saw none of these. His glasses were fixed beyond the oasis and the town of Oasis on the dry lake. The gliders were clear and vivid to him, and the uniformed men busy with them were as sharply and minutely visible as a nest of ants under glass. The training school was more than usually active. One glider in particular, strange to Tallant, seemed the focus of attention. Men would come and examine it and glance back at the older models in comparison.

Only the corner of Tallant's left eye was not preoccupied with the new glider. In that corner something moved, something little and thin and brown as the earth. Too large for a rabbit, much too small for a man. It darted across that corner of vision, and Tallant found gliders oddly hard to concentrate on.

He set down the bifocals and deliberately looked about him. His pinnacle surveyed the narrow, flat area of the crest. Nothing stirred. Nothing stood out against the sage and rock but one barrel of rosy spikes. He took up the glasses again and resumed his observations. When he was done, he methodically entered the results in the little black notebook.

His hand was still white. The desert is cold and often sunless in winter. But it was a firm hand, and as well trained as his eyes, fully capable of recording faithfully the designs and dimensions which they had registered so accurately.

Once his hand slipped, and he had to erase and redraw, leaving a smudge that displeased him. The lean, brown thing had slipped across the edge of his vision again. Going toward the east edge, he would swear, where that set of rocks jutted like the spines on the back of a stegosaur.

Only when his notes were completed did he yield to curiosity, and even then with cynical self-reproach. He was physically tired, for him an unusual state, from this daily climbing and from clearing the ground for his shack-to-be. The eye muscles play odd nervous tricks. There could be nothing behind the stegosaur's armor.

There was nothing. Nothing alive and moving. Only the torn and half-plucked carcass of a bird, which looked as though it had been gnawed by some small animal.

It was halfway down the hill—hill in Western terminology, though anywhere east of the Rockies it would have been considered a sizable mountain—that Tallant again had a glimpse of a moving figure.

But this was no trick of a nervous eye. It was not little nor thin nor brown. It was tall and broad and wore a loud red-and-black lumberjack. It bellowed "Tallant!" in a cheerful and lusty voice.

Tallant drew near the man and said "Hello." He paused and added, "Your advantage, I think."

The man grinned broadly. "Don't know me? Well, I daresay ten years is a long time, and the California desert ain't exactly the Chinese rice fields. How's stuff? Still loaded down with Secrets for Sale?"

Tallant tried desperately not to react to that shot, but he stiffened a little. "Sorry. The prospector getup had me fooled. Good to see you again, Morgan."

The man's eyes had narrowed. "Just having my little joke," he smiled. "Of course you wouldn't have no serious reason for mountain-climbing around a glider school, now would you? And you'd kind of need fieldglasses to keep an eye on the pretty birdies."

"I'm out here for my health." Tallant's voice sounded unnatural even to himself.

"Sure, sure. You were always in it for your health. And come to think of it, my own health ain't been none too good lately. I've got me a little cabin way to hell-and-gone around here, and I do me a little prospecting now and then. And somehow it just strikes me, Tallant, like maybe I hit a pretty good lode today."

"Nonsense, old man. You can see—"

"I'd sure hate to tell any of them army men out at the field some of the stories I know about China and the kind of men I used to know out there. Wouldn't cotton to them stories a bit, the army wouldn't. But if I was to have a drink too many and get talkative-like—"

"Tell you what," Tallant suggested brusquely. "It's getting near sunset now, and my tent's chilly for evening visits. But drop around in the morning and we'll talk over old times. Is rum still your tipple?"

"Sure is. Kind of expensive now, you understand—"

"I'll lay some in. You can find the place easily—over by the oasis. And we . . . we might be able to talk about your prospecting, too."

Tallant's thin lips were set firm as he walked away.

The bartender opened a bottle of beer and plunked it on the damp-circled counter. "That'll be twenty cents," he said, then added as an afterthought, "Want a glass? Sometimes tourists do."

Tallant looked at the others sitting at the counter—the red-eyed and unshaven old man, the flight sergeant unhappily drinking a coke—it was after army hours for beer—the young man with the long, dirty trench coat and the pipe and the new-looking brown beard—and saw no glasses. "I guess I won't be a tourist," he decided.

This was the first time Tallant had had a chance to visit the Desert Sport Spot. It was as well to be seen around in a community. Otherwise people begin to wonder and say, "Who is that man out by the oasis? Why don't you ever see him any place?"

The Sport Spot was quiet that night. The four of them at the counter, two army boys shooting pool, and a half-dozen of the local men gathered about a round poker table, soberly and wordlessly cleaning a construction worker whose mind seemed more on his beer than on his cards.

"You just passing through?" the bartender asked sociably.

Tallant shook his head. "I'm moving in. When the Army turned me down for my lungs I decided I better do something about it. Heard so much about your climate here I thought I might as well try it."

"Sure thing," the bartender nodded. "You take up until they started this glider school, just about every other guy you meet in the desert is here for his health. Me, I had sinus, and look at me now. It's the air."

Tallant breathed the atmosphere of smoke and beer suds, but did not smile. "I'm looking forward to miracles."

"You'll get 'em. Whereabouts you staying?"

"Over that way a bit. The agent called it 'the old Carker place.'"

Tallant felt the curious listening silence and frowned. The bartender had started to speak and then thought better of it. The young man with the beard looked at him oddly. The old man fixed him with red and watery eyes that had a faded glint of pity in them. For a moment Tallant felt a chill that had nothing to do with the night air of the desert.

The old man drank his beer in quick gulps, and frowned as though trying to formulate a sentence. At last he wiped beer from his bristly lips and said, "You wasn't aiming to stay in the adobe, was you?"

"No. It's pretty much gone to pieces. Easier to rig me up a little shack than try to make the adobe livable. Meanwhile, I've got a tent."

"That's all right then, mebbe. But mind you don't go poking around that there adobe."

"I don't think I'm apt to. But why not? Want another beer?"

The old man shook his head reluctantly and slid from his stool to the ground. "No thanks. I don't rightly know as I—"

"Yes?"

"Nothing. Thanks all the same." He turned and shuffled to the door.

Tallant smiled. "But why should I stay clear of the adobe?" he called after him.

The old man mumbled.

"What?"

"They bite," said the old man, and went out shivering into the night.

The bartender was back at his post. "I'm glad he didn't take that beer you offered him," he said. "Along about this time in the evening I have to stop serving him. For once he had the sense to quit."

Tallant pushed his own empty bottle forward. "I hope I didn't frighten him away?"

"Frighten? Well, mister, I think maybe that's just what you did do. He didn't want beer that sort of came, like you might say, from the old Carker place. Some of the old-timers here, they're funny that way."

Tallant grinned. "Is it haunted?"

"Not what you'd call haunted, no. No ghosts there that I ever heard of." He wiped the counter with a cloth, and seemed to wipe the subject away with it.

The flight sergeant pushed his coke bottle away, hunted in his pocket for nickels, and went over to the pinball machine. The young man with the beard slid onto his vacant stool. "Hope old Jake didn't worry you," he said.

Tallant laughed. "I suppose every town has its deserted homestead with a grisly tradition. But this sounds a little different. No ghosts, and they bite. Do you know anything about it?"

"A little," the young man said seriously. "A little. Just enough to—"

Tallant was curious. "Have one on me and tell me about it."

The flight sergeant swore bitterly at the machine.

Beer gurgled through the beard. "You see," the young man began, "the desert's so big you can't be alone in it. Ever notice that? It's all empty and there's nothing in sight, but there's always something moving over there where you can't quite see it. It's something very dry and thin and brown, only when you look around it isn't there. Ever see it?"

"Optical fatigue—" Tallant began.

"Sure. I know. Every man to his own legend. There isn't a tribe of Indians hasn't got some way of accounting for it. You've heard of the Watchers? And the twentieth-century white man comes along, and it's optical fatigue. Only in the nineteenth century things weren't quite the same, and there were the Carkers."

"You've got a special localized legend?"

"Call it that. You glimpse things out of the corner of your mind, same like you glimpse lean, dry things out of the corner of your eye. You encase 'em in solid circumstance and they're not so bad. That is known as the Growth of Legend. The Folk Mind in Action. You take the Carkers and the things you don't quite see and you put 'em together. And they bite."

Tallant wondered how long that beard had been absorbing beer. "And what were the Carkers?" he prompted politely.

"Ever hear of Sawney Bean? Scotland—reign of James First or maybe the Sixth, though I think Roughead's wrong on that for once. Or let's be more modern—ever hear of the Benders? Kansas in the 1870s? No? Ever hear of Procrustes? Or Polyphemus? Or Fee-fi-fo-fum?

"There are ogres, you know. They're no legend. They're fact, they are. The inn where nine guests left for every ten that arrived, the mountain cabin that sheltered travelers from the snow, sheltered them all winter till the melting spring uncovered their bones, the lonely stretches of road that so many passengers traveled halfway— you'll find 'em everywhere. All over Europe and pretty much in this country too before communications became what they are. Profitable business. And it wasn't just the profit. The Benders made money, sure; but that wasn't why they killed all their victims as carefully as a kosher butcher. Sawney Bean got so he didn't give a damn about the profit; he just needed to lay in more meat for the winter.

"And think of the chances you'd have at an oasis."

"So these Carkers of yours were, as you call them, ogres?"

"Carkers, ogres—maybe they were Benders. The Benders were never seen alive, you know, after the townspeople found those curiously butchered bodies. There's a rumor they got this far West. And the time checks pretty well. There wasn't any town here in the eighties. Just a couple of Indian families, last of a dying tribe living on at the oasis. They vanished after the Carkers moved in. That's not so surprising. The white race is a sort of super-ogre, anyway. Nobody worried about them. But they used to worry about why so many travelers used to stop over at the Carkers, you see, and somehow they often never got any farther. Their wagons'd be found maybe fifteen miles beyond in the desert. Sometimes they found the bones, too, parched and white. Gnawed-looking, they said sometimes."

"And nobody ever did anything about these Carkers?"

"Oh, sure. We didn't have King James Sixth—only I still think it was First—to ride up on a great white horse for a gesture, but twice army detachments came here and wiped them all out."

"Twice? One wiping-out would do for most families." Tallant smiled.

"Uh-huh. That was no slip. They wiped out the Carkers twice because you see once didn't do any good. They wiped 'em out and still travelers vanished and still there were gnawed bones. So they wiped 'em out again. After that they gave up, and people detoured the oasis. It made a longer, harder trip, but after all—"

Tallant laughed. "You mean these Carkers were immortal?"

"I don't know about immortal. They somehow just didn't die very easy. Maybe, if they were the Benders—and I sort of like to think they were—they learned a little more about what they were doing out here on the desert. Maybe they put together what the Indians knew and what they knew, and it worked. Maybe Whatever they made their sacrifices to, understood them better out here than in Kansas."

"And what's become of them—aside from seeing them out of the corner of the eye?"

"There's forty years between the last of the Carker history and this new settlement at the oasis. And people won't talk much about what they learned here in the first year or so. Only that they stay away from that old Carker adobe. They tell some stories—The priest says he was sitting in the confessional one hot Saturday afternoon and thought he heard a penitent come in. He waited a long time and finally lifted the gauze to see was anybody there. Something was there, and it bit. He's got three fingers on his right hand now, which looks funny as hell when he gives a benediction."

*   *   *

Tallant pushed their two bottles toward the bartender. "That yarn, my young friend, has earned another beer. How about it, bartender? Is he always cheerful like this, or is this just something he's improvised for my benefit?"

The bartender set out the fresh bottles with great solemnity. "Me, I wouldn't've told you all that myself, but then he's a stranger, too, and maybe don't feel the same way we do here. For him it's just a story."

"It's more comfortable that way," said the young man with the beard, and took a firm hold on his beer bottle.

"But as long as you've heard that much," said the bartender, "you might as well—It was last winter, when we had that cold spell. You heard funny stories that winter. Wolves coming into prospectors' cabins just to warm up. Well, business wasn't so good. We don't have a license for hard liquor and the boys don't drink much beer when it's that cold. But they used to come in anyway because we've got that big oil burner.

"So one night there's a bunch of 'em in here—old Jake was here, that you was talking to, and his dog Jigger—and I think I hear somebody else come in. The door creaks a little. But I don't see nobody and the poker's game going and we're talking just like we're talking now, and all of a sudden I hear a kind of a noise like crack! over there in that corner behind the jukebox near the burner.

"I go over to see what goes and it gets away before I can see it very good. But it was little and thin and it didn't have no clothes on. It must've been damned cold that winter."

"And what was the cracking noise?" Tallant asked dutifully.

"That? That was a bone. It must've strangled Jigger without any noise. He was a little dog. It ate most of the flesh, and if it hadn't cracked the bone for the marrow it could've finished. You can still see the spots over there. The blood never did come out."

There had been silence all through the story. Now suddenly all hell broke loose. The flight sergeant let out a splendid yell and began pointing excitedly at the pinball machine and yelling for his payoff. The construction worker dramatically deserted the poker game, knocking his chair over in the process, and announced lugubriously that these guys here had their own rules, see?

Any atmosphere of Carker-inspired horror was dissipated. Tallant whistled as he walked over to put a nickel in the jukebox. He glanced casually at the floor. Yes, there was a stain, for what that was worth.

He smiled cheerfully and felt rather grateful to the Carkers. They were going to solve his blackmail problem very neatly.

Tallant dreamed of power that night. It was a common dream with him. He was a ruler of the new American Corporate State that should follow the war; and he said to this man "Come!" and he came, and to that man "Go!" and he went, and to his servants "Do this!" and they did it.

Then the young man with the beard was standing before him, and the dirty trench coat was like the robes of an ancient prophet. And the young man said, "You see yourself riding high, don't you? Riding the crest of the wave—the Wave of the Future, you call it. But there's a deep, dark undertow that you don't see, and that's a part of the Past. And the Present and even your Future. There is evil in mankind that is blacker even than your evil, and infinitely more ancient."

And there was something in the shadows behind the young man, something little and lean and brown.

Tallant's dream did not disturb him the following morning. Nor did the thought of the approaching interview with Morgan. He fried his bacon and eggs and devoured them cheerfully. The wind had died down for a change, and the sun was warm enough so that he could strip to the waist while he cleared land for his shack. His machete glinted brilliantly as it swung through the air and struck at the roots of the brush.

Morgan's full face was red and sweating when he arrived.

"It's cool over there in the shade of the adobe," Tallant suggested. "We'll be more comfortable." And in the comfortable shade of the adobe he swung the machete once and clove Morgan's full red sweating face in two.

It was so simple. It took less effort than uprooting a clump of sage. And it was so safe. Morgan lived in a cabin way to hell-and-gone and was often away on prospecting trips. No one would notice his absence for months, if then. No one had any reason to connect him with Tallant. And no one in Oasis would hunt for him in the Carker-haunted adobe.

The body was heavy, and the blood dripped warm on Tallant's bare skin. With relief he dumped what had been Morgan on the floor of the adobe. There were no boards, no flooring. Just the earth. Hard, but not too hard to dig a grave in. And no one was likely to come poking around in this taboo territory to notice the grave. Let a year or so go by, and the grave and the bones it contained would be attributed to the Carkers.

The corner of Tallant's eye bothered him again. Deliberately he looked about the interior of the adobe.

The little furniture was crude and heavy, with no attempt to smooth down the strokes of the ax. It was held together with wooden pegs or half-rotted thongs. There were age-old cinders in the fireplace, and the dusty shards of a cooking jar among them.

And there was a deeply hollowed stone, covered with stains that might have been rust, if stone rusted. Behind it was a tiny figure, clumsily fashioned of clay and sticks. It was something like a man and something like a lizard, and something like the things that flit across the corner of the eye.

Curious now, Tallant peered about further. He penetrated to the corner that the one unglassed window lighted but dimly. And there he let out a little choking gasp. For a moment he was rigid with horror. Then he smiled and all but laughed aloud.

This explained everything. Some curious individual had seen this, and from his account burgeoned the whole legend. The Carkers had indeed learned something from the Indians, but that secret was the art of embalming.

It was a perfect mummy. Either the Indian art had shrunk bodies, or this was that of a ten-year-old boy. There was no flesh. Only the skin and bone and taut dry stretches of tendon between. The eyelids were closed; the sockets looked hollow under them. The nose was sunken and almost lost. The scant lips were tightly curled back from the long and very white teeth, which stood forth all the more brilliantly against the deep-brown skin.

It was a curious little trove, this mummy. Tallant was already calculating the chances for raising a decent sum of money from an interested anthropologist—murder can produce such delightfully profitable chance by-products—when he noticed the infinitesimal rise and fall of the chest.

The Carker was not dead. It was sleeping.

Tallant did not dare stop to think beyond the instant. This was no time to pause to consider if such things were possible in a well-ordered world. It was no time to reflect on the disposal of the body of Morgan. It was time to snatch up your machete and get out of there.

But in the doorway he halted. There coming across the desert, heading for the adobe, clearly seen this time, was another—a female.

He made an involuntary gesture of indecision. The blade of the machete clanged ringingly against the adobe wall. He heard the dry shuffling of a roused sleeper behind him.

He turned fully now, the machete raised. Dispose of this nearer one first, then face the female. There was no room even for terror in his thoughts, only for action.

The lean brown shape darted at him avidly. He moved lightly away and stood poised for its second charge. It shot forward again. He took one step back, machete-arm raised, and fell headlong over the corpse of Morgan. Before he could rise, the thin thing was upon him. Its sharp teeth had met through the palm of his left hand.

The machete moved swiftly. The thin dry body fell headless to the floor. There was no blood.

The grip of the teeth did not relax. Pain coursed up Tallant's left arm—a sharper, more bitter pain than you would expect from the bite. Almost as though venom—

He dropped the machete, and his strong white hand plucked and twisted at the dry brown lips. The teeth stayed clenched, unrelaxing. He sat bracing his back against the wall and gripped the head between his knees. He pulled. His flesh ripped, and blood formed dusty clots on the dirt floor. But the bite was firm.

His world had become reduced now to that hand and that head. Nothing outside mattered. He must free himself. He raised his aching arm to his face, and with his own teeth he tore at that unrelenting grip. The dry flesh crumbled away in desert dust, but the teeth were locked fast. He tore his lip against their white keenness, and tasted in his mouth the sweetness of blood and something else.

He staggered to his feet again. He knew what he must do. Later he could use cautery, a tourniquet, see a doctor with a story about a Gila monster—their heads grip, too, don't they?—but he knew what he must do now.

He raised the machete and struck again.

His white hand lay on the brown floor, gripped by the white teeth in the brown face. He propped himself against the adobe wall, momentarily unable to move. His open wrist hung over the deeply hollowed stone. His blood and his strength and his life poured out before the little figure of sticks and clay.

The female stood in the doorway now, the sun bright on her thin brownness. She did not move. He knew that she was waiting for the hollow stone to fill.

The Red Man

by Eric Martin

The hut sat up on a high bank above the river, overlooking the jungle in both directions like a sniper's nest. Its roof was a tight overlap of dried palo leaves, row after row, tied to the bamboo rafters with black wire. The walls were bamboo, too, and the floor inside was dirt. Two raised wooden platforms stood side by side against the wall. The others had already carved out their space and were settling into their blankets and bags, sleeping or almost there.

I smoked cigarettes outside under the unfamiliar stars, first alone and then with Thip, our guide. He was 41 years old, learned English "a long time ago," he said, been a guide "a long time, too." Thip was a quiet man, and didn't say much more than that. On the trail, during the day, he barely talked to us as he led the way through the dense vegetation, or through the small strange villages where children stared at us with huge, resentful eyes. I'd watched him in the towns and in the jungle, and watched the way he listened and searched, moving his head slowly in the direction of sounds or movements that I could not hear or see.

By the time Thip and I went back inside, the others were already asleep in the kerosene light, exhausted by the hiking or Thip's opium or the strangeness of being far from home. The room was filled with the smell and sound of their collected breath. Thip moved quickly over their still forms, examining them like a den mother, pausing only to lift the long opium pipe out of the half-clenched fist of a tall, pale Brit. I sat on the rough wooden bench near the door and watched Thip take the pipe to the other side of the hut. He lay down on his side, heated the opium, and began to smoke, filling the pipe again and again. His eyes swelled and puffed and finally closed, slowly, like a fireside cat's.

They hadn't been closed for long when the red man entered the hut. He was tall and thin, a white man but with skin so boiled by the years that I couldn't tell if he was in his thirties or his sixties. His face was deeply wrinkled around the eyes; his pants were frayed and dirty; he wasn't wearing any shoes. He stepped by me into the middle of the room without speaking, looking down at the dirt floor of the hut and rubbing his hands together slowly. When he finally looked up, he turned, and his eyes hit me hard in a flash of cold, deep blue. "Rain," he said. He nodded at me as if we'd agreed on something.

I stood up.

"It's coming," the red man said. He smiled at me, stretching his raw, dry lips tight and revealing a row of small, fulvous teeth. "You think it's not, but the weather here is not like the weather there."

I said something that wasn't quite a word, not knowing whether to talk to him or ignore him or tell him to go away. To wake somebody else up, maybe. I didn't know what to do.

The red man sat down in a chair in the middle of the room, watching me watch him until I looked away. Then he laughed, a short small sound that sounded like a laugh and a question at the same time. "Maybe you think it's ridiculous to be all the way out here talking about the weather." I sat down again on the bench against the wall. "But in this case you're wrong," he continued. "The weather here is interesting." He moved his chair swiftly and silently over the dirt floor in my direction, pulling up close, and I slid down the bench a few feet, away from him.

I was about to get up again and wake Thip up when I heard the rain start outside. The first isolated drops rattled the roof, and then it really started raining. I could hear water pounding the dirt into mud outside.

"It's raining," I said. He nodded. "How did you . . ." I started, spreading my arms out in question, hoping he would take it from there, but he didn't say anything. "You live here? You're not travelling?"

"Yes," he said. He was distracted, looking carefully around the hut.

"Do you like it?" I tried again. "It seems like a pretty good place."

"It's a place," he said. "There are things that belong and things that don't." He leaned forward and glanced over at the still form of Thip, and I looked too. Thip's body was limp next to the pipe, his mouth slack and open in a wide, dark oval.

"I've been here for twenty years," the red man said. "I guess I belong, by now."

"Twenty years."

He nodded. "I came up like you. There weren't many travelers here then, but there were some. We hired a guide, me and Jay and this other student. Jay was from Florida. The student was born Thai." He shook his head. "I can never remember his name."

"Twenty years is a long time."

"Yes," he said. "We stayed right here, in this hut. It's a long time but it isn't. Some things don't change."

The rain was coming down harder now, louder, and we had to speak up to be heard.

"I was just outside," I told him, "there wasn't even a cloud."

"That's the way it is," he said. "My first night was the same. We were out there talking to our guide, and all of a sudden he looks up at the sky and tells us to get inside. But we stayed out there. The sky was clear but you could see the river swelling, and hear it rumbling, low and hard. Then we saw the stars disappearing upriver, swallowed up. It was only a few minutes before it started to rain."

"Like this," I said.

"It was worse than this," the red man said. "The wind ripped the cigarette out of my hand, and Jay lost his hat, and then the water hit all at once, like a whole sky full of fists. The three of us were drenched by the time we got inside. Our guide was sitting over there. You smoke opium?"

"No."

"Someone does though. That sticky sweet smell."

"A couple of the others. The guide." I nodded towards Thip lying limp and still across the room.

"Our guide smoked opium too. He was smoking when we came in. We were wet and a little scared and he was stoned, he was elsewhere. We all sat down at a table, and listened to the rain and wind. It felt like we were going to blow away, and Jay got up and said he's leaving."

"Going where?"

"Well. I don't know exactly, he was kind of irrational about things. Jay would get an idea he wanted to do something and then he just had to do it. I guess he thought we'd be better off up the hill a bit, in the trees. That's what he was talking about, trying to convince us, when our guide starts laughing, shaking his head and talking in Thai. We didn't understand him. The student did, though. The student was Thai, but he'd lived in America, he was travelling just like us. His English was good. What was his name?" The red man stared at the wall for a moment, and then shook his head. "He told us our guide kept saying 'It doesn't matter, it doesn't matter,' over and over. It was a creepy thing to hear. Jay started yelling at our guide, about how he'd been out in hurricanes worse than this. And our guide laughed, and Jay got madder and madder. Something might have happened between them, but right then the door opened, and that shut everyone up. Can I get a cigarette from you?"

"Sure." I found my pack and shook out two cigarettes, handing both to the red man. He thanked me, put one of them in his pocket, lit the other and sucked a third of it away in one take. He tilted the glowing butt to the ceiling, the ashes stacked high like a leaning tower until his hand shook and they flaked away.

"Five people came crowding through that door, all at once," he said. "They were dripping and caked in mud. This little boy and a young woman were last, and they had to struggle against the wind to close the door behind them. The other three men stopped and stared at us. The tallest of them was an older wiry man, thin, with strong, outdoor arms. When he saw our guide he put his hands together and made a little bow. They started talking. 'They've come from up the river,' the student told us, '. . . house swept away . . . his wife . . . his wife got swept away. They were praying in a temple, it collapsed into the river.'

"When Jay heard that, he almost jumped out of his skin. 'Let's go,' Jay said. 'Let's go get her, come on, we'll find her.' He grabbed me by the arm, started pulling me over to the door. 'Hey' he told the student, 'tell that guy we going to find his wife! Tell him!' He was excited and proud, ready for some big adventure."

The red man lit his second cigarette with the first, and leaned towards me. "The wiry man, the husband, was talking to our guide, but the student interrupted him and pointed over at me and Jay. The husband looked at us, an ugly look. He didn't say a word, and then turned back to our guide and kept talking in a low voice. 'Did you tell him?' Jay asked the student, 'Come on, tell him, tell him.' 'I told him already.' The student was getting mad, too. I tried to calm everyone down. 'Jay,' I told him, 'I understand your feeling, you know, but the fact is, it's bad out there, it's dark, we don't know our way around. I sure don't want to go out there.' Jay wasn't even listening. 'Well y'all can just hide in here,' he said, 'I'll go out there by myself. I'm gonna find her, you watch.'

"He headed for the door, and then, without warning, the three men grabbed him. They threw him against the wall and the husband took a big knife from his belt. He held the point steady, right in front of Jay's eyes. No one moved. The only sound in the room was the young woman saying something in an even, soft voice. I don't know what she was saying, but the husband shouted once and she shut up.

"'All right,' I said, 'let's just talk about this,' but the husband looked at me and then flicked the knife over Jay's eyes. The knife passed so close I was sure I'd see blood, but there was none. I stepped back towards the wall, and watched the men drag Jay to a chair in the center of the room. They forced him to sit down, and tied him up. I was watching the husband, nodding at him, trying to calm him down. 'Someone needs to tell me what's going on,' I whispered to the student. 'They say that he's going to pay,' he told me. 'Jay?' 'Yes.' 'For what?' 'For that man's wife,' the student said, looking down at the ground. 'They say the storm is because of you.' 'Us?' 'Yes,' he said, 'because you are white.' 'No,' I said, 'no, no, no. That's ridiculous.'

"I turned away from the student and took a few steps towards the husband, patting my hands in the air, palms down, shaking my head. The husband waved the knife at me, and I stopped. 'He says for you to be quiet,' the student said, 'and if you're not quiet you will die.' The student wasn't doing well, now, he was shaking all over.

"'Now you tell him to listen.' I said. 'You tell him we're innocent, we've done nothing to him or his family.' 'I can't say that,' the student said. I was losing him. 'Say it,' I shouted, and I grabbed him by the arm, hard. 'Say it now!'"

The red man leaned back in his chair, kneading the back of his neck with one wide hand. He pointed to a space in the middle of the room.

"There," he said, "Jay was in a chair right there while the two men tightened the ropes around his arms and legs. It didn't take long, and when they finished they turned to face me. The husband took a step towards me, and I got ready. The odds were bad but at least I had a chance. The two other men tried to flank me, but I had a little bit of room to back up. I kept my eye on the knife. Just as I was about to lunge for it, someone shoved me sharply from behind." The red man jerked his body forwards, hitting the bench with his knees, hard, rocking me. "After that it was over. They got me, and bound me tight, tied me to a chair, and dragged me next to Jay."

"Who pushed you?" I asked.

"It was our guide. I've thought about it, since, and I guess I think he did it to save my life." The red man rubbed his nose with both hands, like he was praying. He shrugged. "I don't know what he thought." The red man was quiet then, for a long moment, and I saw the muscle of his jaw bulge and tighten and then relax.

"They grabbed the student, too, and all three of us were trussed up like chickens in the middle of the room. Then they started arguing. It went on for a few minutes and when our guide turned to us he finally said, 'Okay. Now you will go into trial.' He held a finger up to stop us before we could say anything. 'You must explain first why you are here. Then why you are not responsible for the storm.' 'That's insane,' I told him, but he shook his head. The student said something, too, but our guide told him to speak English. When he tried again in Thai the husband started shouting. 'No,' our guide said. 'You are them,' he said. 'You speak like them. You begin.'

"The husband shouted again, and the student started to speak, slowly, in English, with our guide translating. 'I was born in the south of this country,' the student said. He named a village, I don't remember which. 'I have lived elsewhere,' he said, 'but I have always considered Thailand my home.' The husband stepped forward then slapped him very hard across the cheek. He shouted again at the student, and the kid closed his eyes. Then he opened them and said, not afraid, but sadly, 'Okay, if you want, that's what I'll say. Maybe it's true. Maybe I don't belong here. You can see if I'm to blame.'

"'I left our country when I was fourteen years old,' the student said. 'I went with my father and my brother to live in Los Angeles, and I learned to speak English. But I learned other things too. Before I left Thailand, a young girl had been promised to me, a girl who I knew since I was small. I even loved her, and I think she loved me too. But in the American high schools there were so many girls.' One of the men hissed, then, and the student stopped. 'Go on,' our guide said. 'There was a girl in my English class,' the student continued. 'She was a tall white American girl with blue eyes and yellow hair and straight teeth. We became friends.'

"'I knew that my real place was here, with my childhood girl, but I was also young and not going to deny myself. I didn't expect to fall in love in America, but that is what happened. I fell in love with the tall blue-eyed girl. I did not know what was happening to me at first. I couldn't sleep. I waited outside her window on cold nights, hoping to see her shadow. Sometimes I felt sick. I knew that in the American books I was reading, all these were symptoms of love. Western love. Selfish love. A love that is all about you and no one else.'

"The rain was so loud that I could barely hear the student as he spoke. I couldn't see him, either; the three men were surrounding him on all sides, listening. Then one moved and I had a view of the student's face. He was calm, his eyes were closed, his head bowed.

"'I forgot the girl back home,' the student continued. 'I forgot my family. I chased my tall blue-eyed girl until at last I got her. I did not worry about how I was going to take care of her; I did not think about how the match would help my family; I did not think about our chances of a life together. I just lived for every moment with her. I never told my family, for fear of what they might say. I knew what they would say. My family, even in America, was deeply set in our traditions.

"'Then a strange thing happened. One morning I woke up and I didn't love the tall blue-eyed girl anymore. There was another girl in my math class, a girl with a thin nose and long red-brown hair, and very white skin. That morning I woke up and found myself thinking about her instead. And after the red-brown haired girl there was another girl, and another and another. At first I blamed it on youth, but when I turned 21 and it hadn't stopped, I knew that this new love had ruined me.'

"The student opened his eyes, then, and looked up at the men standing over them. 'It is a terrible thing,' he said. 'It is not simply the desire to be with another woman; we all know that will not go away, not ever, and how we decide to act on that will be our decision. But western love is not for us. It makes you believe that true happiness is in tomorrow, in the skirts of the next love, the next woman. I came back to our country four months ago because it was the only way out I could see. My childhood girl has wisely married someone else. I have some family here. After this trip I will stay with them and work. I thought to take a trip, to see the parts of this country I didn't know. I thought that might help me understand what I did wrong. And that is how I come to be here this night. That is my story.'"

The red man paused for a moment, and reached for his breast pocket, but there was nothing there. As I held out another cigarette to him, he looked up and seemed surprised to see me, as if he had been expecting someone else. He glanced over my shoulder, and when I turned, I saw Thip sitting up against the wall, watching us.

"It's raining," I said to Thip, as if that explained something. "He . . ." I started. But Thip just shook his head, slowly, and I turned back to the red man.

He'd lit his cigarette and put his elbow on the table, rolling up his sleeve. There, on the wide biceps, green tattooed letters were etched in gothic script: "Born to Suffer."

"Vietnam," the red man said, nodding at his tattoo. "I signed up the day I turned eighteen. I don't know why. I couldn't have told you then, either. But I was there at the end. It was all I could think about as the student was telling his story. I started to think that maybe they were right, I shouldn't be there, maybe I had brought the bad with me, maybe I did cause the storm. I don't know how that sounds to you. I felt like I really was facing these judges or fates.

"The men nodded when the student finished, and suddenly it was like they'd understood him. So I decided right then that I had to tell the truth, even though it seemed like there was a chance that it wouldn't work out." He stared at me, and I looked away.

"I explained to them about going to Vietnam," the red man continued, "putting in my two tours of duty, returning to the States when it was over. How I only lasted three months in California before packing my small bags and getting on a plane that brought me here." He banged his knee with his fist, twice. "No, what I mostly talked about was how, on my first night in Bangkok, I had walked through the streets, looking for a shave. That had always been something I'd liked back when I was in Vietnam: getting a shave.

"I found the perfect place. It was a clean, mirrored room, small, facing the street with floor-to-ceiling windows. There was a big pile of hair sweepings in the corner; in the States there would have been a little spiral pole out front. An older man was talking inside, lathering a customer, and a young man sat in the other chair, waiting his turn. I entered and pantomimed a shave to the old barber, and then sat down myself to wait. I was surprised when the young man, who I had mistaken for an expectant customer, rose and grinned at me, motioning for me to sit down in the extra barber chair. He must have been a few years younger than me; he looked like he hadn't even started to shave yet. I sat down and watched him remove a straight razor from a steaming cup of water and check the edge with his finger. He lathered my face. Without hesitation or ceremony, he began to shave me quickly. He wasn't bad, but it felt too fast, and I was uneasy about it.

"He shaved my face, then tilted back my head and worked on my neck. From that position the room did not seem as clean as it had first appeared. There were cobwebs on the ceiling, and strange stains on the walls. As he moved my head to one side with a strong hand, my eye caught the yellow flash of a poster, and when my eyes focused I realized that it was a map. I tried not to move, the razor was on the curve of my cheek. It was a map of Vietnam. Right then, the man looked down at me and said, 'You, U.S.A.?' His huge face was right in front of mine, staring at me, and I saw in his eyes, in his cheekbones, I saw the faces of men I killed during the war. I was so frightened then, more frightened than I had ever been before, even more frightened than when I was getting shot at in the trees. I was more afraid in the barber's chair, there in that strange city, far from everything and everybody I knew, where I'd come back to a continent I'd cursed with all my heart. I waited for him to slit my throat. It seemed to me, at that moment in history, both the world's and mine, that if he did, that would be justice. His hand came up over my eyes and shut them, like an undertaker. But nothing happened. He sprayed me with a light film of alcohol, wiped my face, pulled the bib away and stepped back. I stood, a little dazed, and paid him. As I made for the door he stopped me with one hand on the middle of my chest, and pointed at himself. 'Me, Vietnam,' he said. 'Yes, I know,' I answered. He looked at me, like he was thinking, and then took his hand back. He did not smile, but he nodded once. 'Okay,' he said. Then I was out in the streets, where I touched my smooth cheeks, the alcohol still stinging my neck, and I walked away. I could feel the fear welling up inside me, but instead of rage—at myself, at him, at his or my country, at what had been—I experienced only a sense of space. That was why I was there that night, I told them, because I had found a space in Thailand which seemed real, where the past and the present and the future could all exist without denying one another. It wasn't forgiveness; it wasn't understanding. It was a common acknowledgment of the way things stood. And that was the story I told."

The red man stood up suddenly. I turned to see Thip standing behind me, shaking his head at the red man, shooing him with both hands like one might a neighbor's dog.

"Okay," the red man said. "I'm going."

"But what happened?" I said. "What happened then?"

"There was no then," the red man replied. He was still looking at Thip.

"I stayed here."

"They let you go."

"Yes." He took a step towards the door, and I followed him. "It was the right story. They let us go. We went and we found his wife."

"But why did you stay?"

"Because I told the truth," the red man said. "The truth, you know." He took a deep breath, let it out slowly, and then opened the door and went out into the rain. As the door swung shut behind him, I started to follow when a hand caught me from behind. It was Thip. His eyes were wide and sober, now, and something in his face made me push his arm away, and back up to the door. I felt my way to the catch without turning around and opened the door and backed outside.

The rain was still coming down, hard. I put my hands over my eyes, straining to see through the gloom, but there was nothing there. I thought about calling out, but I realized I didn't know the red man's name. "Hey," I yelled. "Hello." But he didn't call back.

Thip was waiting for me when I went back inside.

"He's gone," I said.

Thip nodded. Slowly, he stood up and latched the door behind me. "I apologize," he said. "I forgot to lock it. He comes sometimes, when I'm here."

"You know him?"

Thip nodded. "When I smoke, sometimes, I forget to lock the door, I'm sorry."

"Where does he live? What does he do?" I was still thinking about the story, about what the red man had said to his inquisitors, and wondering: what would I say? What would I say if my time were to come? But Thip was shaking his head, and his face was dark and serious.

"He never gives me a name. That's my punishment. To hear this story again and again and to never have a name."

"What do you mean?"

"The student," he said. "Do I look like a student to you?" He didn't.

He looked old and worn and gray. He looked like he was at the end of something. "But yes, once I was a student."

"That was you?"

"Yes," he said.

"Is it true?"

"Some is true," he said. "But not the end." Thip looked at his hands. "I'm sorry," he said, "I do not mean to be mysterious. It's not comfortable to explain. He's harmless."

"What do you mean?" I said, but he shook his head. I looked around at my sleeping companions and lowered my voice to a whisper. "I won't tell anyone."

"These stories," he said, "stories. My western love. His shave. Do you know how many times I've heard them? But not like the first time."

"Did it really happen?"

"You want to know what happened?"

"Yes."

He nodded. "It happened. It was here, and it happened. But the men didn't like his story. It made them angry. When he finished they took him and the other American and they cut their throats. We were outside near the river and they had me watch. They cut their throats and they threw the bodies down into the river. And then you know what happened?" I didn't move. Thip almost laughed, but it couldn't be called a laugh, anymore. "They threw the bodies in and the rain stopped."

I stepped back from him, and went to the door and opened it. Outside, the rain was gone. Stars were out again, and a slim moon was coming up over the trees. I ran to the edge of the river bank, looking down, trying to see something. But there was only the flood-swelled water of the river rushing south on its long, inevitable journey to the sea, and from the sea to the oceans, and out to every part of the world. Where the water finally ended I did not know.

PART IV:

ELVES

Hunters in the Snow

by Tobias Wolff

Tub had been waiting for an hour in the falling snow. He paced the sidewalk to keep warm and stuck his head out over the curb whenever he saw lights approaching. One driver stopped for him but before Tub could wave the man on he saw the rifle on Tub's back and hit the gas. The tires spun on the ice.

The fall of snow thickened. Tub stood below the overhang of a building. Across the road the clouds whitened just above the rooftops, and the street lights went out. He shifted the rifle strap to his other shoulder. The whiteness seeped up the sky.

A truck slid around the corner, horn blaring, rear end sashaying. Tub moved to the sidewalk and held up his hand. The truck jumped the curb and kept coming, half on the street and half on the sidewalk. It wasn't slowing down at all. Tub stood for a moment, still holding up his hand, then jumped back. His rifle slipped off his shoulder and clattered to the ice, a sandwich fell out of his pocket.

He ran for the steps of the building. Another sandwich and a package of cookies tumbled onto the new snow. He made the steps and looked back.

The truck had stopped several feet beyond where Tub had been standing. He picked up the sandwiches and his cookies and slung the rifle and went up to the driver's window. The driver was bent against the steering wheel, slapping his knees and drumming his feet on the floorboards. He looked like a cartoon of a person laughing, except that his eyes watched the man on the seat beside him. "You ought to see yourself," the driver said. "He looks just like a beach ball with a hat on, doesn't he? Doesn't he, Frank?"

The man beside him smiled and looked off.

"You almost ran me down," Tub said. "You could've killed me."

"Come on, Tub," said the man beside the driver. "Be mellow. Kenny was just messing around." He opened the door and slid over to the middle of the seat.

Tub took the bolt out of his rifle and climbed in beside him. "I waited an hour," he said. "If you meant ten o'clock why didn't you say ten o'clock?"

"Tub, you haven't done anything but complain since we got here," said the man in the middle. "If you want to piss and moan all day you might as well go home and bitch at your kids. Take your pick." When Tub didn't say anything he turned to the driver. "Okay, Kenny, let's hit the road."

Some juvenile delinquents had heaved a brick through the windshield on the driver's side, so the cold and snow tunneled right into the cab. The heater didn't work. They covered themselves with a couple of blankets Kenny had brought along and pulled down the muffs on their caps. Tub tried to keep his hands warm by rubbing them under the blanket but Frank made him stop.

They left Spokane and drove deep into the country, running along black lines of fences. The snow let up, but still there was no edge to the land where it met the sky. Nothing moved in the chalky fields. The cold bleached their faces and made the stubble stand out on their cheeks and along their upper lips. They stopped twice for coffee before they got to the woods where Kenny wanted to hunt.

Tub was for trying someplace different; two years in a row they'd been up and down this land and hadn't seen a thing. Frank didn't care one way or the other, he just wanted to get out of the god-damned truck. "Feel that," Frank said, slamming the door. He spread his feet and closed his eyes and leaned his head way back and breathed deeply. "Tune in on that energy."

"Another thing," Kenny said. "This is open land. Most of the land around here is posted."

"I'm cold," Tub said.

Frank breathed out. "Stop bitching, Tub. Get centered."

"I wasn't bitching."

"Centered," Kenny said. "Next thing you'll be wearing a nightgown, Frank. Selling flowers out at the airport."

"Kenny," Frank said, "you talk too much."

"Okay," Kenny said. "I won't say a word. Like I won't say anything about a certain babysitter."

"What babysitter?" Tub asked.

"That's between us," Frank said, looking at Kenny. "That's confidential. You keep your mouth shut."

Kenny laughed.

"You're asking for it," Frank said.

"Asking for what?"

"You'll see."

"Hey," said Tub, "are we hunting or what?"

They started off across the field. Tub had trouble getting through the fences. Frank and Kenny could have helped him; they could have lifted up on the top wire and stepped on the bottom wire, but they didn't. They stood and watched him. There were a lot of fences and Tub was puffing when they reached the woods.

They hunted for over two hours and saw no deer, no tracks, no sign. Finally they stopped by the creek to eat. Kenny had several slices of pizza and a couple of candy bars; Frank had a sandwich, an apple, two carrots, and a square of chocolate; Tub ate one hard-boiled egg and a stick of celery.

"You ask me how I want to die today," Kenny said, "I'll tell you burn me at the stake." He turned to Tub. "You still on that diet?" He winked at Frank.

"What do you think? You think I like hard-boiled eggs?"

"All I can say is, it's the first diet I ever heard of where you gained weight from it."

"Who said I gained weight?"

"Oh, pardon me. I take it back. You're just wasting away before my very eyes. Isn't he, Frank?"

Frank had his fingers fanned out, tips against the bark of the stump where he'd laid his food. His knuckles were hairy. He wore a heavy wedding band and on his right pinky another gold ring with a flat face and an "F" in what looked like diamonds. He turned the ring this way and that. "Tub," he said, "you haven't seen your own balls in ten years."

Kenny doubled over laughing. He took off his hat and slapped his leg with it.

"What am I supposed to do?" Tub said. "It's my glands."

* * *

They left the woods and hunted along the creek. Frank and Kenny worked one bank and Tub worked the other, moving upstream. The snow was light but the drifts were deep and hard to move through. Wherever Tub looked the surface was smooth, undisturbed, and after a time he lost interest. He stopped looking for tracks and just tried to keep up with Frank and Kenny on the other side. A moment came when he realized he hadn't seen them in a long time. The breeze was moving from him to them; when it stilled he could sometimes hear Kenny laughing but that was all. He quickened his pace, breasting hard into the drifts, fighting away the snow with his knees and elbows. He heard his heart and felt the flush on his face but he never once stopped.

Tub caught up with Frank and Kenny at a bend of the creek. They were standing on a log that stretched from their bank to his. Ice had backed up behind the log. Frozen reeds stuck out, barely nodding when the air moved.

"See anything?" Frank asked.

Tub shook his head.

There wasn't much daylight left and they decided to head back toward the road. Frank and Kenny crossed the log and they started downstream, using the trail Tub had broken. Before they had gone very far Kenny stopped. "Look at that," he said, and pointed to some tracks going from the creek back into the woods. Tub's footprints crossed right over them. There on the bank, plain as day, were several mounds of deer sign. "What do you think that is, Tub?" Kenny kicked at it. "Walnuts on vanilla icing?"

"I guess I didn't notice."

Kenny looked at Frank.

"I was lost."

"You were lost. Big deal."

They followed the tracks into the woods. The deer had gone over a fence half buried in drifting snow. A no hunting sign was nailed to the top of one of the posts. Frank laughed and said the son of a bitch could read. Kenny wanted to go after him but Frank said no way, that people out here didn't mess around. He thought maybe the farmer who owned the land would let them use it if they asked. Kenny wasn't so sure. Anyway, he figured that by the time they walked to the truck and drove up the road and doubled back it would be almost dark.

"Relax," Frank said. "You can't hurry nature. If we're meant to get that deer, we'll get it. If we're not, we won't."

They started back toward the truck. This part of the woods was mainly pine. The snow was shaded and had a glaze on it. It held up Kenny and Frank but Tub kept falling through. As he kicked forward, the edge of the crust bruised his shins. Kenny and Frank pulled ahead of him, to where he couldn't even hear their voices any more. He sat down on a stump and wiped his face. He ate both the sandwiches and half the cookies, taking his own sweet time. It was dead quiet.

When Tub crossed the last fence into the road the truck started moving. Tub had to run for it and just managed to grab hold of the tailgate and hoist himself into the bed. He lay there, panting. Kenny looked out the rear window and grinned. Tub crawled into the lee of the cab to get out of the freezing wind. He pulled his earflaps low and pushed his chin into the collar of his coat. Someone rapped on the window but Tub would not turn around.

He and Frank waited outside while Kenny went into the farmhouse to ask permission. The house was old and paint was curling off the sides. The smoke streamed westward off the top of the chimney, fanning away into a thin gray plume. Above the ridge of the hills another ridge of blue clouds was rising.

"You've got a short memory," Tub said.

"What?" Frank said. He had been staring off.

"I used to stick up for you."

"Okay, so you used to stick up for me. What's eating you?"

"You shouldn't have just left me back there like that."

"You're a grown-up, Tub. You can take care of yourself. Anyway, if you think you're the only person with problems I can tell you that you're not."

"Is something bothering you, Frank?"

Frank kicked at a branch poking out of the snow. "Never mind," he said.

"What did Kenny mean about the babysitter?"

"Kenny talks too much," Frank said. "You just mind your own business."

Kenny came out of the farmhouse and gave the thumbs-up and they began walking back toward the woods. As they passed the barn a large black hound with a grizzled snout ran out and barked at them. Every time he barked he slid backwards a bit, like a cannon recoiling. Kenny got down on all fours and snarled and barked back at him, and the dog slunk away into the barn, looking over his shoulder and peeing a little as he went.

"That's an old-timer," Frank said. "A real graybeard. Fifteen years if he's a day."

"Too old," Kenny said.

Past the barn they cut off through the fields. The land was unfenced and the crust was freezing up thick and they made good time. They kept to the edge of the field until they picked up the tracks again and followed them into the woods, farther and farther back toward the hills. The trees started to blur with the shadows and the wind rose and needled their faces with the crystals it swept off the glaze. Finally they lost the tracks.

Kenny swore and threw down his hat. "This is the worst day of hunting I ever had, bar none." He picked up his hat and brushed off the snow. "This will be the first season since I was fifteen I haven't got my deer."

"It isn't the deer," Frank said. "It's the hunting. There are all these forces out here and you just have to go with them."

"You go with them," Kenny said. "I came out here to get me a deer, not listen to a bunch of hippie bullshit. And if it hadn't been for dimples here I would have, too."

"That's enough," Frank said.

"And you—you're so busy thinking about that little jailbait of yours you wouldn't know a deer if you saw one."

"Drop dead," Frank said, and turned away.

Kenny and Tub followed him back across the fields. When they were coming up to the barn Kenny stopped and pointed. "I hate that post," he said. He raised his rifle and fired. It sounded like a dry branch cracking. The post splintered along its right side, up towards the top. "There," Kenny said. "It's dead."

"Knock it off," Frank said, walking ahead.

Kenny looked at Tub. He smiled. "I hate that tree," he said, and fired again. Tub hurried to catch up with Frank. He started to speak but just then the dog ran out of the barn and barked at them. "Easy, boy," Frank said.

"I hate that dog." Kenny was behind them.

"That's enough," Frank said. "You put that gun down."

Kenny fired. The bullet went in between the dog's eyes. He sank right down in the snow, his legs splayed out on each side, his yellow eyes open and staring. Except for the blood he looked like a small bearskin rug. The blood ran down the dog's muzzle into the snow.

They all looked at the dog lying there.

"What did he ever do to you?" Tub asked. "He was just barking."

Kenny turned to Tub. "I hate you."

Tub shot from the waist. Kenny jerked backward against the fence and buckled to his knees. He folded his hands across his stomach. "Look," he said. His hands were covered with blood. In the dusk his blood was more blue than red. It seemed to belong to the shadows. It didn't seem out of place. Kenny eased himself onto his back. He sighed several times, deeply. "You shot me," he said.

"I had to," Tub said. He knelt beside Kenny. "Oh God," he said. "Frank. Frank."

Frank hadn't moved since Kenny killed the dog.

"Frank!" Tub shouted.

"I was just kidding around," Kenny said. "It was a joke. Oh!" he said, and arched his back suddenly. "Oh!" he said again, and dug his heels into the snow and pushed himself along on his head for several feet. Then he stopped and lay there, rocking back and forth on his heels and head like a wrestler doing warm-up exercises.

Frank roused himself. "Kenny," he said. He bent down and put his gloved hand on Kenny's brow. "You shot him," he said to Tub.

"He made me," Tub said.

"No no no," Kenny said.

Tub was weeping from the eyes and the nostrils. His whole face was wet. Frank closed his eyes, then looked down at Kenny again. "Where does it hurt?"

"Everywhere," Kenny said, "just everywhere."

"Oh God," Tub said.

"I mean where did it go in?" Frank said.

"Here." Kenny pointed at the wound in his stomach. It was welling slowly with blood.

"You're lucky," Frank said. "It's on the left side. It missed your appendix. If it had hit your appendix you'd really be in the soup." He turned away and threw up into the snow, holding his sides as if to keep warm.

"Are you all right?" Tub said.

"There's some aspirin in the truck," Kenny said.

"I'm all right," Frank said.

"We'd better call an ambulance," Tub said.

"Jesus," Frank said. "What are we going to say?"

"Exactly what happened," Tub said. "He was going to shoot me but I shot him first."

"No sir!" Kenny said. "I wasn't either!"

Frank patted Kenny on the arm. "Easy does it, partner." He stood. "Let's go."

Tub picked up Kenny's rifle as they walked down toward the farmhouse. "No sense leaving this around," he said. "Kenny might get ideas."

"I can tell you one thing," Frank said. "You've really done it this time. This definitely takes the cake."

They had to knock on the door twice before it was opened by a thin man with lank hair. The room behind him was filled with smoke. He squinted at them. "You get anything?" he asked.

"No," Frank said.

"I knew you wouldn't. That's what I told the other fellow."

"We've had an accident."

The man looked past Frank and Tub into the gloom. "Shoot your friend, did you?"

Frank nodded.

"I did," Tub said.

"I suppose you want to use the phone."

"If it's okay."

The man in the door looked behind him, then stepped back. Frank and Tub followed him into the house. There was a woman sitting by the stove in the middle of the room. The stove was smoking badly. She looked up and then down again at the child asleep in her lap. Her face was white and damp; strands of hair were pasted across her forehead. Tub warmed his hands over the stove while Frank went into the kitchen to call. The man who had let them in stood at the window, his hands in his pockets.

"My friend shot your dog," Tub said.

The man nodded without turning around. "I should have done it myself. I just couldn't."

"He loved that dog so much," the woman said. The child squirmed and she rocked it.

"You asked him to?" Tub said. "You asked him to shoot your dog?"

"He was old and sick. Couldn't chew his food anymore. I would have done it myself but I don't have a gun."

"You couldn't have anyway," the woman said. "Never in a million years."

The man shrugged.

Frank came out of the kitchen. "We'll have to take him ourselves. The nearest hospital is fifty miles from here and all their ambulances are out anyway."

The woman knew a shortcut but the directions were complicated and Tub had to write them down. The man told them where they could find some boards to carry Kenny on. He didn't have a flashlight but he said he would leave the porch light on.

It was dark outside. The clouds were low and heavy-looking and the wind blew in shrill gusts. There was a screen loose on the house and it banged slowly and then quickly as the wind rose again. They could hear it all the way to the barn. Frank went for the boards while Tub looked for Kenny, who was not where they had left him. Tub found him farther up the drive, lying on his stomach. "You okay?" Tub said.

"It hurts."

"Frank says it missed your appendix."

"I already had my appendix out."

"All right," Frank said, coming up to them. "We'll have you in a nice warm bed before you can say Jack Robinson." He put the two boards on Kenny's right side.

"Just as long as I don't have one of those male nurses," Kenny said.

"Ha ha," Frank said. "That's the spirit. Get ready, set, *over you go,*" and he rolled Kenny onto the boards. Kenny screamed and kicked his legs in the air. When he quieted down Frank and Tub lifted the boards and carried him down the drive. Tub had the back end, and with the snow blowing into his face he had trouble with his footing. Also he was tired and the man inside had forgotten to turn the porch light on. Just past the house Tub slipped and threw out his hands to catch himself. The boards fell and Kenny tumbled out and rolled to the bottom of the drive, yelling all the way. He came to rest against the right front wheel of the truck.

"You fat moron," Frank said. "You aren't good for diddly."

Tub grabbed Frank by the collar and backed him hard up against the fence. Frank tried to pull his hands away but Tub shook him and snapped his head back and forth and finally Frank gave up.

"What do you know about fat," Tub said. "What do you know about glands." As he spoke he kept shaking Frank. "What do you know about me."

"All right," Frank said.

"No more," Tub said.

"All right."

"No more talking to me like that. No more watching. No more laughing."

"Okay, Tub, I promise."

Tub let go of Frank and leaned his forehead against the fence. His arms hung straight at his sides.

"I'm sorry, Tub." Frank touched him on the shoulder. "I'll be down at the truck."

Tub stood by the fence for a while and then got the rifles off the porch. Frank had rolled Kenny back onto the boards and they lifted him into the bed of the truck. Frank spread the seat blankets over him. "Warm enough?" he asked.

Kenny nodded.

"Okay. Now how does reverse work on this thing?"

"All the way to the left and up." Kenny sat up as Frank started forward to the cab. "Frank!"

"What?"

"If it sticks don't force it."

The truck started right away. "One thing," Frank said, "you've got to hand it to the Japanese. A very ancient, very spiritual culture and they can still make a hell of a truck." He glanced over at Tub. "Look, I'm sorry. I didn't know you felt that way, honest to God I didn't. You should have said something."

"I did."

"When? Name one time."

"A couple of hours ago."

"I guess I wasn't paying attention."

"That's true, Frank," Tub said. "You don't pay attention very much."

"Tub," Frank said, "about what happened back there, I should have been more sympathetic. I realize that. You were going through a lot. I just want you to know it wasn't your fault. He was asking for it."

"You think so?"

"Absolutely. It was him or you. I would have done the same thing in your shoes, no question."

The wind was blowing on their faces. The snow was a moving white wall in front of their lights; it swirled into the cab through the hole in the windshield and settled on them. Tub clapped his hands and shifted around to stay warm, but it didn't work.

"I'm going to have to stop," Frank said. "I can't feel my fingers."

Up ahead they saw some lights off the road. It was a tavern. Outside in the parking lot there were several jeeps and trucks. A couple of them had deer strapped across their hoods. Frank parked and they went back to Kenny. "How you doing, partner," Frank said.

"I'm cold."

"Well, don't feel like the Lone Ranger. It's worse inside, take my word for it. You should get that windshield fixed."

"Look," Tub said. "he threw the blankets off." They were lying in a heap against the tailgate.

"Now look, Kenny," Frank said, "it's no use whining about being cold if you're not going to try and keep warm. You've got to do your share." He spread the blankets over Kenny and tucked them in at the corners.

"They blew off."

"Hold on to them then."

"Why are we stopping, Frank?"

"Because if me and Tub don't get warmed up we're going to freeze solid and then where will you be?" He punched Kenny lightly in the arm. "So just hold your horses."

The bar was full of men in colored jackets, mostly orange. The waitress brought coffee. "Just what the doctor ordered," Frank said, cradling the steaming cup in his hand. His skin was bone white. "Tub, I've been thinking. What you said about me not paying attention, that's true."

"It's okay."

"No. I really had that coming. I guess I've just been a little too interested in old number one. I've had a lot on my mind. Not that that's any excuse."

"Forget it, Frank. I sort of lost my temper back there. I guess we're all a little on edge."

Frank shook his head. "It isn't just that."

"You want to talk about it?"

"Just between us, Tub?"

"Sure, Frank. Just between us."

"Tub, I think I'm going to be leaving Nancy."

"Oh, Frank. Oh, Frank." Tub sat back and shook his head.

Frank reached out and laid his hand on Tub's arm. "Tub, have you ever been really in love?"

"Well—"

"I mean *really* in love." He squeezed Tub's wrist. "With your whole being."

"I don't know. When you put it like that, I don't know."

"You haven't then. Nothing against you, but you'd know it if you had." Frank let go of Tub's arm. "This isn't just some bit of fluff I'm talking about."

"Who is she, Frank?"

Frank paused. He looked into his empty cup. "Roxanne Brewer."

"Cliff Brewer's kid? The babysitter?"

"You can't just put people into categories like that, Tub. That's why the whole system is wrong. And that's why this country is going to hell in a rowboat."

"But she can't be more than—" Tub shook his head.

"Fifteen. She'll be sixteen in May." Frank smiled. "May fourth, three twenty-seven p.m. Hell, Tub, a hundred years ago she'd have been an old maid by that age. Juliet was only thirteen."

"Juliet? Juliet Miller? Jesus, Frank, she doesn't even have breasts. She doesn't even wear a top to her bathing suit. She's still collecting frogs."

"Not Juliet Miller. The real Juliet. Tub, don't you see how you're dividing people up into categories? He's an executive, she's a secretary, he's a truck driver, she's fifteen years old. Tub, this so-called babysitter, this so-called fifteen-year-old has more in her little finger than most of us have in our entire bodies. I can tell you this little lady is something special."

Tub nodded. "I know the kids like her."

"She's opened up whole worlds to me that I never knew were there."

"What does Nancy think about all of this?"

"She doesn't know."

"You haven't told her?"

"Not yet. It's not so easy. She's been damned good to me all these years. Then there's the kids to consider." The brightness in Frank's eyes trembled and he wiped quickly at them with the back of his hand. "I guess you think I'm a complete bastard."

"No, Frank. I don't think that."

"Well, you *ought* to."

"Frank, when you've got a friend it means you've always got someone on your side, no matter what. That's the way I feel about it, anyway."

"You mean that, Tub?"

"Sure I do."

Frank smiled. "You don't know how good it feels to hear you say that."

Kenny had tried to get out of the truck but he hadn't made it. He was jackknifed over the tailgate, his head hanging above the bumper. They lifted him back into the bed and covered him again. He was sweating and his teeth chattered. "It hurts, Frank."

"It wouldn't hurt so much if you just stayed put. Now we're going to the hospital. Got that? Say it—I'm going to the hospital."

"I'm going to the hospital."

"Again."

"I'm going to the hospital."

"Now just keep saying that to yourself and before you know it we'll be there."

After they had gone a few miles Tub turned to Frank. "I just pulled a real boner," he said.

"What's that?"

"I left the directions on the table back there."

"That's okay. I remember them pretty well."

The snowfall lightened and the clouds began to roll back off the fields, but it was no warmer and after a time both Frank and Tub were bitten through and shaking. Frank almost didn't make it around a curve, and they decided to stop at the next roadhouse.

There was an automatic hand-dryer in the bathroom and they took turns standing in front of it, opening their jackets and shirts and letting the jet of hot air breathe across their faces and chests.

"You know," Tub said, "what you told me back there, I appreciate it. Trusting me."

Frank opened and closed his fingers in front of the nozzle. "The way I look at it, Tub, no man is an island. You've got to trust someone."

"Frank—"

Frank waited.

"When I said that about my glands, that wasn't true. The truth is I just shovel it in."

"Well, Tub—"

"Day and night, Frank. In the shower. On the freeway." He turned and let the air play over his back. "I've even got stuff in the paper towel machine at work."

"There's nothing wrong with your glands at all?" Frank had taken his boots and socks off. He held first his right, then his left foot up to the nozzle.

"No. There never was."

"Does Alice know?" The machine went off and Frank started lacing up his boots.

"Nobody knows. That's the worst of it, Frank. Not the being fat, I never got any big kick out of being thin, but the lying. Having to lead a double life like a spy or a hit man. This sounds strange but I feel sorry for those guys, I really do. I know what they go through. Always having to think about what you say and do. Always feeling like people are watching you, trying to catch you at something. Never able to just be yourself. Like when I make a big deal about only having an orange for breakfast and then scarf all the way to work. Oreos, Mars Bars, Twinkies. Sugar Babies. Snickers." Tub glanced at Frank and looked quickly away. "Pretty disgusting, isn't it?"

"Tub. Tub." Frank shook his head. "Come on." He took Tub's arm and led him into the restaurant half of the bar. "My friend is hungry," he told the waitress. "Bring four orders of pancakes, plenty of butter and syrup."

"Frank—"

"Sit down."

When the dishes came Frank carved out slabs of butter and just laid them on the pancakes. Then he emptied the bottle of syrup, moving it back and forth over the plates. He leaned forward on his elbows and rested his chin in one hand. "Go on, Tub."

Tub ate several mouthfuls, then started to wipe his lips. Frank took the napkin away from him. "No wiping," he said. Tub kept at it. The syrup covered his chin; it dripped to a point like a goatee. "Weigh in, Tub," Frank said, pushing another fork across the table. "Get down to business." Tub took the fork in his left hand and lowered his head and started really chowing down. "Clean your plate," Frank said when the pancakes were gone, and Tub lifted each of the four plates and licked it clean. He sat back, trying to catch his breath.

"Beautiful," Frank said. "Are you full?"

"I'm full," Tub said. "I've never been so full."

Kenny's blankets were bunched up against the tailgate again.

"They must have blown off," Tub said.

"They're not doing him any good," Frank said. "We might as well get some use out of them."

Kenny mumbled. Tub bent over him. "What? Speak up."

"I'm going to the hospital," Kenny said.

"Attaboy," Frank said.

The blankets helped. The wind still got their faces and Frank's hands but it was much better. The fresh snow on the road and the trees sparkled under the beam of the headlight. Squares of light from farmhouse windows fell onto the blue snow in the fields.

"Frank," Tub said after a time, "you know that farmer? He told Kenny to kill the dog."

"You're kidding!" Frank leaned forward, considering. "That Kenny. What a card." He laughed and so did Tub. Tub smiled out the back window. Kenny lay with his arms folded over his stomach, moving his lips at the stars. Right overhead was the Big Dipper, and behind, hanging between Kenny's toes in the direction of the hospital, was the North Star, Pole Star, Help to Sailors. As the truck twisted through the gentle hills the star went back and forth between Kenny's boots, staying always in his sight. "I'm going to the hospital," Kenny said. But he was wrong. They had taken a different turn a long way back.

For Everything
Its Season

by John Long

It's been seven years since Steve Alexander broke this story down at a Mexican restaurant in the mountain hamlet of Idyllwild, after a day's climbing at Tahquitz Rock. The Cochran brothers were there, big strapping twins who the next winter were swept off Peak 60 in the Pamirs by an avalanche. And Art DeSaussure was there too. That was before he became an international star, before Nuptse and K2. He was 20 or 21 then and was overwhelming for all his energy and questions but we put up with him because he reminded us of ourselves at that age, so anxious to make a name for himself and ready to try any climb, anywhere. Four years later, Art died trying to repeat the very climb which he hounded Steve Alexander into telling us about: the landmark first ascent of the Citadel in Sequoia National Park, California.

Art put the question right to him. What about the Citadel? Steve had made the first ascent with Russ Owens, another legendary climber who had vanished after the Citadel climb. Some say Russ simply quit climbing and went to Spain where his mother was born or was a beachcomber in the Solomon Islands, for he was a known loner; but no one ever saw him again. Twelve years has passed since the Citadel climb and no one had repeated it, though many tried. And twelve years had never gotten Steve to say one word about it. But that Art got right in Alexander's face—the kid had to know— and we all thought Alexander was going to go off on him because Alexander was like that. Maybe it was the beer, or the fact that Steve's climbing career was virtually over that made him freeze the kid with a stare and, palms up, say: "You got to know, do you?!" Art nodded slowly. Alexander looked toward the ceiling, cackled, and yelled out for another beer. He glowered at us all in turn, then laughed in our faces.

"Yea, I'll tell you bastards all right, because I don't care what comes of it anymore." Alexander didn't care about anything—we all knew that—so I was surprised that he once cared about something, whatever it was. He turned his palms over, glared at us all again, and after the beers came, started his story.

"Everyone knows who Russ Owens was and what he did but there's hardly anyone around now who remembers what he was like. I'm not sure I remember, or ever really knew, because I only did the one climb with him. But I'll tell you right now, these young hotshots today aren't the shit on his boots. None of them. All the pink jump-suits and diamond earrings and funk diets and Olympian workouts. And just look what they're doing wanking around these scrappy little cliffs, where every toehold's chalked and all the gamble's been engi-neered away. And they call it 'worldclass'. She-it . . . Now Russ, he couldn't be bothered with anything but the biggest, wildest stuff,

stuff you'd look up at and want to dig yourself a hole and crawl inside just to hide from it. Stuff like the Citadel.

"Anyhow, climbers back then were all broke and they all drove junkers. I remember starting for the Citadel in Russ's old Volkswagen van and how it backfired all the way up the Grapevine Pass. He threw it into neutral and we started the long coast into the Bakersfield basin and man, it had to be 100 degrees in that van. He hadn't said one word since we'd left Los Angeles, two hours back. He never talked much. I guess that's why people thought he was arrogant.

"I was 22 then and his invitation to join him on the Citadel caught me totally off-guard. I knew that the Citadel had twice defeated Russ and my brother Vic. You'll remember that the previous winter, Russ and Vic had gone to the Karakoram to climb Nameless Tower. They did all their climbing together, though they never hung out off the cliffside. Some say theirs was the best alpine partnership of all time, but who knows. Well, Vic got killed on Nameless Tower. Russ claimed Vic had slipped off an easy shelf near the summit, and fell to his death. Now my brother was one of the best alpinists in the world—he and Russ had done the most outrageous stuff anyway— so I never could buy that business about slipping off easy ground. Whatever. After Vic fell Russ went ahead and climbed the last ice field and bagged the summit. It was probably this climb, the first ascent of the peak, and the North face at that, which made Russ Owens so legendary. He descended in a whiteout, or so he said, and he never found Vic's body. But I wonder if he ever even looked. I thought that was really cold for Russ to just leave my brother like that so he could make the climb. The climbing community didn't know what to make of it, but a few besides myself wondered about the whole affair. But you can't prove anything, so in a few months the whole thing was just another alpine tragedy, a statistic.

"So there I was, heading to attempt the Citadel; and I didn't give a damn about it. I came to find out about Vic. The truth had to come out over the next few days. I'd feel things out and force the issue if I had to. Who could say what was going through Russ's head, or why he'd invited me? It was plenty awkward just sitting there— no music or nothing. Every few minutes I'd glance over at him but his eyes never left the road and he never said a word.

"We finally got to Sequoia National Park around midnight and Russ parked behind the annexe because he knew someone there. Right off he dragged the packs out of the van and asked, 'You ready?' Ready? Ready for what? Here the van was still dieseling and this guy's set to thrash the four miles into the Citadel! I couldn't reckon what was driving him. I shouldered my pack and we hit the trail and the guy takes off like a deer. The sixty-pound packs and his wicked pace were so gruelling I thought he was trying to hike me to death. But so be it, I wouldn't eat this guy's dust so I stayed right on his heels. In half an hour we were both sweat-soaked and steaming, stumbling through a dark pine forest, tripping over roots and stones and my heart was aflame in my chest. Then the trail left the trees and we were fairly jogging out in the open.

"The sky was a high dome of thin clouds, and burning through it was a three-quarter moon with a big red ring around it. The left side of the valley was all steep ramps and towers and minarets. The polished granite shone silver but the hollows and chimneys of the escarpment were jet black and the whole place resembled a weird moonscape. The right side of the valley was a void of dark ramparts but a mile or so beyond, my eyes were yanked straight to the gleaming Citadel. And, man, I couldn't tear my eyes away no matter how hard I tried and I really wanted to because the thing looked so damn awesome. There's a 1,000-foot slab leading right to the base, then it rears vertical for 2,000 feet. We dashed through a wet meadow to a stream below the slab to fill our water bottles. And now there was no escaping it. I could stare straight up and tremble, or gaze into the stream and see its reflection. I closed my eyes and started the ceremony we all go through before a frightening climb, assuring myself that I'd done big climbs before, hard ones, impossible ones, some certainly harder than what lay overhead, which didn't look so bad after all. All the way up the long slab I kept telling myself there was no place on earth I'd rather be. But when we got to the base and I stared up I knew I'd been talking lies.

"The thing stabbed the sky like a giant sabre and I felt sick knowing I had to climb it. 'The climb starts in that corner,' was all Russ said. Then he dumped his pack and sat down. I looked into the shadows and before I could spot the corner, Russ was laid out and snoring. I was so amped I couldn't think of knocking off, so I slumped back and studied the rock and several times took an elbow just to look at Russ sleeping. The guy spooked me. When again I looked up I knew some part of me was desperate to find out about Vic because only desperation could have gotten me on that bloody cliff. Otherwise I'd have been sprinting away as fast as my legs could take me. I guess I went out but I started dreaming about not being able to sleep and when Russ woke me at dawn I didn't know if I'd slept or not and felt like I hadn't. He handed me a cup of coffee. He still had his headlamp on and in the first light he's already packed the haul bag and gotten all the gear together because there it was—the ropes all flaked out and the pitons racked. 'I'm ready whenever you are,' he told me, and turned off the stove."

Steve paused there. His face was blank and he drained the rest of his beer in one draw and ordered another, again barking at the waitress. Art didn't care about the business with Russ and Vic, he only wanted to hear about the Citadel; but for all his fidgeting, Steve's scowl told him what it told me and the silent Cochran brothers. If you interrupted him, that might be all you'd hear. More beers came, and Steve carried on.

"While I wrestled into boots and harness Russ just gazed across the valley real tranquil like. But once he started climbing there was no stopping him and I knew we were going to scale that bastard or die trying. The first two ropelengths followed a vertical crack in a huge, white corner. I got the second lead, a vicious, leaning thin crack I could barely get my fingers into. But I made it okay and felt pretty good about it. But just above, a huge ceiling shot out overhead and a shallow crack marked the way. This roof had twice defeated Russ and my brother, and a few pitons part way out marked their high-point. Now Russ led this pitch like it was nothing, dangling in his stirrups and casually banging in pitons that didn't sound so good and, of course, he never said a word. Only after he had turned the roof and I started following the lead, cleaning all the pegs, did I realize they were all so wretched that had he fallen no piton could have checked his fall and he'd 've crashed into the lower wall and died as sure as I'm sitting here. I wondered if my anchor would have held such a fall, so maybe he would have yanked me off as well. If the dupe wanted to risk his life, fine. But we were in this thing together and I didn't fancy his risking my ass as well. I was going to let him hear about it, but after I turned the roof I went dumb.

"There wasn't a ledge above the roof, so we were just hanging there, lashed to a cluster of suspect pitons just over the lip, the ropes looped down and dangling in free space below us. Russ was Buddha-calm and just surveyed the steep wall above. A vertical, wafer-thin flake curved up to a big ledge about six hundred feet above us. I don't know what was holding that flake to the wall. We were committed now. Irreversibly. We couldn't get down because if we tried, the end of the ropes would just be hanging in space below the overhang, four hundred feet off the deck. And since we still had about 1,600 feet to go and it hardly looked easy, I wondered if we'd ever get off that wall. I'd started out dead serious but just then I found it all the funniest thing. I didn't care. I laughed. I laughed so hard it echoed across the valley. I figured if we got stranded, it'd give me that much more time to find out about Vic. But my mind wasn't working quite right. I laughed again. It was better to lose it that way than to freeze up, I guess.

"We climbed the rest of that day and I was never in better form. I was climbing unconscious. But as invincible as I felt I saw just how much better Russ was. You know how the best guys stay alive. They know just where their limit is and they might go right to it but they never cross the line. Not Russ. He'd cross the line every time. He'd get irreversibly committed and he'd just rise to it because he didn't have a limit. It was madness of course, and it was terrifying duty to climb with him because you knew one day he would take a fall that no man could hold, a fall that would take you with him. But I didn't care just then. I must have been scared though I don't remember.

"Anyway, about four that first day, Russ led a really wild pitch up the flake which was creaking and flexing as he jammed behind it. The few pitons he got in were bunk. He reached a point not far below that ledge, less than a rope's length we reckoned. When I gained Russ's stance I saw right off that we were dead-ended. The flake, pinched down so thin you could only get fingertips behind it, was too brittle for pitons, and everything else just rattled around inside, though Russ was trying to slot some wire nuts behind it. When I realized we were stuck my mind cleared and I got really angry—crazy, I guess. Russ still looked calm, and for a moment I thought the clown didn't realize he had finally overreached himself.

There was no way up and no way down. So Russ starts rubbing chalk into his hands, taking deep breaths, like he's psyching to actually lead this impossible flake. He was insane; anyone could see that by the way he climbed. Then he unclips from the anchor and hands me the belay rope, like he's set to cast off. 'Whenever you're ready,' he says to me. I lost it. 'We're stuck you fool,' I yelled, 'don't you see that?!' Nobody could climb that bloody flake. I was sure of it. But Russ is going to try anyway so I've got to go along, right? What else can I do? The only way off is up. But before he kills us both I come right out and ask, 'What happened with you and Vic?' 'We'll talk about it on the ledge.' 'The ledge?! We're never going to make that ledge,' I screamed. But he just keeps looking straight up, rubbing chalk into his hands. 'Whenever you're ready,' he tells me again. And he just keeps staring up, waiting. . . ."

Steve paused again here. His face was flushed and wringing wet and he swilled down two half-filled glasses of water left on the table. You could have heard a candle flicker just then. Steve was so lost in the telling he seemed to have rolled back sixteen years and was hanging on the Citadel. A silent minute passed. None of us moved.

"An army couldn't have held him back, so Russ takes off up the flake and like I said you could only get your fingertips behind it, so even Russ was straightaway desperate, his feet skedaddling all over the polished wall and his arms quaking from the strain. And there's no way to get a piton or anything in the flake—it's just too thin and brittle. He couldn't have let go with one hand anyway and there's not a single foothold, but the maniac just keeps going, laybacking up this flake, his feet pasted right up by his fingertips now. And damn if he's not fifty, sixty, seventy feet above me, and looking to pitch off every move. Soon he's a hundred feet out and I'm thinking: when he falls, he'll rip out my anchor and we'll both plunge 1,000 feet into the talus. At least he's lost in the function but I'm just watching him, and then I just can't look any longer. I glance down and imagine us both plummeting like ragdolls, the talus racing up and then the impact, and I screamed out loud. 'I don't want to die,' I yelled. I'm so scared I can hardly breathe and I'll do anything to live. And hell if Russ isn't just below that ledge and I'm screaming that he's got to make it or I'll kill him and babbling all kind of nonsense 'cause I'm so terrified I pissed my pants. That's right, and I'm not afraid to admit it.

"Then the rope came tight. I hadn't been paying attention to the rope and he's got none left and he's only a few feet below the ledge, hanging on for both our lives. He claws up a couple more moves and the rope comes tight against the anchor pitons. I untie from the anchor and this gives him enough slack to get his hands on the ledge; but he can't get on it and he's running out of gas and gasping and his feet are bicycling and I see his hands slowly buttering off. So I clip a sling into the anchor and stand in it and this gives Russ just enough slack to claw onto the ledge. I looked down between my legs, got dizzy, and puked. When he finally shouts down that I'm anchored off I'm still shaking pretty bad and can't move for ten minutes.

"When I finally crawled onto that ledge—a big one—I went to the wall, slammed home another four pitons, tied myself in with zero slack and just death-gripped the sling. I hated Owens for dragging me onto that wall, and would have sold my soul to get off it. I couldn't have climbed another inch, I was that fried. We'd get off all right. A single crack shot straight to the summit. No doubt we could climb it. It looked a lot easier than what we'd just done.

"We were finished for the day. The sun was sinking over the jagged ridge across the valley. We were both trashed so we bivouacked on the ledge. I tried to relax but I still hated being convict to both Russ and the Citadel. I stared at him as he emptied the haul bag. He needed a partner to climb this bastard, but there was more to me being there than that; and knowing we could get off made me that much more anxious to find out what the thing was all about. But I was too gassed to press things. Russ got some food out and I ate a few sardines.

"'You're a better rock climber than your brother was,' he told me, citing the thin crack I'd led lower down on the wall. What a load of crap. I'd come around in the last year because I wanted to be a player like they were. A big player. But I couldn't have carried Vic's pack. I knew that. Then he says he wants me to be his new partner, that we could do things wilder than even the Citadel, and I started shaking again because I didn't want any part of the Citadel, even less of something harder. Then I thought about Vic and I just went off thinking how brazen Russ was. So I jumped up and started yelling:

"'I'm just going to take over where Vic left off, am I?' And I grabbed him and kept yelling at him and he never resisted, never said anything. I let him loose and went across the ledge and laid down.

"Then Russ unties from the rope, wanders over toward the edge and starts staring straight down. I remember these big white clouds had crept in and carpeted the whole valley. He takes a step forward to where his toes are curled over the very brink.

"'You could drop a piton here and it wouldn't even hit the wall,' he said in that calm, measured voice. 'It'd free-fall all the way to the base—1,300 feet.' I could breathe on him and he'd fall off. 'It's easy to believe something when you want to, or when you need to,' he continued. I leapt up. 'No matter how outrageous it is,' he added. I stood there, staring at his back. He didn't move an inch and never looked back. The truth was outrageous. Russ had pushed Vic off, and now his conscious was begging me to return the favour. I'd known it all along, ever since I'd first heard that lie about Vic slipping on easy ground, and I'd hidden it in my heart like a bullet in a healed wound; and like Vic's death, I was too scared to carve it out and examine it for what it was. No more.

"'But when something's utterly meaningless—even a cold fact—it's almost impossible to believe.' His voice was sad but it didn't matter. I took a step toward him, but suddenly froze up.

"'Shut up!', I started. 'Shut up or I'll push you off, just like you pushed Vic!!' Suddenly Russ spun around and we were eye to eye, his heels now hanging off the ledge.

"'No you won't Steve, you won't because you're not a killer, and neither am I.' I shook horribly, not so sure of either count. 'Your brother fell, Steve, slipped right off an easy ledge. God knows how, but that's what happened.' And looking into his eyes, I knew it was so. Russ had brought me along, had risked both our lives a dozen times, just to prove it.

"If I'd been right about Russ it would have taken some of the edge off Vic's death. There would have been some sense to it, and some comfort in seeing Russ pay. Instead, Vic has simply slipped off an easy ledge, and died. Nothing could have seemed more absurd. I sank down and put my head on my knees. The moment just hung there.

"I slept like a dead man and arose okay, but my nerves were shot so Russ did all the leading. The wall actually got steeper. The crack was hard, but good, and the few times it petered out Russ pendulumed over to another crack. Toward the top the exposure was really there because the whole wall just dropped away, 2,000 feet straight to the talus.

"Late that afternoon we finally got to a ledge just below the summit. An easy chimney led 40 feet to the top and I could climb off without a rope. I sat back and started laughing again though I didn't know why. Russ coiled up the ropes and stuffed all the hardware into the daypack. He shouldered the pack and the ropes, then looked up at the last bit to the top.

"'You take it, partner,' he told me. He was going to let me scramble off, so I'd be the first on top. A nice gesture, but I wasn't ready. Russ walked back out the ledge and started gazing at the clouds billowing below. He said we had climbed one of the world's great routes, and in only two days. We were partners now and his career was finally back on track. Without the right partner, the last months had hardly been worth living, he said. He had me, we were partners now, and I'd have to climb a lot of others worse than the Citadel, and I couldn't fathom that. Russ, he keeps talking about this new partnership, what it will mean to both of us and it slowly dawned on me that what he was really describing, what he needed and now thought he had, was that magic he once had going with my brother. They really had something, something I couldn't bring back to life any more than I could resurrect Vic. So I'm thinking: the guy doesn't realize that they'd had their season, Russ and Vic, and it had passed.

"Then it all came together for me. I wasn't his man and I didn't want to be his man. He deserved more. He deserved Vic, and I knew, I tell you I knew he'd never be happy so long as that partnership was denied him. And as Russ kept talking calmly about all that awaited us, as he gazed across the valley breathing in the clear air, I stepped over to the brink and pushed him off. And you know the wall was better than vertical so he probably free-fell the whole way down. And he never even screamed—not a peep—because he knew I'd done him proud. Him and Vic, together forever.

"Forty feet of easy ground and I was on the summit. I went back to the base and found the body, or what was left of it, and buried it on the flanks, in a patch of soot. Then I spread gravel over it and dragged some boulders on top. You'll never find it, but you can look if you want."

This last detail was said matter-of-factly, not as a challenge, for Steve's voice and face and everything behind it was clearly played out. He simply got up and left.

McTeague

by Frank Norris

from *McTeague*

At the end of this novel, written in 1899, a San Francisco dentist named McTeague kills his wife in a fit of greed and flees with her money. He is finally caught by his erstwhile friend and neighbor, Marcus, as he tries to make his way across the vast expanse of Death Valley.

At Marcus's shout McTeague looked up and around him. For the instant he saw no one. The white glare of alkali was still unbroken. Then his swiftly rolling eyes lighted upon a head and shoulder that protruded above the low crest of the break directly in front of him. A man was there, lying at full length upon the ground, covering him with a revolver. For a few seconds McTeague looked at the man stupidly, bewildered, confused, as yet without definite thought. Then he noticed that the man was singularly like Marcus Schouler. It *was* Marcus Schouler. How in the world did Marcus Schouler come to be in that desert? What did he mean by pointing a pistol at him that way? He'd best look out or the pistol would go off. Then his thoughts readjusted themselves with a swiftness born of a vivid sense of danger. Here was the enemy at last, the tracker he had felt upon his footsteps. Now at length he had "come on" and shown himself, after all those days of skulking. McTeague was glad of it. He'd show him now. They two would have it out right then and there. His rifle! He had thrown it away long since. He was helpless. Marcus had ordered him to put up his hands. If he did not, Marcus would kill him. He had the drop on him. McTeague stared, scowling fiercely at the levelled pistol. He did not move.

"Hands up!" shouted Marcus a second time. "I'll give you three to do it in. One, two—"

Instinctively McTeague put his hands above his head.

Marcus rose and came towards him over the break.

"Keep 'em up," he cried. "If you move 'em once I'll kill you, sure."

He came up to McTeague and searched him, going through his pockets; but McTeague had no revolver; not even a hunting knife.

"What did you do with that money, with that five thousand dollars?"

"It's on the mule," answered McTeague sullenly.

Marcus grunted, and cast a glance at the mule, who was standing some distance away, snorting nervously, and from time to time flattening his long ears.

"Is that it there on the horn of the saddle, there in that canvas sack?" Marcus demanded.

"Yes, that's it."

A gleam of satisfaction came into Marcus's eyes, and under his breath he muttered:

"Got it at last."

He was singularly puzzled to know what next to do. He had got McTeague. There he stood at length, with his big hands over his head, scowling at him sullenly. Marcus had caught his enemy, had run down the man for whom every officer in the State had been looking. What should he do with him now? He couldn't keep him standing there forever with his hands over his head.

"Got any water?" he demanded.

"There's a canteen of water on the mule."

Marcus moved toward the mule and made as if to reach the bridle-rein. The mule squealed, threw up his head, and galloped to a little distance, rolling his eyes and flattening his ears.

Marcus swore wrathfully.

"He acted that way once before," explained McTeague, his hands still in the air. "He ate some loco-weed back in the hills before I started."

For a moment Marcus hesitated. While he was catching the mule McTeague might get away. But where to, in heaven's name? A rat could not hide on the surface of that glistening alkali, and besides, all McTeague's store of provisions and his priceless supply of water were on the mule. Marcus ran after the mule, revolver in hand, shouting and cursing. But the mule would not be caught. He acted as if possessed, squealing, lashing out, and galloping in wide circles, his head held high in the air.

"Come on," shouted Marcus, furious, turning back to McTeague. "Come on, help me catch him. We got to catch him. All the water we got is on the saddle."

McTeague came up.

"He's eatun some loco-weed," he repeated. "He went kinda crazy once before."

"If he should take it into his head to bolt and keep on running—"

Marcus did not finish. A sudden great fear seemed to widen around and inclose the two men. Once their water gone, the end would not be long.

"We can catch him all right," said the dentist. "I caught him once before."

"Oh, I guess we can catch him," answered Marcus, reassuringly.

Already the sense of enmity between the two had weakened in the face of a common peril. Marcus let down the hammer of his revolver and slid it back into the holster.

The mule was trotting on ahead, snorting and throwing up great clouds of alkali dust. At every step the canvas sack jingled, and McTeague's bird cage, still wrapped in the flour-bags, bumped against the saddle-pads. By and by the mule stopped, blowing out his nostrils excitedly.

"He's clean crazy," fumed Marcus, panting and swearing.

"We ought to come up on him quiet," observed McTeague.

"I'll try and sneak up," said Marcus; "two of us would scare him again. You stay here."

Marcus went forward a step at a time. He was almost within arm's length of the bridle when the mule shied from him abruptly and galloped away.

Marcus danced with rage, shaking his fists, and swearing horribly. Some hundred yards away the mule paused and began blowing and snuffing in the alkali as though in search of feed. Then, for no reason, he shied again, and started off on a jog trot toward the east.

"We've *got* to follow him," exclaimed Marcus as McTeague came up. "There's not water within seventy miles of here."

Then began an interminable pursuit. Mile after mile, under the terrible heat of the desert sun, the two men followed the mule, racked with a thirst that grew fiercer every hour. A dozen times they could almost touch the canteen of water, and as often the distraught animal shied away and fled before them. At length Marcus cried:

"It's no use, we can't catch him, and we're killing ourselves with thirst. We got to take our chances." He drew his revolver from its holster, cocked it, and crept forward.

"Steady, now," said McTeague; "it won' do to shoot through the canteen."

Within twenty yards Marcus paused, made a rest of his left forearm and fired.

"You *got* him," cried McTeague. "No he's up again. Shoot him again. He's going to bolt."

Marcus ran on, firing as he ran. The mule, one foreleg trailing, scrambled along, squealing and snorting. Marcus fired his last shot. The mule pitched forward upon his head, then, rolling sideways, fell upon the canteen, bursting it open and spilling its entire contents into the sand.

Marcus and McTeague ran up, and Marcus snatched the battered canteen from under the reeking, bloody hide. There was no water left. Marcus flung the canteen from him and stood up, facing McTeague. There was a pause.

"We're dead men," said Marcus.

McTeague looked from him out over the desert. Chaotic desolation stretched from them on either hand, flaming and glaring with the afternoon heat. There was the brazen sky and the leagues upon leagues of alkali, leper white. There was nothing more. They were in the heart of Death Valley.

"Not a drop of water," muttered McTeague; "not a drop of water."

"We can drink the mule's blood," said Marcus. "It's been done before. But—but—" he looked down at the quivering gory body— "but I ain't thirsty enough for that yet."

"Where's the nearest water?"

"Well, it's about a hundred miles or more back of us in the Panamint hills," returned Marcus, doggedly. "We'd be crazy long before we reached it. I tell you, we're done for, by damn, we're *done* for. We ain't ever going to get outa here."

"Done for?" murmured the other, looking about stupidly. "Done for, that's the word. Done for? Yes, I guess we're done for."

"What are we going to do *now?*" exclaimed Marcus, sharply, after a while.

"Well, let's—let's be moving along—somewhere."

"*Where,* I'd like to know? What's the good of moving on?"

"What's the good of stopping here?"

There was a silence.

"Lord it's hot," said the dentist, finally, wiping his forehead with the back of his hand. Marcus ground his teeth.

"Done for," he muttered; "done for."

"I never *was* so thirsty," continued McTeague. "I'm that dry I can hear my tongue rubbing against the roof of my mouth."

"Well, we can't stop here," said Marcus finally; "we got to go somewhere. We'll try and get back, but it ain't no manner of use. Anything we want to take along with us from the mule? We can—"

Suddenly he paused. In an instant the eyes of the two doomed men had met as the same thought simultaneously rose in their minds. The canvas sack with its five thousand dollars was still tied to the horn of the saddle.

Marcus had emptied his revolver at the mule, and though he still wore his cartridge belt, he was for the moment as unarmed as McTeague.

"I guess," began McTeague coming forward a step, "I guess, even if we are done for, I'll take—some of my truck along."

"Hold on," exclaimed Marcus, with rising aggressiveness. "Let's talk about that. I ain't so sure about who that—who that money belongs to."

"Well, I *am,* you see," growled the dentist.

The old enmity between the two men, their ancient hate, was flaming up again.

"Don't try an' load that gun either," cried McTeague, fixing Marcus with his little eyes.

"Then don't lay your finger on that sack," shouted the other. "You're my prisoner, do you understand? You'll do as I say." Marcus had drawn the handcuffs from his pocket, and stood ready with his revolver held as a club. "You soldiered me out of that money once, and played me for a sucker, an' it's *my* turn now. Don't you lay your finger on that sack."

Marcus barred McTeague's way, white with passion. McTeague did not answer. His eyes drew to two fine, twinkling points, and his enormous hands knotted themselves into fists, hard as wooden mallets. He moved a step nearer to Marcus, then another.

Suddenly the men grappled, and in another instant were rolling and struggling upon the hot white ground. McTeague thrust Marcus backward until he tripped and fell over the body of the dead mule. The little bird cage broke from the saddle with the violence of their fall, and rolled out upon the ground, the flour-bags slipping from it. McTeague tore the revolver from Marcus's grip and struck out with it blindly. Clouds of alkali dust, fine and pungent, enveloped the two fighting men, all but strangling them.

McTeague did not know how he killed his enemy, but all at once Marcus grew still beneath his blows. Then there was a sudden last return of energy. McTeague's right wrist was caught, something licked upon it, then the struggling body fell limp and motionless with a long breath.

As McTeague rose to his feet, he felt a pull at his right wrist; something held it fast. Looking down, he saw that Marcus in that last struggle had found strength to handcuff their wrists together. Marcus was dead now; McTeague was locked to the body. All about him, vast interminable, stretched the measureless leagues of Death Valley.

McTeague remained stupidly looking around him, now at the distant horizon, now at the ground, now at the half-dead canary chittering feebly in its little gilt prison.

Author Biographies

BERYL BAINBRIDGE is the critically acclaimed author of *Master Georgie, The Birthday Boys,* and *Every Man for Himself.* Ms. Bainbridge was a five-time nominee for the Booker Prize and two-time winner of the Whitbread Book Award for fiction.

ANTHONY BOUCHER is the author of numerous books of mystery, fantasy, and science fiction including *The Compleat Werewolf, The New Adventures of Sherlock Holmes,* and *Rocket to the Morgue.* Mr. Boucher won three Edgar Allan Poe Awards from the Mystery Writers of America for criticism.

PAUL BOWLES was the world-renowned composer, translator, and author of essays, travel writing, short stories, and novels, including *Let It Come Down* and *Up Above the World.* He was perhaps best known for his first published novel, *The Sheltering Sky.* He died in 1999.

JUDITH M. BRUESKE holds a Ph.D. in cultural anthropology and is the publisher of *The Desert Candle,* a quarterly newspaper in which her articles on the "mystery" lights occasionally appear. She is a resident of Alpine, Texas.

GREG CHILD has written, edited, and compiled numerous books on mountaineering and climbing. His works include *Postcards from the Ledge: Collected Mountaineering Writings of Greg Child; Thin Air: Encounters in the Himalayas;* and *Climbing: The Complete Reference to Rock, Ice and Indoor Climbing.*

LARRY KANUIT is an adventurer and author who has brought to the page true stories of encounters between bears and humans in *Alaska Bear Tales* and *More Alaska Bear Tales.* He is also the author of *Cheating Death: Amazing Survival Stories from Alaska.*

JACK LONDON, born in San Francisco in 1876, wrote the well-known and loved adventure novels *Call of the Wild, White Fang,* and *The Sea Wolf,* as well as numerous other books and short stories. Based on his own experiences in Alaska and California, and at sea, his stories appeal to millions.

JOHN LONG is the author of *Big Walls* and *Advanced Rock Climbing,* which was the first prize winner at the Banff Book Festival. He has authored and edited numerous other books, including *The Big Drop: Classic Big Wave Surfing Stories* and *Gorilla Monsoon.*

ERIC MARTIN is an author who lives in San Francisco. His novel, *Luck,* is forthcoming from Norton.

PETER MATTHIESSEN, a novelist and naturalist, received the National Book Award in 1978 for *The Snow Leopard,* an account of his trip to the remotest parts of Nepal in search of the Himalayan blue sheep and the rarely seen snow leopard. Another work of nonfiction, *The Tree Where Man Was Born,* and his novel *At Play in the Fields of the Lord,* which was adapted into a film in 1991, were also nominated for the National Book Award. His most recent work of fiction is *Bone by Bone.*

HARUKI MURAKAMI is Japan's most highly regarded novelist and the recipient of the Yomiuri Literary Prize. His works, which include *The Wind-Up Bird Chronicle, Dance Dance Dance,* and *Norwegian Wood,* have been translated into fourteen languages. His latest novel is *South of the Border, West of the Sun.*

FRANK NORRIS is most famous for the cult classic *McTeague,* the true crime story of a dentist and his greedy wife. First published in 1899, *McTeague* depicts the sordid affairs of the quickly developing America and was instantly a literary sensation. Born in 1870, Norris died at age 32 having written seven novels and over 200 poems and essays.

EDGAR ALLAN POE is considered by many to be the father of the mystery/horror genre. *The Tell-Tale Heart, The Murders in the Rue Morgue,* and *The Fall of the House of Usher,* along with many more tales, have given chills to generations of readers. Poe is also known for his poetry, perhaps most famously for "The Raven" and "Annabel Lee," as well as for literary criticism.

MARC REISNER is the author of *Cadillac Desert: The American West and Its Disappearing Water,* which was nominated for the National Book Critics Circle Award. Mr. Reisner, former staff writer for the Natural Resources Defense Council, is also the author of *Game Wars: The Undercover Pursuit of Wildlife Poachers.*

ROBERT W. SERVICE was born in England in 1874, but lived in Canada much of his life. His poems often recall colorful adventures set in mining camps and saloons in the Yukon. They can be found in the volumes *The Spell of the Yukon and Other Verses, Ballads of a Cheechako,* and *Rhymes of a Rolling Stone.*

GEORGE R. STEWART was the first winner of the International Fantasy Award. He has published numerous works of history, biography, and fiction, as well as studies of natural catastrophe, including *Ordeal by Hunger: The Story of the Donner Party* and *Fire.* His only work of science fiction is *Earth Abides.*

TOBIAS WOLFF has received numerous awards for his writing, including the PEN/Faulkner Award for his novel *The Barracks Thief,* the Los Angeles Times Book Award for his childhood memoir *This Boy's Life,* and the Rea Award for excellence in the short story. His most recent work is *The Night in Question,* a collection of short stories.

Acknowledgments

"The Snow-Shoers" from *Ordeal by Hunger* by George R. Stewart. Copyright © 1936, 1960, and © renewed 1963 by George R. Stewart. Copyright © renewed 1988 by Theodosia B. Stewart. Reprinted with permission of Houghton Mifflin Company. All rights reserved. "The Birthday Boys" from *The Birthday Boys* by Beryl Bainbridge. Copyright © 1994 by Carroll & Graf. Reprinted by permission of Kent Carroll, Publisher. "The Other Side of Luck" from *Thin Air: Encounters in the Himalayas* by Greg Child. Copyright © 1988 by Greg Child. Reprinted with permission of the publisher from *Thin Air: Encounters in the Himalayas* by Greg Child, published by The Mountaineers, Seattle, WA. "Cadillac Desert" from *Cadillac Desert,* revised and updated by Marc P. Reisner. Copyright © 1986, 1993 by Marc P. Reisner. Used by permission of Viking Penguin, a division of Penguin Putnam, Inc. *The Seventh Man* by Haruki Murakami. Copyright © 1998 by Haruki Murakami. Reprinted by permission of International Creative Management, Inc. "The Hyena" Copyright © 1979 by Paul Bowles. Reprinted from *Collected Stories 1939–1976* with the permission of Black Sparrow Press. "Come Quick! I'm Being Eaten by a Bear!" from *Alaska Bear Tales,* Alaska Northwest Books, 1983. Copyright © 1983 by Larry Kanuit. Reprinted with permission of Alaska Northwest Books, an imprint of Graphic Arts Center Publishing Co., Portland, Oregon. "The Wolves of Aguila" from *On the River Styx* by Peter Matthiessen. Copyright © 1989 by Peter Matthiessen. Reprinted by permission of Random House, Inc. "The Marfa Lights" by Judith M. Brueske. Copyright © 1989 by Judith M. Brueske. Reprinted and adapted with permission of Judith M. Brueske. "They Bite" from *Far and Away* by Anthony Boucher. Copyright © 1943, 1951, and 1953 by Anthony Boucher. Reprinted by permission of Ballantine Books, a Division of Random House, Inc. "The Red Man" by Eric Martin. Copyright © 1999. "Hunters in the Snow" from *In the Garden of the North American Martyrs* by Tobias Wolff. Copyright © 1976, 1978, 1980, 1981 by Tobias Wolff. Reprinted by permission of The Ecco Press. "For Everything Its Season" by John Long. Copyright © 1982 by John Long. Reprinted with permission of the author.